Special thanks to the following people for helping breathe life into the Godsverse:

Adam Goldstein, Alejandro Lee, Anna Carlson, Azia MacManus, Becky Fuller, Ben Coleman, Beth C, Brian Pickering, Bugz, Caledonia, Carl Bradley, Chad Bowden, Chris B, Chris Call, Daniel Groves, Dave Baxter, Deaven Shade, Dustin Cissell, Ed Vreeburg, Edward Nycz Jr., Emerson Kasak, Eva M., Gary Phillips, Harry Van den Brink, Hollie Buchanan II, Jake Schroeder, Janice Jurgens, Jason Crase, Jeff Lewis, Jennifer & Charlie Geer, Johnny Britt, Jonathan, Joshua Bowers, Journee Gautz, Jude M, Kenny Endlich, Logan Waterman, Louise Mc, Luis Bermudez, Matt Selter, Matthew Johnson, Michael Bishop, Moana McAdams, Nari Muhammad, Nick Smith, Celeste, Brian, and Niobe Cornish, Paul Nygard, Rhel ná DecVandé, Richard A Williams, Rick Parker, Rob MacAndrew, Robert Williams, Ronald, Rosalie Louey, Ruth, Stacy Shuda, Talinda Willard, Tamara Slaten, Tony Carson, tvest, Viannah E. Duncan, Victoria Nohelty, Walter Weiss, and Zachary.

GODSVERSE PLANETS

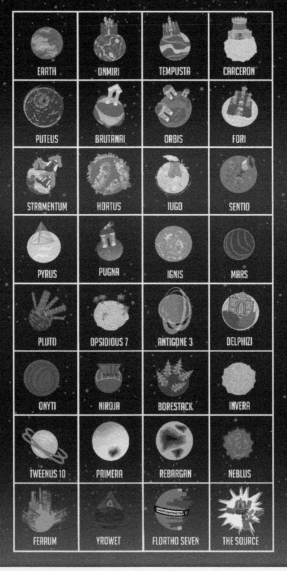

1000 BC – BETRAYED [HELL PT 1]
/PIXIE DUST

500 BC – FALLEN [HELL PT 2]

200 BC – HELLFIRE [HELL PT 3]

1974 AD – MYSTERY SPOT [RUIN PT 1]

1976 AD – INTO HELL [RUIN PT 2]

-1984 AD – LAST STAND [RUIN PT 3]-

1985 AD – CHANGE

1985 AD – MAGIC/BLACK MARKET HEROINE

1989 AD – DEATH'S KISS
[DARKNESS PT 1]

1985 AD – EVIL

2000 AD – TIME

2015 AD – HEAVEN

2018 AD – DEATH'S RETURN [DARKNESS PT 2]

2020 AD – KATRINA HATES THE DEAD
[DEATH PT 1]

2176 AD – CONQUEST

2177 AD – DEATH'S KISS
[DARKNESS PT 3]

12,018 AD – KATRINA HATES THE GODS
[DEATH PT 2]

12,028 AD – KATRINA HATES THE UNIVERSE
[DEATH PT 3]

12,046 AD – EVERY PLANET HAS A GODSCHURCH
[DOOM PT 1]

12,047 AD – THERE'S EVERY REASON TO FEAR
[DOOM PT. 2]

12,049 AD – THE END TASTES LIKE PANCAKES
[DOOM PT 3]

12,176 AD – CHAOS

ALSO BY RUSSELL NOHELTY

NOVELS
My Father Didn't Kill Himself
Sorry for Existing
Gumshoes: The Case of Madison's Father
Invasion
The Vessel
The Void Calls Us Home
Worst Thing in the Universe
Anna and the Dark Place
The Marked Ones
The Dragon Scourge
The Dragon Champion
The Dragon Goddess
The Obsidian Spindle Saga

COMICS and OTHER ILLUSTRATED WORK
The Little Bird and the Little Worm
Ichabod Jones: Monster Hunter
Gherkin Boy
How NOT to Invade Earth

www.russellnohelty.com

DARKNESS

Book 10 of The Godsverse Chronicles

By:
Russell Nohelty

Edited by:
Leah Lederman

Proofread by:
Katrina Roets & Toni Cox

Cover by:
Psycat Covers

Planet chart and timeline design by:
Andrea Rosales

BOOK 1

"Death's Kiss"

CHAPTER 1

It was five years ago when a bloody cult murdered my best friend and mentor, Julia Freeman.

No. That's not true.

She wasn't murdered. She was sacrificed at the altar of a demon, a mhrucki, so the cultists could attain longer lives and fill their coffers.

The only bright side to the whole affair was the mhrucki lied about helping their cause and, after being brought to Earth, she slaughtered each and every one of them and escaped, but not before sucking the soul from my body, leaving me in a coma.

I shouldn't have survived. I wouldn't have survived, except that Julia somehow came back from the bowels of Hell, possessed my comatose body, and used it to track down the mhrucki and kill it, sending my soul back into my body and jolting her back to Hell. I can still feel her sometimes, in the darkness—or at least the remnants she left behind inside of me. Just a hint here, or a moment there, but I always smile when I feel her.

I should be dead, but she gave everything to save me. Since then, I have been obsessed with finding her and saving her soul from the pits of Hell. I don't have any problem saying that I'm obsessed. What would you do if somebody came back from the dead to save you from eternal torment? If you wouldn't give up everything for them, I question your morality.

I still wake up in the middle of the night, remembering the feeling of a million pins and needles ripping my soul apart inside the stomach of the evil mhrucki. I've never been the same since that horrible experience, never had a worse experience than that—and I've been to Hell.

Yes, that's right. I've had a crappy life, all things considered. I've quite literally been to Hell and back.

I was only a child when a banshee kidnapped me and brought me to Hell as an offering to Lucifer. I was lucky there, too, because Lucifer did not accept me as a sacrifice. It was better than I deserved and more decency than I thought Old Scratch capable of, given the stories about him.

I was lucky because Julia came for me then, too.

She'd saved me twice, which is all the more reason why I won't rest until I rescue her.

After she saved me from the banshee, she took me under her wing and taught me all she knew. She showed me how to fight and how never to be scared again.

I was a violent child, filled with rage, and she showed me how to channel my righteous anger and turn it against the demons who deserved it. We saved a lot of fairies together. I still work to save fairy kind every chance I get. I carried on Julia's legacy or tried to, and I hoped she would be proud. Still, I wouldn't rest, I couldn't truly rest until I knew Julia was safe, and she could never be safe in Hell.

After I graduated high school as valedictorian of my class, I went to North Larchmont University in Havenbrook, Connecticut, to study under Doctor Reginald Dankworth, the foremost occult scholar in the world. My mother thought I was crazy for turning down scholarships to Duke and Notre Dame. She told me a thousand times that I was throwing my life away, but I knew what I was doing. By all rights, I shouldn't have even had a life. Julia saved me twice, so I made my decision about where and what to study based on what was the best way to help her.

The least I could do was save her, just once. If it took the rest of my days—if I died without finding her, then at least I could die knowing I tried to help her. I couldn't let her burn in the pits.

I could have been a normal kid. I could still be normal, I guess. I heard people talking about the new *Batman* movie directed by the guy who brought us *Peewee's Big Adventure*, and I just couldn't care about it at all. I didn't care about watching the Ghostbusters jazz up the Statue of Liberty, and I certainly didn't want to talk about whether George Bush was going to raise taxes or not. I didn't care about any of it. I only cared about getting Julia back and protecting magical creatures from demons and other things that went bump in the night.

My life became a cycle. I spent my days studying every bit of demonology and Christian theology I could find while I spent my nights tracking down leads, protecting fairy folk, and looking for anything that could give me a clue on how to summon Julia from the abyss or bring her back from the dead.

I was set to meet one of my informants later in the evening for intel on where to find Julia, and I was frantic to finish a paper on microeconomics before then. It was a class I didn't even care a little bit about, except that it was essential to graduate.

In my first semester at school, I forced my way into an independent study degree with Doctor Dankworth on occultism. I quickly rose to become his star pupil and most trusted aid, but I still needed a lot of gen ed classes to graduate, even though I hated them. I mean, when would I ever need to understand the efficacy of the stock market, really? It's not like money was even going to matter once the Apocalypse descended upon us, and it would descend on us eventually, but until then…I had to act the part of a good student if only to make my mother happy.

"How is the paper coming, Kimberly?" my roommate, Molly, asked as she passed my room, her body and head wrapped in two different white towels that accented her dark complexion. She had just finished a shower, and her skin glistened from the water. Her bright smile filled any room she entered. Everybody loved her. Somehow, she tolerated me, even though I hated everybody she liked.

"It's going," I said. "Honestly, if I have to look at stock symbols for one more minute, I might scream."

She smiled even wider when she laughed, which she almost always did like the world was filled with overabundant joy. Everything seemed to work in her favor without her even trying. Nothing seemed to get her down. "At least wait until my date gets here before you go postal. I don't care that you scare off any boy who gets close to you, but I do care if you scare them off when they come around for me."

I couldn't help but chuckle. I wasn't much of a laugher, but Molly brought it out of me. I hadn't gotten close to anyone since Julia. If I didn't scare Molly off pretty soon, maybe she would even succeed at winning me over. "Deal. Where is Ted taking you?"

"Ha!" She belted out a laugh. "That boy is last week's spoiled potatoes. I think this new guy's name is Ernie or Jordan. I have it in my planner. I have a date with one of them tonight and the other one tomorrow." She leaned in closer and whispered, "I can't really tell them apart."

Molly went through boys like I went through knives, and for the same reason—because they became dull and uninteresting. I hadn't been on a date since high school, and then just barely. In high school, it was hard enough to be that girl who got abducted by a cult and used in a ritual sacrifice. I didn't want to be a freak because I didn't date, too. Eventually, I grew out of caring what other people thought of me.

"If you get done, I'll probably be at Patty's later." Patty's was a bar and a diner, the kind that only existed in college towns. They served terrible food and watered-down drinks, but they were cheap, making them a popular hangout. It was the kind of place that sounded great while you were in school, but you quickly realized it was a sty after you graduated. I realized it earlier than most, but Molly loved it because it was always filled with drunk boys, and drunk boys showered her with attention. Molly's battery ran on attention.

"I'll think about it," I said with a polite smile. I knew I wouldn't be showing up. She knew it too but was too kind to say anything. Instead, she left with a knowing nod. The door to her room slammed a couple of seconds later, and I heard loud bass thumping through the walls as she got ready for her date.

It had been a lonely road since Julia left. It's not that I didn't try to get close to other people, but every time I did, my stomach curled up in knots as I realized what horrors they would experience if they got close to me.

My life was filled with demons, hellhounds, and all manner of undead creatures hunting me as I hunted them. I couldn't subject anyone to that, no matter how much I yearned for connection. I had already lost one friend to the darkness, and I wasn't about to lose any more, which meant I needed to close myself off.

Molly was the exception. She had been my roommate since freshman year, and when she wanted to move off campus junior year, it made sense we would room together. We lived two separate lives, but we could cohabitate well enough together. Still, even after three years, I wouldn't call us friends.

Fifteen minutes later, I heard a knock. Molly turned off the music and skittered to the front door, where a deep male voice greeted her. They exchanged muffled pleasantries, and a moment later, I heard the door close again, this time with Molly on the other side of it with her date. I was alone in the dark silence, which had become the only true friend I had left.

***

My meeting was at 2 am. Demons did not like the heat of the sun. I always thought that was weird, as they were creatures born and molded in Hell. Maybe it was because the night bred mischief, and demons oozed chaos out of every pore.

Charlie was no different. I met him a year ago, and he'd helped me slowly piece together Julia's life in Hell. He would have been a friend if you could make friends with demons without them stabbing you in the back, literally. He understood how the world worked and knew a lot about the occult, a subject more people shied away from in polite society.

I met him outside the large library that dominated the middle of the campus. I spent many hours in the basement of the library, which housed one of the greatest collections of occult literature from the 1600–1900s, culled from decades of Doctor Dankworth's obsessive quest to track them down.

"You're late, Kimberly," a gruff grumble came from behind a giant bronze statue of a hippopotamus, the school's mascot.

He startled me, and I instinctively went for the daggers I kept sheathed on my hip. When I saw the yellow of his eyes, I softened and looked down at my watch. 1:55 am. "I'm five minutes early."

"That's not what my watch says," Charlie grumbled, choosing to stay in the shadows instead of stepping into the soft light shining through the library windows. "You know how I feel about punctuality."

I looked up at the top of the library, which steepled in a clock tower. The tower read the same time as I had on my watch. I let it go. It wasn't worth the argument. I let most things roll off my back. It made getting through life easier.

"I'm sorry, Charlie. I'm here now."

"I guess that's something. Do you have it?"

I reached into my leather coat and pulled out a vial of ashes from the grave of Peter, the first pope of the Catholic church. As a pixie, I was able to teleport anywhere in the world as long as I could paint a complete picture of it in my mind. That made me valuable to Charlie, especially since he liked to collect weird pieces of Catholic theology. Demons couldn't step into churches, especially the Vatican where Saint Peter was buried. It was dirty work, digging up a two-thousand-year-old grave, but I was used to dirty work.

Charlie held out his thin, red, clawed hand and snatched the vial from my hand. "Not very much, is there?"

I scoffed. I'd spent four days trying to get that tiny vial. "You asked for ashes. It was hard enough to get that much."

"Yeah? How'd you get them, anyway?"

I didn't want to think about it. "What matters is that I got it. Do you have what I need? I didn't just dig that vial up for my health."

The light hit Charlie's bald, red head as he moved reluctantly into the light. He was short, barely waist-high, with a bulbous paunch and two little horns poking out from his forehead. His teeth were yellow and pointed, and his arms dangled low on his body. He pulled out a piece of parchment from his belt. "It wasn't easy to get this either, you know. I hope you appreciate it."

The corners of my mouth twisted into a scowl. "Just give me the paper."

He handed the paper over, and I unfolded it. It was an address in Queens. "You sure about this?"

"Who you askin'?" Charlie said with a growl. "Of course, I'm sure. That demon worked the same pit Julia was assigned. I'm sure of it. If imps know anything, it's bureaucracy."

I clasped the paper close in my hand. "Finally. Thank you, Charlie."

"Don't thank me yet," Charlie said, holding up his hands and backing away. "That demon's a real asshole."

I smirked. "Aren't they all?"

CHAPTER 2

Julia taught me to travel without using pixie dust. It wasn't quite as accurate, but it was a whole lot more convenient. The pink powder was temperamental and stuck to your fingers, and in the middle of a fight, it was a pain to have to go digging in your pocket for it. It was even more annoying to carry it around your belt.

To teleport between locations, it helped if you'd been to your intended destination before. A picture would do in a pinch. I spent years training myself on landmarks around the world, from luxurious places like the Eiffel tower to the more unimpressive First Reformed Church in Jamaica, Queens. You never knew where you would have to travel and needed to bank and recall as many places as possible quickly. I spent many nights with cue cards quizzing myself on the landmarks of the world...because, of course, I did. I was always a good student. Before she died, Julia taught me to study and analyze every situation. I did this obsessively to always make sure that I wasn't walking into a trap.

I closed my eyes and pictured the town hall in Flushing, Queens. When it was vivid in my mind, I vanished in a puff of purple air. A moment later, I was standing outside of the town hall. The building looked a bit like a medieval castle, replete with towers around it that, in a different time and place, could have housed little imps with arrows.

The address I was given was a half-mile away. I could have pulled out my wings and flown, but I liked to keep a low profile, even in the dead of night. It would be light soon, and that meant the demon would likely be home, safe from the breaking of the dawn. Their apartments were filled with blackout curtains to blot out the sun, and they kept their lairs dark.

The fact that this particular demon had an apartment meant he probably had a job nearby. Perhaps he was on a mission for Lucifer, or the ever-elusive Lilith, queen of the demons, whom I had been trying to track for half a decade. She was my white whale. There was no one as knowledgeable as to the workings of Hell as she was. Since being kicked out of the Garden of Eden, she had seen thousands, perhaps millions of demons pass through Earth. Her writings became the cornerstone of everything else I knew about demons, the bedrock of my studies.

After about ten minutes of walking, I arrived at a dump of a building. The façade was cracked, and the walls seemed to sway in the stiff breeze of the autumn evening. It didn't surprise me that a demon would choose a rundown hole. They preferred decrepit places.

I expected it to be locked, but when I tried the front door, the knob turned for me. I pushed open the door and strode inside. When I took another step, my foot brushed past something that tugged at the cuff of my pants. I heard the "click" and looked down. A tripwire. *That's not good.* I closed my eyes and vanished just as the flames licked my face, and an explosion rocked the walls.

I had been set up, and that little imp Charlie was going to pay for it.

***

In a small town in Scotland, there was a bar. The place looked like a plain house, like any other house on any other unassuming block in the country, except it was filled with angels and demons drinking themselves stupid. Legend had it that hundreds of years ago, a man accidentally summoned a demon while making his dinner. He and the demon got to talking and became friends over a beer. That beer led to another, and those beers led to dozens more over the next few years. Eventually, the word got out that the man was a hospitable host and more demons showed up. Those demons brought the suspicion of angels, who came to investigate and ended up joining in on the fun. They were all having such a good time that it became a sort of neutral zone for demons and angels visiting Earth.

A forcefield protected the house, turning away anybody who didn't know the place existed. In order to move through the forcefield, you had to hit it head-on at full gait, brimming with confidence. Even then, it stung.

I took a running start and passed through the forcefield without incident. My hands and feet went numb from the intense shock, but after a minute, I could feel them again, and I marched inside the house. The place also happened to be the favorite hiding space of an imp who I was about to send back to Hell in a body bag.

A group of angels was shouting off-key, "You take a whiskey drink, you take a lager drink!" Some gruff demons joined them, growling, "You sing the songs that remind you of the good times, you sing the songs that remind you of the best times!"

As they splashed their drinks together, their arms flailing in the air, I craned my neck, looking for the imp in the sea of demons and angels. Their commingling was really a mind screw if you hadn't seen it before. Mortal enemies sharing a drink like they were best friends, even though their job was basically to kill each other.

I walked up to the wooden bar at the far end of the pub. A ginger-haired man with a thick, bristly beard smiled at me.

"What can I get ya?"

"Charlie," I hollered clearly over the screams of the denizens.

He shook his head. "Don't know that drink, I'm afraid."

"It's not a drink." I pressed my hands on the bar. "He's an imp. A real squirrely one. Likes to hang out here."

"Oh yeah," the barkeep said. "He's got quite a tab. I haven't seen him for a while. If you find him, send him this way before you kill him, will ya? He needs to settle up."

"I'll do that," I said, my eyes narrowing. "You sure you haven't seen him?"

The barkeep shrugged. "There's a lot of demons that come through here, but Charlie's a right git. I try to keep track of him whenever he's around. I'm telling you I ain't seen him for a fortnight, maybe two."

"Any idea where he might be?"

"I'm not his keeper." He turned to a hefty angel seated nearby. "Get you a refill, love?"

I grabbed the burly barkeep by his hairy arm. "Please."

The angel spun around angrily. "Get off of him."

The barkeep smiled. "I'd listen if I were you. I'm a bit of a universal treasure, don't ya know?"

I held up my arms, and the barkeep pulled away. "I don't want to fight. Please, the as—Charlie nearly killed me tonight. Anything you can do to help me would be appreciated."

The barkeep thought for a moment. "There's a girl. Cherub girl. He used to take up with her a bit if I recall." The barkeep looked at the angel as he finished a beer, teetering to one side and then the other. "You remember her? Pudgy girl. Stocky build. Beautiful hair."

"Yeah, I know her." The angel belched. "Clarice."

"Can you tell me where she is?" I asked.

"That depends," the angel said, slurring his words. "Is this next round on you?"

I nodded. "You got it."

"Then, yes. Pull up a chair, and let's get sloshed."

***

I walked out of the bar bleary-eyed the next morning. The angels and demons there sure knew how to throw a party. By the end of it, I was stumbling over my own feet, trying to find my way through the forcefield. When I tried to rush toward it, I tripped over my feet and fell in the grass. I was lying there, splayed out in the grass when a large shadow moved in front of the sun and blocked my view.

"This is unbecoming of you," the voice growled. When I pushed myself up, I saw Aziolith, the dragon who Julia begged to look after me before her untimely death. I recognized him even in his more palatable human form. He had a hefty supply of morphing syrup which he used to mingle among the mortals. In his true form, he was a 30-foot-tall red dragon with impressive scales and potent fire breath. As a human, he chewed a lot of mint gum.

"Come on, Kimberly," he said, wrapping his arm around my shoulder. "Let's get some food in you."

***

You would think that baked beans didn't go with breakfast, but you would be wrong. They were delicious alongside my bacon, eggs, sausage, and tomatoes. I enjoyed going full English whenever I was in the UK. I turned down the haggis, though, pushing it over to Aziolith. He who would eat anything that ever had a pulse.

"Feel better?" Aziolith asked as he munched on a chewy piece of a sheep's lung. "Hrm…I prefer raw."

"No. I feel way worse," I said, chomping down a spoonful of baked beans. "I'm less drunk now, but I have a splitting headache."

Aziolith pulled out a bottle of aspirin from his jacket and placed it on the table. I took it without saying a word and swallowed four pills. Aziolith wasn't really a friend. He was more like the father I never had, down to the withering stare he gave me whenever he disapproved of my life choices, which was often.

"What are you doing here anyway?" I said.

Aziolith leaned forward. "When you didn't come home last night, your roommate called your mother, who called me."

"Oof," I replied. "She must be worried. She hates you."

Aziolith smiled. "The feeling's mutual, but I told her I would find you, and I have."

"You would think after years she would get a grip on the idea that I'm not a child."

"Give her some credit. She just wants you to be safe. She knows you're doing something dangerous, taking risks."

I shoveled a forkful of eggs into my mouth and barely chewed before swallowing them. "The world isn't safe. My risks are mine to take."

"That is what your mentor said too, and look what happened to her."

"Low blow."

"I suppose this is about her, then?" Aziolith sighed. "What am I talking about? It's always about her."

"Not always," I replied, indignant. "But yes, this was about her and nearly getting my ass blown up last night."

"Hrm," Aziolith said. His right eyebrow lifted. "And you really think that your mother has no reason to be worried?"

I growled. "Fine. Maybe she does. Can you just please help me find the asshole who nearly killed me so I can figure out why?"

"Of course," Aziolith said. "Why else would I be here?"

CHAPTER 3

"Open up!" I shouted, pounding on the door to Clarice's apartment. It was nicer than the slums where demons usually hung out, but angels had more expensive tastes than demons.

I slammed on the door until I finally heard the creaking of a bed and feet dragging on the other side of the door. There was a long sigh, and the door opened. A blinding light emanated from the other side like I was staring into the surface of the sun from two feet away.

"How can I help you, child?" a pleasant, heavenly voice said.

"Are you Clarice?" I asked, squinting.

"That's correct," she replied sweetly. "What can I do for you, my love?"

I nearly gagged. I was very comfortable around demons, which were filled with piss and bile, but the piety of angels always turned my stomach. "I'm looking for Charlie."

"WHAT?" Her voice nearly cracked. "That scumbag?"

The light flicked off, and Clarice hovered into the doorway. Hardly bigger than a child, she was unkempt, her hair matted against her head. Smeared makeup covered her face, and her toga was stained and ripped, revealing thick belly rolls underneath.

She jammed her pudgy hands onto her hips. "Why would you say that name here? Don't you know what he did to me?"

I shook my head. "No clue."

"He got me kicked out. Of Heaven. Now I'm stuck pulling miracles out of my ass to make ends meet." She looked back at the kitchen, where a naked man was sneaking out of a back room and skittering across the hallway. "Be right back, doll!"

"Miracles?" Aziolith said. "That's what you're calling it?"

"Hey!" Clarice protested. "You ever been kicked out of Heaven? Huh?" Aziolith shook his head, and the angel turned to me. "What about you?"

"No, I haven't."

She pointed her finger in my face. "Well, it sucks. I used to be bathed in the light of the Lord and now look at me. I look like somebody just smashed me with a two-by-four. How could he?"

"What did he do?" I asked.

"I don't wanna talk about it," she said, pouting.

"That's ok—"

"Did you know a demon and a cherub can have a kid?" Clarice asked. "Cuz I didn't, but apparently we're descended from the same line or somethin', so yeah. He knocked me up, and I was not about to have his kid. So, he gave me money to—take care of it…"

"You mean an ab—"

Clarice cut her hand through the air. "Don't say the word. God didn't like that. He didn't think it was a good look for one of his pure, chaste cherubs to have a child with a demon, but when he found out I had…well that I had an…well, you know, one those things that the whole Catholic Church is up in arms about." She sighed. "It sucks, though. I didn't even have anything to do with getting pregnant!"

"I mean, it seems like you had something to do with it," Aziolith said. "It takes two to tango, as they say."

"Watch it, mister," Clarice said. "You don't know me. I was a slave to Heaven, doing every little thing they asked. I had a moment of fun…and…just one moment of fun in a million years…"

"I'm sorry that happened to you. I really am." I held up my hands. "But listen, we really need to see Charlie. I promise to wring his neck for you. You have my word on that."

She smiled a little. "Really? That would be swell."

"I promise," I said. "So, do you have any way to contact him?"

Clarice flew toward her kitchen and pulled a piece of paper from the fridge. She turned and handed it to me. "He said if I ever needed him, just to use this, and he'll come running."

I looked down to see a demonic summoning circle with a series of symbols around it. "Thanks. This is perfect."

"Perfect? That's a word I haven't heard in a while." Clarice went to close the door. "Hey, if you do find him, can you kick him in the balls for me, too?"

I nodded. "You got it."

***

After a trip to a butcher to pick up lamb's blood, Aziolith and I made our way to a large cavern. I often used the place to shelter fae children from demonic attacks. It was warded up the ass, which meant Charlie couldn't escape or pull any funny business. Having a dragon on my side was a helpful bonus in case it all went to pot.

Aziolith cracked his neck and stretched his arms out in front of him. As he did, they lengthened until they were longer than any humans could be, and his legs morphed into thick, stocky dragon legs. He arched his back and a pair of large red wings extended from his spine. His head expanded into a long neck and his enormous jaw emerged from it, followed by his snout and the rest of his face. When he was done, he towered over me.

"Better?" I asked.

"So much better," he replied, rolling his neck and shoulders. "You have no idea how cramped it is in one of those bodies. I mean, it's nice to see people, I suppose, but at what cost, you know?"

"Let's get this over with and then we can go back and figure out our next move."

"That sounds lovely," Aziolith said, looking around. "By the way, this is a very nice cave. It's not the top of the Swiss Alps, but it's nice."

"You would know," I said before kneeling on the ground.

I spent the next hour drawing the sigils for the summoning circle. Demons were quite particular. You needed the right blood, the right sigils, and the right chant, otherwise, they wouldn't come when you called, or if they did, they were prone to slaughter you. I wasn't worried about that, but I certainly didn't want Charlie to ignore my call.

When it was done, I sat outside the circle. "*Imp mundana magne, potens bestiarum genus daemoniorum. Veni ad me.*" I looked back at Aziolith. "This doesn't make any sense. Can you tell me what it means?"

Aziolith bent down and peered at the markings. "This was clearly found on Google Translate. If I had to guess,

I'd say it means something like 'Oh great worldly imp, all-powerful among beasts and demonkind. Come to me.' It's really a dreadful translation, though."

"Ha!" I said. "Leave it to Charlie to self-aggrandize his own incantation. That's just like him. Are you ready?"

"Ready."

I turned to the circle and closed my eyes, focusing all concentration on summoning Charlie. "*Imp mundana magne, potens bestiarum genus daemoniorum. Veni ad me. Imp mundana magne, potens bestiarum genus daemoniorum. Veni ad me. Imp mundana magne, potens bestiarum genus daemoniorum. Veni ad me.*"

Wind whipped through the cave, and the circle glowed red. The ground shook beneath my feet. It would have been very impressive if I wasn't completely over Charlie's theatrics. Lightning cracked onto the ground, and when it was over, the imp Charlie stood naked in front of me. "I'm here, baby. Let's get frea—" He saw us and snarled. "Oh, come on!"

I rushed him, grabbing his hands to prevent him from snapping away from me. No matter how many wards I had up, I didn't trust demons not to wriggle away. "You tried to kill me, Charlie! Why?"

He kicked and screamed as I lifted him into the air. "It wasn't personal!"

"Let me have him," Aziolith said, opening his mouth.

I placed Charlie's hands inside Aziolith's mouth, and the dragon bit down on them, putting just enough pressure so that the duplicitous imp couldn't escape. Green blood oozed down Charlie's arms as Aziolith held him in the air.

"Of course, it's personal, Charlie." I kicked him in the balls. "That's for Clarice." I punched him across the face. "That one was for me. Nothing personal."

"You don't understand!" Charlie shouted. "You're getting too close!"

"Too close to what?"

"To everything!" Charlie shouted. "And she doesn't want you getting any closer, so she put a price on your head."

"Who's she?" I asked, furrowing my brow.

Charlie shook his head fervently. "I don't wanna say. You're not gonna like it."

I punched him across the jaw. "I don't like not knowing, either. Now TELL ME!"

"Lilith!" he screamed. "It's Lilith. She told me if I couldn't kill you, she was gonna send in real muscle to finish the job. I was just trying to protect you."

"By killing me?"

"And sending you to Hell, where I could protect you!"

I socked him in the stomach. "Are you insane? That's not how any of this works! You don't protect somebody by killing them!"

"How would I know? I ain't never had a human-type friend before."

"We are not friends," I growled. "You gave up any chance of that when you tried to kill me. Now, where is Lilith?"

Charlie smirked at me. "Why would I tell you if we're not friends?"

I looked up at Aziolith and nodded. He clamped down harder, and Charlie screamed bloody murder.

"You probably don't know this, but dragons can actually kill demons by eating them. It takes a while, but it can be done."

"Ith'z Twhoo," Aziolith said. "They're delithioth."

"Don't talk with your mouth full. Thanks, though." I looked down at Charlie. "So, you have to decide if you want to be stuck disintegrating in a dragon's stomach for the next century or if you want to help me and live."

"Get out of here. How am I gonna live?" Charlie scoffed. "I tried to kill you, and now you're gonna kill me. I know the score, so let's just get it over with."

"You're right." I sighed. "I was going to kill you, but you said about the only thing that could have saved your puny, insignificant life. You know I've been searching for Lilith, so this is clearly a manipulation, but I don't care. Tell me what you know."

"She'll kill me."

"It's either her or us." I asked, "Who do you think has a better shot? The one with a dragon that's literally eating you right now, or the demon queen?"

He snarled. "I guess I'll take my chances with you."

I laughed. "Don't do me any favors." I walked toward him. "Now tell me, where is the demon queen?"

"I don't know," he said. "She moves around all the time. I only know the cipher she sent me."

"Give it to me," I said.

"I'll bring it to you."

"No," I said. "You'll bring me to it." I nodded, and Aziolith crunched down on Charlie's hands, ripping them from Charlie's arms. The weaselly imp fell to the ground, screaming and clutching his bloody stumps to his chest.

"My hands!" he screamed. "Do you know how long those will take to grow back?"

I pulled him to his feet. "The better for me to make sure you can't escape." I looked up at Aziolith. "Can you do something about this, so he's not dripping blood everywhere?"

"My pleasure." Aziolith spewed a light stream of fire and cauterized Charlie's wounds at the wrists. Charlie squealed some more.

"Thanks." I squeeze the imp's ear. "Now, where are we going?"

"You're merciless. Do you know that?"

"I do know that," I replied in an even tone. "How about you tell me something I don't know? Lead me to the cipher."

"How am I gonna do that, genius?" Charlie said. "I ain't got no hands to snap away!"

"You're right." I sighed. "Wait here."

CHAPTER 4

In my studies of ancient books, I came across an advanced technique in which pixies used other people's memories to teleport. I'd only managed to perform it successfully twice before, and it required something I never kept with me—pixie dust.

Most of my supplies were in Aziolith's cave high in the Swiss Alps. That way, it was only a teleportation away when I needed it, and I didn't need to worry about Molly or somebody else finding it and asking all sorts of valid but uncomfortable questions about what I was doing with a bag of pink crystals.

In a puff of purple smoke, I arrived at Aziolith's cavern. Even though the cold was brutal outside of the cave, he always had several fires lit so that the inside was toasty enough for even the most discerning dragons and cold-blooded people. I took a deep breath, sucking in the fresh, crisp mountain air, and looked at the hordes of gold. There must have been billions in bullion scattered haphazardly throughout the cave.

Aziolith had accumulated untold wealth during his first tour of Earth before Akta slaughtered him and before Julia's blood brought him back. After my mentor's death, he allowed me access to as much of the treasure as I wanted. Even a single chest of gold was plenty to live on for the rest of my natural life, and there were thousands of chests' worth, from ancient rune swords to gems, to gold, to armor, to magical artifacts. One might wonder why I needed a roommate if I had access to untold riches, but I kind of just wanted a normal college experience, especially since nothing else about my life was normal.

I spent a lot of time in the stacks, cataloging what artifacts and weapons I could, trying to learn any of the occult properties the objects might possess. Often, I fell asleep on the same bed that Julia had set up on the far side of the cave, where shelves full of books rested and where I felt most at home in the whole world. Many times, Molly thought I was out all night with a boy, but I had really just fallen asleep reading one ancient manuscript or another. Aziolith often curled up at the foot of my bed to keep me warm and to listen to me read from his many books, most of which were boring enough that they could put anyone to sleep.

Next to the bed, I had built a wardrobe which I filled with the best weapons and armor I'd found rummaging through the stacks, along with bags upon bags of pixie dust. Learning how to mix pixie dust was an ancient rite of passage to my people, but the knowledge had been lost through the ages, making the pouches full of the dust more precious than any amount of gold.

I opened the wardrobe and pulled out a blue pouch adorned with moons and stars. It was Julia's pouch and Akta's before her, so it held a special place in my heart. I tied it around my belt and closed my eyes, a picture of the cave where we were holding Charlie in my mind, and with a flash, I vanished there.

"All right," I said, slapping my hands together. "Let's do this."

"You're still missing the point, honey," Charlie said, waving his stumps. "I don't have any hands. I can't take you anywhere."

I took a pinch of the pixie dust from the pouch. Instead of throwing it on the floor, I rubbed it along my gums. Pixie dust was a powerful stimulant to pixies, and much of the dust was lost by fairies snorting it like cocaine for a boost of power. I felt my fingers tingle, and that tingling traveled up my arms and into my chest. A jolt shocked through me, and I felt more powerful than I had in a long time.

"Holy shit!" Charlie stammered. "Your eyes are glowing pink, Kimberly. You're crazy."

I grabbed his head with both hands as he struggled against me. "Stay still."

"What are you gonna do to me?"

He fought against me, but I was more powerful in that moment than I had ever been before, and I steadied him quickly. "Think of the place you want to take me."

"I—"

"Do it!" I screamed.

"I would listen to her," Aziolith said. "There's no arguing with her when she's like this."

"Fine, fine," Charlie said. "I'm thinkin'. Gimme a second."

I closed my eyes, and images from Charlie's mind flashed through my brain. I saw his debauchery, his lecherousness, and his callous disregard for humanity until he finally settled on the image of a house, looking out upon the ocean.

"Is that it?" I asked.

He nodded slightly. "Yeah, yeah, yeah. That's where we gotta go."

"You realize if you're lying to me and try to escape, I'll find you and feed you to Aziolith, right?"

"I'm tellin' the truth," Charlie sniveled. "I swear to ya."

I pressed my eyes closed. "Then let's go."

***

Several people screamed when we reappeared in front of the house. I usually preferred discretion, but I was just so tired of Charlie's bull and so amped up on pixie dust that I couldn't care less about being seen by normals. It's not like anyone would believe them anyway. There were plenty of legit pictures of magic and monsters in the world, but they are all discounted as fakes.

"Open it," I said.

"How?" Charlie grunted. "No hands."

I had to give him that one. "Where's the key?"

"It's…umm…in my other pants."

I groaned. The front door was framed around a big window in the center. I peered inside the house, studying everything there, from the books on the shelf to the woodgrain on the floor. When I closed my eyes, we flashed inside.

The alarm began to blare the second we entered. "Find it."

I pushed Charlie toward the white couch in the center of the room. He shrugged. "Why? If I just wait long enough, my security company will send officers to investigate, and I'll be saved."

I stuck one of my daggers to Charlie's neck. "No, you'll be dead, and I'll be long gone. How long until somebody summons a miserable son of a bitch like you? A hundred years? A thousand? You have thirty seconds before I gut you."

Charlie skittered to the bookshelf, where he reached for a piece of parchment and a golden amulet—a crescent moon with a cross under it, the symbol of Lilith. They slipped out of his nubs as he tried to move them toward me, clattering onto the floor.

"Here!" he shouted, kicking them to me. "Now, leave me alone."

"How do they work?" I asked.

"Wouldn't you like to know? That's not part of our deal." Charlie looked out the front window. The sound of police sirens was getting closer, and he smiled. "Looks like you need to leave, so I guess you'll never know."

"I hate you."

"Back at you, kid."

I closed my eyes and vanished from the room just as a pair of police officers slammed through the front door, guns drawn. If only I could have stuck around to see how Charlie talked himself out of that one like I knew he would. But I had other things to do, like find Lilith, and I had my first real clue in years. I was not going to let it go to waste.

CHAPTER 5

The letter was written in longhand cursive and didn't make much sense in the original text. That was the point of ciphers and secret codes. I had read it a dozen times, looking for potential clues.

> *Antipathy was the mother of regret*
>
> *Never be sure of the taste*
>
> *Fraught with patience*
>
> *Pain to come.*
>
> *Regrets,*
>
> *-L*

The golden amulet Charlie gave me didn't do anything to help me, either. I should have gone to find him and slit his throat for sending me on a wild goose chase, but I was too tired.

I slid the amulet over every inch of the parchment, trying to replace letters, take the letter that the moon was pointing to and replace it with the one that the cross pointed to. I tried replacement ciphers. I tried symmetric key, asymmetric key, and even Kerberos architecture, but all to no avail. Nothing that I tried made any sense.

"Any luck?" Aziolith asked, stomping over to my bed. I could hear the concern in his voice. I saw it in his face every time he looked at me. I hadn't eaten in two days.

"Not yet."

"Perhaps you need to take a break," he said. "Maybe if you put your mind to something else, then you'll be able to concentrate better on this, and the secret will unlock itself."

I pushed myself up to my knees. "There's a demon witch after me, an imp tried to kill me, and you want me to just go on like nothing happened? I can't do that. I need to figure it out before I can rest."

"I'm not saying go on like nothing happened. I'm saying that you're thinking too hard, and often if you just think about something else, the answer might present itself. You need new inputs. Go read a book, or play minigolf, or screw a boy. You're not doing yourself any good staring at that parchment like you're going to burn a hole through it."

I had to admit, the more I looked at the paper, the further the answer seemed to get. I rubbed my eyes. "Maybe you're right. I should probably go back to the apartment. People are worried about me."

"I told your mother you were staying with me, but I would think your roommate would be concerned that you haven't been home in days."

I pushed off the bed. "Nah. I'll bet she didn't even notice. She's got her head up her own ass, or perhaps somebody else has their head up there right about now." Then, I remembered that I had a paper due days ago in economics. "Crud."

"Something wrong?" Aziolith asked.

"Yes. Everything's wrong. I got so carried away here I kind of forgot I had a life back at school. I forgot about my stupid paper." I groaned. "Let's just hope my professor understands whatever excuse I can come up with."

"I'm sure she will. Time is relative."

I laughed. "You've clearly never been in school."

***

Professor Lowell scoffed, gathering her papers after class. "I can't give you an extension." She was short, with fire red hair cut into a bob. The glasses on her wide face made her eyes look even further apart than they really were. "I'm sorry."

I held the paper in my hands up. "I'm not asking for an extension. I'm asking for you to accept the paper as it is, right here."

"That would mean moving the due date for you, which is tantamount to an extension, which I didn't give anyone else. What kind of message would that send?"

"I don't know. That you have a heart."

She was putting books in her satchel and stopped short. "It's not wise to insult the person you're asking for a favor."

I threw my hands in the air. "Well, being nice didn't help much since you're telling me I am going to fail this class since you won't accept my paper two days late."

"Missing one paper won't fail you, but yes, you'll be unlikely to receive higher than a C in this class."

"And what about my scholarship, huh?" I said.

"I'm sorry you're in a tough spot. I did not fail you. You failed to turn in the paper." She sighed. "You will soon, very soon, be out in the real world, and in the real world, they don't accept things late."

I let out a high-pitched laugh. "That's complete horse plop. My mother is constantly talking about people who blow deadlines and how projects have to get shuffled around because of it."

Professor Lowell blinked. "And is she talking about these people in a positive fashion?"

I looked down at the ground. "Well, no."

"We are trying to instill good habits into the students at this university. Telling them they can just willy-nilly turn their papers in late is not instilling in you good habits."

I stepped closer to her. "Listen, I'm telling you. I swear to you that I had this paper done on time, but then I got caught up on research for my dissertation, and I just…forgot to come to class."

Professor Lowell shook her head, disgusted. "That sounds like a you problem. I will not bend my rules because of your ineptitude."

I sighed. "So, there's nothing I can do to get you to take this paper?"

"I suppose if you can get your advisor to give you a note that you were truly working on research for your dissertation, then I will consider it," Professor Lowell said. "However, it better be a convincing note."

"And how is that a positive message for us? That you won't believe us, but you'll believe white men in authority."

She shrugged. "It's showing you the way of the world, Kimberly. Now, if you'll excuse me, I have a lecture."

***

I stomped past the students playing frisbee and smoking weed on the campus mall, making my way towards Doctor Dankworth's office in the anthropology department. His office was in the basement of the campus museum, where hundreds of prehistoric artifacts were on display. He'd found many of them himself during his travels around the world. The faculty indulged Doctor Dankworth's predilection for the occult because his digs often brought back millions in rare objects and untold prestige for the university, as well as priceless endowments to the museum and the library.

Doctor Dankworth's published literature focused mainly on comparative religion and the origins of Christianity, and he was one of the most famous researchers in his field. His penchant for the occult fueled all his research, a fact the university preferred to sweep under the rug. However, if it hadn't been for his book, *How Demons Invaded Our Culture: A Pop-Culture Study of the Occult,* I never would have chosen their esteemed university.

I stepped through the thick wooden doors into the museum and moved across the polished wooden floors. I loved the building's smell of leather and oak. Often I spent long afternoons there mulling over the turn of the century crucifix at its entrance, but today I was grouchy and on a mission not to fail out of school or have to repeat economics. If anybody could talk some sense into Professor Lowell, it was my advisor.

I took a left at the ancient plates from the Etruscan period and hopped down the stairs to the basement and Doctor Dankworth's lab, where he was hard at work cleaning a series of relics that he had gathered on his last dig in Turkey over the Christmas holiday.

"Afternoon, Doc," I said.

He turned to me and smiled. He had been working in anthropology since before I was born, and yet he still beamed when he was working with ancient objects. I wished I had as much unrepentant joy for anything as he had for his work.

He removed the thick glasses that allowed him to do intricate cleaning work. "I haven't seen you in a while, Kimberly. Did you forget we had a meeting yesterday?"

"Yikes. Yes, I did, but you will not believe what I found."

Doctor Dankworth was one of the few people in the world I trusted with my secret about being a fairy, and my brushes with demons, though he had never seen one in the flesh. I figured that even if he told people I was a pixie, nobody would believe him.

"It had better be good if you skipped class," he said. "I had a very interesting relic to share with you."

I held up the parchment and the amulet. "I don't know. Is a letter written by Lilith and this decoder big enough for you to forgive me?"

His eyebrows lifted high onto his forehead. "My, my. If that's true, I suppose I can forgive you. Where did you find it?"

"An imp named Charlie gave it to me."

He smiled. "You have the craziest adventures when I'm not around. Oh, to be young and a pixie." He reached out for the parchment. "May I?"

I handed it to him. "That's why I brought it here. The amulet is supposed to decode the message, but I can't figure it out."

He walked the parchment over to the metal table, carefully unrolling the scroll. I handed him the amulet before he asked for it, and he dragged it across the parchment. "Gibberish."

"That's what I thought. I've tried a hundred different types of cryptography, and none of them worked."

"Hrm," the doctor said. He put his glasses back on and studied the amulet, pulling gently at his hair as he often did when he was concentrating. "Ah yes, I thought so. There is a piece missing. That's why you can't read it."

"Of course," I snarled. "That scumbag. I knew he was going to double-cross me. Any idea what it could be that I'm looking for?"

He nodded. "Interestingly, there is a lot of symbolism in the early church that combines the idea of Lilith with that of Eve. Did you know that?"

"Oh?" Of course, I knew, but when the doctor got into a mood to pontificate, it was best to just let him go.

Doctor Dankworth walked to his massive bookshelf. "Yes, with Eve being Adam's second wife, and Lilith being his first, there are some theories that they are really two halves of the same whole."

"Yes, but there is no symbol specifically tied to Eve, is there?" I was egging him on. He'd had so little fun after the death of his beloved wife.

"No, but I think I have a possible…" He pulled down a book—no, this was more than just a book. It was expansive and enormous, an epic tome. He set it on the table and flipped through it. "Ah, here it is."

He spun the book around and pointed to a picture of a golden apple with a bite taken out of it.

"This is what I'm looking for?" I asked.

"Oh no, this is a book I wrote on pieces from our collection. We have this one upstairs. Once the museum is closed, I will take you up there, and we'll see if it works. Won't that be nice?"

I smiled. That would be nice. "Thanks. Hey, do you think you can talk to Professor Lowell for me?"

CHAPTER 6

We didn't have to sneak around in the museum after hours since Doctor Dankworth was a professor and responsible for its upkeep, and especially since he was the person who found a lot of the pieces in the museum.

"Here it is," the professor said, stepping up to a glass case lit from underneath with a soft blue light. He pulled out his key and opened the lock on the side before sliding it open. Doctor Dankworth was giddy like a schoolchild when he picked up the small golden apple, the size of a quarter, and held it up to the light. "When we found this piece, I noticed this small groove around the middle of the apple. I always thought there was a story to it, as if it were a part of a bigger whole. Here, let me see the amulet."

I placed the amulet in his outstretched palm and watched as he slid the apple into it. The apple snapped into place perfectly. The professor shook with excitement. "That's it! Do you have the parchment?"

I shook my head. "No. It's downstairs."

"Well, go get it. Go get it, woman!"

"Fine, fine." I didn't question him when he held a wildfire in his eyes. Besides, thanks to him, in a few minutes, I would be able to find Lilith and, through her, save Julia.

Down in the lab, I carefully rolled up the parchment so that it didn't rip and walked back upstairs. I was hardly at the top of the stairs when I heard the sounds of a struggle and then a crash. I pushed open the door to find Doctor Dankworth on the floor, three demons hovering around him.

"Give it to us!" The biggest demon shouted as it spotted me and grabbed for the parchment.

I pulled my daggers out of my belt and rushed for them. Before the two smaller demons could turn and defend themselves, I stabbed them through their necks. They screamed out in gurgled pain before falling onto the ground.

The third demon slashed at me, and I blocked his attack. It grabbed me by the shoulder, digging its long talons into my skin, and I kicked it back against a display of medieval plates.

"Watch it!" Doctor Dankworth said. "Those are irreplaceable."

"So am I!" I yelled over my shoulder. "Create a summoning circle. Anarchist cross in the middle and the Greek letters for alpha, omega, rho, and pi counterclockwise around the outside at three, six, nine, and twelve o'clock!"

"With what?" he asked frantically.

I pointed to the green bile leaking out of the demons. "With their blood. And hurry!"

The third demon charged, smashing me into a pane glass window so hard that I dropped my daggers. I pushed the demon off me and ducked as it sliced at my face. I weaved left and punched the creature in its rock-hard gut. I wasn't stupid enough to believe that I would hurt the demon without my daggers, but I needed to make some space so I could punt it away. The sock to the gut did the trick. I managed to wedge my legs between us and shove the demon away.

I scrambled to my feet and leaped for my daggers, grabbing one by the handle and spinning around just as the demon dug its claws into my leg and pulled me closer. I stabbed the dagger into its side. The demon let out a howl.

"How's it going over there?" I shouted.

"Done!" Dankworth said, his face lit up with a smile. At least he was enjoying himself. "Let's hope I did it right."

"Pull the dead demons into the middle of the circle!" I smashed my hands against the dagger in the demon's side, and it howled in pain again. I clocked it across the face, once, twice, three times, and then looked back over at Doctor Dankworth.

He finally managed to pull the second demon into the circle, though he stumbled to his knees when he dropped the body. "There you go!" He brushed his hands off. "What now?"

I yanked my dagger out of the demon and tossed its flailing body into the pile. "Get out of the circle." Doctor Dankworth scrambled to his feet and ran out of the circle, his pants stained with green demon blood. I pressed my hand against the edge of the circle just as the demon stood up. "*Daemonium ego mittam te!*" The circle lit up in green, and the demon screamed as it disintegrated into a million pieces, and the other two vanished as well.

"I'd never seen one before," Doctor Dankworth said after a moment of silence. "Where did they go?"

"The pits of Hell. The question is, how did they know we were here in the first place?"

Doctor Dankworth shrugged.

"Well, at least that's over." I sheathed my daggers and looked up. "Where is the amulet?"

Doctor Dankworth's eyes went big as saucers as he patted his pockets. "I don't have it. I must have dropped it making the circle."

"So now it's in the pits of Hell, too?" I said with a sigh. "Awesome. All right, let's clean this up at least. Can't have the janitors finding it."

Doctor Dankworth looked at the mess, frowning. "I didn't think your line of work would have so much blood."

"I kill demons. What did you think it was like?"

"I mean, I'm not sure. I never thought about the blood, I guess. Maybe I didn't even know they had blood."

"Oh, they have blood. Heaps and heaps of it."

***

It took us two hours to mop up all the blood and replace the cabinet so that the room looked untouched. Nobody would ever know what had happened there. Luckily, none of the plates had gotten broken.

"Thank you," I said as I threw a pile of bloody rags into the incinerator. "I usually don't have help cleaning up."

Doctor Dankworth smiled. "Fastidiousness is my life."

If they found even a drop of demon blood upstairs, it would unleash an investigation onto the school I wasn't ready to deal with at the present moment. The government first learned about the existence of demons in the 70s, and more than once, I'd come in contact with the FBI as they worked to hide the fact there were monsters and mythological creatures everywhere. They didn't think the public could deal with it. I had to agree with them.

"Last thing," I said. "I have to destroy the surveillance tapes."

"Somebody's going to notice that, won't they?" the doctor asked.

"Probably," I replied. "They'll notice a little more if the tape shows a big fight with demons in their museum."

"Good point."

He led me upstairs to the security office next to the front entrance. Even though they had the tapes running all the time, they were too cheap to hire nighttime security. Thank goodness for budget cuts. One of the campus guards came by once an evening, and otherwise, they simply patrolled outside.

Doctor Dankworth opened the door and hit the tape deck to eject the tape, but nothing happened. "Weird."

I pushed him aside and opened the flap on the deck. "There's no tape in here."

"What does this mean?" the doctor asked.

"I don't know." Blinking slowly, I stared at the empty tape deck. I wasn't fully processing the situation. I was as tired as I had ever been. It was more than the adrenaline crash after the fight; I'd also come down from a pixie dust high and hadn't slept for days before that. I needed to rest. "I'll go back and call some contacts to see if it's turned up anywhere."

"Sounds like a plan."

Doctor Dankworth walked me to my car, asking a few times if I was okay to drive. I pushed past him and started up my beat-up, red Honda Civic hatchback. He waved as I pulled into the street. He was right to be worried.

When I sat down on my bed, I smashed against something hard and plastic. "Ow! What the hell?" I rolled over to find what it was I'd landed on. It was a videotape.

Written across the top of it in green demon blood was *"Heard you were looking for me – L."*

It was written in the same cursive as the parchment.

Lilith.

CHAPTER 7

I didn't have a TV or a VCR in my room, and there wasn't one at Aziolith's cavern either, since it was a cavern at the top of the Swiss Alps. However, we had one out in the living room, so I took the videotape outside and turned on the TV. I hoped that Molly was out with one of her boy toys or something so she wouldn't hear whatever was on the tape.

I pushed in the tape and used the remote to flip to channel three, then pressed play on the VCR. I leaned back, ready to throttle the volume if it got too loud. Even though Molly was probably gone, I didn't want to take any chances. I had no idea what I was about to watch.

The screen went fuzzy as the VCR spun the tape. Four different screens appeared on the TV showing four different angles of the museum. I watched as the demons strolled into the museum and began to rough up Doctor Dankworth. A few seconds later, I entered and thrashed my way through the demons. I fast-forwarded the fight, as I already knew what had happened, and while I was fine with bloodshed as a necessary evil to achieving my goals, I didn't like watching it.

A minute after I banished the demons back to the underworld, the image on the screen scrambled and was replaced by a pale woman with bright red eyes. She sat straight in a chair against a black background, with just a hint of light popping against the shiny black hair that draped down over her shoulders to her chest.

"Good evening, my dear," she said in a strong, authoritative voice. "I will skip the pleasantries, as I assume you know who I am. I would be very disappointed if you had been looking for me for so long, harassing my poor, sweet babies, and you couldn't recognize the mother of demons by sight alone."

Lilith. It was really her. She had been described a hundred different ways in a hundred different stories, but it was unmistakably her.

"Of course, I tend to change my appearances every few decades, so perhaps I should just confirm that it is I, Lilith, first of my name, the demon queen, and mistress of the dark."

She giggled. "That is quite a mouthful, but I'm sure you understand that ceremony is all we have to separate us from the animals, and I do so love a good ritual." Lilith looked directly at me through the screen. "I don't understand why you've taken so many back channels to find me instead of simply asking. I have never been shy to those who wish to find me."

That was a lie. I had tried every way I could to find Lilith, and yet, no matter what I did, she eluded me. It wasn't until I started roughing up her people that she finally revealed herself.

She shook her head sadly. "You know how much I love my children, and you have maimed them." She stood up and walked across the room. The camera followed her. "And poor Charlie. It makes me wonder if I should maim something that you love."

A whimper rose, faintly at first, but with every step Lilith took, it grew louder until she revealed Molly, tied to a chair, bound and gagged, visibly trembling but still struggling against the ropes. "I believe you know this charming girl, and she knows you, or at least she knows the you that you have shown her. She was so surprised to know that demons roamed the world, my pet, and I was surprised you didn't tell her since she claimed to be your friend. But, can people like you and me really have friends?"

I'll kill her. I'll kill her. I paused the tape and ran to Molly's room. It was trashed like she had gone on a bender with KISS. Her bed was turned over, and her dresser had been tossed across the room, leaving clothes everywhere. I looked down at the ground to see blood, both red and green. *Good, Molly. You defended yourself.*

I stomped back into the living room and hit play again.

"Don't worry, my love. I didn't hurt her, much, though she put up a hell of a fight. She's quite a spitfire. Perhaps if you had warned her what went bump in the night, she might have even fought my demons off. Tsk tsk. You left her woefully unprepared."

I rubbed the sides of my temples. Lilith knew how to drag things on, that was for sure, which meant that I had time to save Molly.

"If you're anything like the others of your kind, you'll want me to get to the point sooner than later, which I think is a shame. I have been on this Earth for thousands of years, and one thing I have learned is the importance of enjoying the journey. After all, you only get one life, no matter how short or long it is.

"Still, I know you are anxious to parlay. Indeed, our inevitable meeting should be hastened. I will meet with you. Please understand that I have not hurt your friend, and it will remain that way if you do as I say."

I couldn't trust a word she said. If I had learned nothing else about the trickster queen, it was that she viewed an agreement as little more than a guideline and enjoyed changing the terms at her leisure.

"Go to the 13th Street bridge, three a.m. on the nose. A car will pick you up. Miss it, and you will lose your chance.

More importantly, your friend will lose her life, and she has such a bright future."

The video cut again, and it returned to images from the security cameras showing us mopping up the disgusting mess of demon blood. Another second and the video cut for a third time, and we were back with Lilith. "Oh, and love, I have many, many copies of this tape. If you cross me, I will make sure every single news outlet in the country gets it, and then you'll have some explaining to do. Be a good, little girl, and we can all get through this without hassle, m'kay?"

***

It wasn't hard to get to the 13th Street bridge on time. I had been there a thousand times before. It was harder to hold my head up as I waited for the car to arrive. Even with the additional adrenaline coursing through my veins, I was still so tired that I could have slept for a hundred years.

The bridge was deserted for the half-hour I stood there, but at 2:58, a black car pulled onto it and slowly inched forward before rolling to a stop in front of me. The tinted passenger window rolled down, and a long-faced demon smiled at me.

"You Kimberly?"

I nodded. "I am."

The back door unlocked, and the demon pointed behind him. "Get in."

I slid into the leather back seat and closed the door, which locked behind me. A glass divider separated me from the demons in the front seat, which was as much for their protection as mine. The passenger wore a studded leather coat, and the stocky driver was wearing sunglasses even though it was the middle of the night.

"Where are we going?" I asked as the car eased into drive and rolled forward.

"That's need to know," the driver said in a low growl. "And you don't need to know."

"Fair enough," I replied, sliding back and trying to get comfortable. Lilith had gone through too much trouble just to kill me, so I tried to relax. If she wanted me dead, she wouldn't be so subtle about it. The demons would have lured me to a warehouse and had a hundred or more of them attack me. Even in that situation, I liked my odds. After all, I had beaten them before.

Before I left home, I had placed a pinch of pixie dust in my inside jacket pocket. As we drove, I reached into the pocket and coated my finger with it. I rubbed it on my gums and felt the dust rush through me for the second time in a day.

It took fifteen minutes to navigate across the city and enter the warehouse district. We pulled up in front of an old, condemned building. *What was I saying about an ambush?*

"Get out," the long-faced demon said.

"Do I just walk in?"

"If you don't want to keep her waiting," the driver said. "And the mistress doesn't like to be kept waiting."

The car drove away as I walked to the front door. At least they weren't waiting to attack me. That was a blessing—two fewer demons to worry about. I pushed the door open and walked inside. In the center of the building was a single light shining down on Molly, strapped to a chair, glistening with sweat, and surrounded by darkness. I rushed over to her and pulled the gag out of her mouth.

"Are you okay?" I asked.

"Are you—are you kidding me?" Her voice was a screech. "Of course, I'm not okay! I've just been captured and tortured by demons!" She had a wild and reckless fire burning in her eyes that I had never seen before. "What is going on here?"

"Oh, please." I heard Lilith's dulcet tones from the back of the warehouse. Her heels clacked against the concrete floor as her shadow moved toward us. "I wouldn't call that torture. It was just a little fun."

"That. Was not. Fun!" Molly screamed.

Lilith chuckled. "Well, it was fun for us."

"Enough, Lilith," I said. "Let her go."

"No, I don't think I'll do that yet," the demon queen said, walking into the light. "I think I'll keep her right where she is for now." I stomped forward, but Lilith snapped her fingers, and a hundred hungry, glowing, yellow eyes lit the dark. "I wouldn't."

"You know I've beaten worse odds than this, right?"

"Yes," Lilith said. "Your stories are legendary. It's quite hard to know where the woman ends, and the myth begins, actually, just like it's hard to separate myself from the legend of myself."

The corner of my lip rose into a sneer. "Oh, I don't think it's that hard. I just take all the stories and assume ten percent of them are true. It doesn't matter which ten percent."

"Oh," Lilith smiled wryly, her red lips curling on the edges. "Knowing which parts are true very much matters. I'm a psychopath out for blood, a scorned woman out for revenge, a gentle mother guarding my babies. Depending on what you read of me, you might think me a monster or a martyr."

I shook my head. "I figure you're a little bit of each of them. One thing I've learned in my travels is that people can be all sorts of things. I have a friend who's a blood-thirsty dragon, an insatiable hoarder, and the nicest being you could ever meet unless you cross him. We all have a capacity for great good and great evil."

"Touché," Lilith said. "You truly are a refreshingly fascinating creature. Most of the time, I meet world-weary adventurers at the end of their lives or treasure-seekers who have no depth, but you are more than that, aren't you?"

I shook my head. "No, I wish I had depth, but I am as obsessed as any of your treasure-seekers. Otherwise, I never would have found you."

"Ha!" Lilith let out a forced laugh. "Obsessive. Yes, that is something all my suitors have. So, my love, what is your obsession? Why would you risk all you love to find me, and please, know that I judge you on the next words out of your mouth."

I swallowed loudly. "My mentor, Julia Freeman, died protecting me. She saved my life—twice. She's the reason I'm here, and she's stuck in Hell, being tortured forever. It's not fair. I want her back, up here, with me. I want to save her, just like she saved me, and I know you can help me."

"Oh, my love," Lilith's voice dropped. "Yes, that is the legend, but I'm afraid it's just not true. I can't do anything to bring the people in Hell back to Earth. I have no power over the dead, only the demons that lurk in the darkness."

"Then what good are you?" My voice broke as I spoke the words. How could I help Julia, then?

Lilith raised a finger into the air. "Watch yourself. I am confident you can hold your own against my demons, but pure, beautiful Molly cannot."

I bit my lip. The power that coursed through my blood needed a release, and I wanted so badly to take my anger out on Lilith's face. It paid to be deferential, I knew. I needed whatever help she could give me.

I dipped my head. "I'm sorry, your grace."

"That's better," she replied. "Now, while I can't help you bring back your friend, I know who can."

I looked up, eyebrows raised in question.

She stroked her chin. "Thanatos, god of death. He is the keeper of the souls in Hell, and only he can bring back your friend."

"How do I find him?"

"I'm afraid that's where the trouble comes in." Lilith pursed her lips and inhaled. "Some time ago, he was banished from this realm after saving the universe from Ragnarok. The gods thought him and his kin too powerful, so they locked them away, never to be heard from again."

I shook my head. "Nothing is forever."

"True. I happen to know there is a spell to bring him back, for a time at least, locked in a long-forgotten book." Lilith brushed her finger through Molly's kinky hair. Molly jerked away. "However, what is lost can be found, and I have heard you are very good at finding things."

"Get off me!" Molly screamed.

Lilith bent down to whisper into Molly's ear. "Tsk, tsk. It takes two to kidnap. The kidnapper and the kidnapped. You have as much to play in this as I do."

Molly knocked her head against Lilith's lip. "That's insane! I didn't—"

Lilith snarled, balled up her fist, and knocked Molly across the faceinst so hard she passed out.

"Molly!" I screamed.

"I can't abide unpleasantness. You understand, don't you?" Lilith gingerly touched her lip with the back of her hand.

I could barely control my rage but knew I had to for Molly's sake and Julia's. "Yes, ma'am."

"Good," Lilith said, dragging her nail across Molly's unconscious lips. "You are much more pliable than I imagined. You must truly love this poor sack of blood and bile."

"I do, and I love Julia. She would do anything for me. The least I can do is swallow my pride."

"Wonderful. You will get far in this life with that attitude." Lilith stepped toward me. "Now, as for the book. I have long sought after it and believe we have discerned its location. However, it is a place no demon can go. You can, though, and you must, if you want to save your friend and earn my assistance."

"Tell me what I need to do."

"I believe the first thing you must do is pull, I believe it's called a caper, yes? I hope you don't mind theft, my love."

I shook my head. "I don't. And what about Molly?"

"If you help me summon Death, then I will let her go. I promise. In the meantime, she will remain here as my honored guest, as long as she can behave."

"What do you want with Death?" I growled.

Lilith chuckled. "That is between him and me, isn't it? Now, run along. I will send my people to you with directions tomorrow night." She stepped forward and grabbed my chin. "Until then, sleep. You look like Hell worn over, and I should know."

CHAPTER 8

I don't know how long I slept, but by the time I woke up again, it was night. I could have slept another dozen hours or dozen years, but an incessant banging on the front door forced me to rise, and when I regained my faculties, I remembered that my roommate was being held prisoner by Lilith, whose minions were likely the ones knocking.

I pushed myself up to standing and made my way through the apartment, rubbing the sleep out of my eyes. With a deep stretch of my body, my back snapped and cracked in a half dozen places, and I let out a groggy sigh of relief. Someone slammed on the door, and I opened it.

Or I tried to. I had barely turned the knob when two burly demons pushed their way into the apartment and made a beeline for our living room. I recognized them as the ones from the car the night before.

"Took you long enough," the long-faced one said, disgust oozing from his lips. He had a poster tube slung across his back. "We were waiting out there forever. You know Lilith don't like being kept waiting."

"I'm sorry. Who are you?" I asked, confused.

"I'm Pete." He pointed to his partner, a more muscular demon wearing frayed jean shorts and a muscle shirt, carrying a bookbag. He wasn't wearing sunglasses, but it was unmistakably the driver from last night. "This is Ivan. We're here to help you break into Eden."

"I'm sorry…Eden?" I shook my head. "You're going to have to run that back again, Pete."

He sighed. "This is not starting well. You need to find a book for my boss so that you can call forth Thanatos and bring back your girlfriend from the dead, yes?"

"Not my girlfriend," I replied. "But sure."

"The girl you're obsessed with," Ivan said, his voice a gurgle. "Same thing."

"Exactly." Pete turned back to me. "We just so happen to know where the book is, but we can't get it."

"Why?" I replied. "You seem capable…ish to me."

"Cuz we're demons," Pete said. "And it's guarded by angels inside a holy shrine. If we enter, we get burned alive. Even if we somehow survive the enchantments, dozens of angels would skewer us alive, and then God gets pissed at Lucifer, and next thing you know, we're in a war with the big man. We've already lost one of those. You, on the other hand, well, you got powers we don't, and I plan to exploit them."

"Wonderful. I love being exploited."

"That's good," Pete said, clearly unable to understand sarcasm. "You don't have a problem stealing from the Lord, do you?"

I thought back to my theft of the urn that held the first pope's ashes. "Not at all. God can eat a big bag of dicks."

"That's a wonderful sentiment," Pete said with as much a smile as a demon could muster. It looked more like a forlorn look of constipation. "You got a kitchen table or something?"

I shook my head. "Nope. Just the coffee table."

"That's pathetic, you know that? Grown woman without a kitchen table." Pete walked over to the coffee table and pushed everything off it. Then he popped open his poster tube and unrolled a set of blueprints. "This is Eden. It's a secure facility deep in the Ural Mountains of Russia. Any intelligent being would have put the base inside the mountains, but God insists that he be able to see everything, so it's just buried deep in the woods, far away from human civilization, guarded by a cadre of the worst angels in the cosmos."

"The worst?"

"Absolutely terrible," Ivan groaned.

Pete nodded in agreement. "It's not a very glamorous position. They're not fighting demons, or even appearing in cheese, so angels don't generally want it. They give it to peons who've only been angels for ten thousand years or anybody they want to get rid of for a while. It's a real 'who's who' of annoying pricks that can barely tie their own shoes."

The blueprints were intricate. The building was a quarter-mile long and a mile wide and set up in the shape of a cross. "Any pictures of the inside?" I asked.

Pete shook his head. "Nothing."

"That's gonna make it harder to get in," I said. "Downright impossible, actually."

"Well, if it was easy, we'd already have the book, wouldn't we?" Ivan growled.

"You're not wrong, mate," Pete said. "Our job is to get you close. Your job is to get in and get the book."

"Where is it located inside the compound?" I asked. Pete pointed to the center of the cross, where all the hallways met. "Of course."

"Good news is that if you can get inside, there will be very little to stop you. Angels have enough wards to keep demons away and enough manpower to kill anybody without a soul who gets inside."

"Without a soul?" I asked.

He shrugged. "Demons don't have souls, at least not in the traditional sense. So, we need somebody like you who has a fresh, juicy one."

"It's not going to be much use to you if I can't see where I'm going."

Ivan grunted. "That's where you're wrong."

Pete dragged his finger down the long hallway. "There's a window, right here. You can see inside from there. Only place in the whole compound."

"Why didn't you tell me that in the first place?"

"Because it's also the most heavily guarded point in the whole complex. If you infiltrate there, you're toast."

"It's a classic Catch 22," Ivan added.

"Good reference," I said. "I assume you have a plan, then?"

Ivan pulled off his backpack and unzipped it. "Kinda." He pulled out a small helicopter with four blades and a remote control. "We have a drone."

"Seriously?" I scoffed. "You're going to infiltrate a heavily guarded, angelic compound with a kid's toy?"

"It's going to revolutionize how humans kill each other in the next few years." Ivan pushed the drone into the air and moved it side to side. "This is state-of-the-art Army tech that we bought on the black market."

Pete pointed to the drone. "Our plan is to jump this little baby inside using your pixie powers and then use it to find a better entry point."

"That thing is inconspicuous as hell."

Pete shook his head. "Nah, we conceal it. We're masters of disguise, but the whole facility is locked up tighter than a virgin during First Communion. However, the one thing that angels hate more than they hate us is technology. They will never believe that humans used their brains to develop something that could be used to hurt them. They're pompous like that."

"Only one problem with that," I said. "I can't jump things that aren't me."

"That's why I'm here," Pete replied. "I'm gonna unlock some latent powers in you."

"How are you gonna do that?" I crinkled my nose. "You an expert in fairies now?"

"I am. Who do you think sculpted you out of clay at the behest of the gods?"

"You?" I chuckled. "Bull."

"Not bull." He shook his head. "I was the original programmer. The gods may have created fairies, but they didn't do the hard work of figuring out what makes you tick. That was me and Ivan. We very literally built you, and now we get to show you how to unlock a part of your brain you never even knew existed."

"Super," I grumbled. "I can't wait to be reprogrammed by demons."

***

"Hold this," Pete said, placing a red apple in my outstretched hands. "Don't eat it."

"I never would. I'm more a Fuji girl myself."

"Don't be a smart ass," Pete said, pulling a pair of sunglasses out of Ivan's bag. "Put these on."

The glasses made the room look like it was covered in an orange film. "You said you created fairies. That means you were an angel once."

"Of course, we were angels once." Pete scoffed. "Lots of us were. Lucifer knew he couldn't take on Heaven with just the demons in his ranks, so he tried to get us to join him. Some of us said yes, and when we lost…after a day, mind you—yeah, that's how long it took for me to lose everything—a single, bloody day. Well, Bacchus looked at us and said that if we wanted so badly to be with the demons, we could look like them, too, and thus, this beautiful mug you see in front of you."

"That sucks."

Pete shrugged. "Hey, it was my choice. Ivan's too. And it's not so bad. Besides the nasty appearance, we get a lot more freedom in Hell than we ever did in Heaven. I came down here exactly one time in my last ten thousand years with the big man, and let me tell you, Mount Olympus is boring as piss. Now, I can be up here as often as I get summoned. You know how many people summon angels?"

"A lot?" I replied.

"Nah, they pray to angels, but they summon demons." Pete snapped his finger in my right ear and then my left. "Concentrate on the apple."

I looked down at the apple. "Explain what I need to do, aside from looking at an apple and not eating it."

"Look at it carefully. Stare at it. Notice every little grain on the surface of it. Turn it in your hands. Make it real in your mind."

I concentrated on the apple as hard as I could, which was admittedly not very hard because it was an apple, but as I looked, I noticed the apple's tiny fibrous hairs and the small grooves that made up its surface. I took in every tiny little imperfection and found myself fascinated, though I felt rather dumb being so enamored with a stupid, inanimate apple.

"Why didn't anyone tell me that looking at things was so fascinating?"

"Cuz it isn't," Ivan grumbled as he pulled a large wand out of his backpack and handed it to Pete.

"He's right." Pete agreed. "The glasses heighten your perception, like being on shrooms but in a focused manner that won't send you on a bad trip. Now, whatever you do, do not blink."

Pete and Ivan both covered their eyes. There was a pop and then a flash, followed by another one. It burned my retinas, but I did everything I could to keep my eyes open until the third flash when Pete opened his eyes again.

"Ow," I said.

"Oh, quit being a baby. It's not so bad." He bent down and looked into my eyes. "Yup, looks like that did it."

"Did what?"

"All right," Pete said. "Now, I want you to close your eyes and imagine the apple in your mind. Can you do that?"

"I mean, it's an apple, so I think so. I've imagined whole cities in my mind."

"Good," Ivan grumbled. "Then quit talking, and let's do it."

I closed my eyes, and the apple materialized in my mind. "All right. It's there."

"Excellent. Now, I assume you remember what your kitchen looks like?"

"Yeah, smartass, I do."

"Then I want you to imagine the apple on the counter of your kitchen. No sass. Just do."

I imagined the apple on my counter. It wasn't hard to think of my kitchen. After all, I had been in it thousands of times, and I had a near-photographic memory. I reconstructed the kitchen around the apple in my hand, and when I was done, I felt a jolt. My hand was suddenly lighter.

"It worked!" Pete nearly squealed.

I opened my eyes and saw that my hand was empty. I looked past Pete and Ivan to see the apple on the counter. "No way."

Pete grabbed the apple and took a bite. "Delicious." He smiled at me, bits of apple in his jagged teeth. "Now, let's go rob God."

CHAPTER 9

I spent the next several hours practicing my new skill by moving stuff all around my apartment. I moved the television into my bedroom, the couch to the near wall instead of the far wall because I never liked it where it was and didn't have the energy to move it by myself. I moved plates and stacked them on top of each other on my counter, then poured spoiled milk into the sink. I moved my trash to the dumpster outside, and when I was done, all my chores were done, and my apartment was half clean and half a disaster from my mercurial whims. It was awesome.

"You got it now?" Pete asked, lying on the couch.

"I think I had it about an hour ago. Now I'm just showing off." I closed my eyes and sent the bathroom soap onto the coffee table next to Ivan, who was sitting on the floor with his head in his hands.

"Then we should go," Pete said, getting up with a groan. "Time is wasting."

Ivan rose like an excited puppy. "Finally."

Pete held out his arm. "Grab on."

I put my hand on Pete's clammy one, and Ivan slapped his sweaty paw on top of ours. With a deep breath, Pete snapped his fingers, and we vanished together. I had never traveled with a demon before, and while the feeling was similar to traveling with a pixie, there was a far harsher jolt to it. When we finally rematerialized, we did so with a violent lurch. It took a moment to steady myself after being ripped through the darkness.

We were in the middle of a forest, the trees around us rising into the heavens. The midday sun shone directly overhead. It was unsettling to leave in the dark of night and arrive in the light of day somewhere on the other side of the world. Once, I'd left a perfectly clear summer day and moved to the middle of a hailstorm. That often happened when I traveled between the north and south hemispheres. At least it was nice out, this time.

"I thought it would be colder," I said as I followed Pete through the trees.

"Yeah, I get that, but Russia has seasons, too, ya know. It's not all fur coats and funny hats."

"How far is it?" I asked.

When we crested the hill, I had my answer. In the valley below stood a gleaming white building shaped like a cross and surrounded by trees. Four angels guarded the roof, and a dozen more marched around the compound.

"They really are out in the open about it, aren't they?"

"I wouldn't call the middle of the forest 'out in the open,' but yes," Ivan said, sitting cross-legged on the ground and retrieving the drone from his pack. He also took out the remote control and a television monitor, which he plugged into a battery and turned on. It flickered and, when it finally settled, showed us an image of the Ural Mountains. As Ivan pushed the drone into the air and it soared higher, the picture changed along with the drone's altitude.

"It's working," Pete said. "Brilliant, bring it down."

The drone lowered into Pete's hand. I couldn't get over how big it was. "How is that monstrosity going to avoid detection?"

"Subterfuge," Pete said. He waved his hand over the drone, and it shrank until it was the size of a pea. With the snap of his fingers, the drone disappeared, replaced by a little mosquito.

"Fascinating," I replied.

Pete placed the mosquito in my hand. It was heavier than I expected.

"Don't confuse yourself," Pete said. "The drone is still the same size it was a moment ago. I'm just masking it. Don't put it into too small a crack because it won't fit."

"Got it, and whatever wards are in there won't wipe away your masking?"

Pete looked at Ivan and then back at me. "I hadn't thought of that, but let's hope not."

"Awesome. So glad you are prepared."

Pete pulled a small telescope from his pocket and extended it until it was the length of my arm. He looked into the eyepiece and moved the telescope around until he found what he was searching for. "There it is."

He beckoned for me to look into the telescope. When I did, I saw through the window of the complex. An angel with shaggy brown hair and a mean scowl stared blankly into space. He turned and, for a moment, I thought he was looking right at me, but then he spun and walked away.

"Got it?" Pete said.

I squinted and studied the room for another moment. "Not quite. This isn't quite as easy as moving stuff around my apartment."

"You can do it." Pete slapped me on the back. "I believe in my design of you, if nothing else."

"Thanks."

I spent a minute studying the mosquito from every angle, then looked into the telescope and studied the room once again. I repeated this a few times before I finally took a deep breath and closed my eyes. I constructed what I saw inside my mind and then placed the mosquito into it. There was a crack, and when I opened my eyes, the mosquito was gone.

I turned to Ivan. "Did it work?"

"Seems to have." He was studying the screen in his lap. The video showed the inside of Eden. "This is as close as we've ever come to Eden. We're all gonna be legends after this."

"Take it slow, mate," Pete said. "If we're right, the book will be at the end of this hallway, right in the middle of the building."

"What's it called?" I asked.

"*El Canon de Benedict of Andelusia*, by a Spanish Saint who cataloged the occult in the early 14th century. He's not viewed by anyone as a very important saint because the angels downplayed him. They didn't want anyone to learn about this book."

"I have access to hundreds, thousands of old texts. It's hard to believe this spell is not in any of them."

"And yet…" Pete said, trailing off at the end as we all watched the monitor. The mosquito buzzed through the security measures set up by the angels and down the hallway, passing several angels as it traveled through the bright white walls adorned with ancient paintings of saints and gods. At the end of the hallway, there was a huge glass case.

"That must be it," I shouted. "Oh, I am legit excited. That's unexpected."

"All right, bring it around for a good look. Once we have confirmation, we'll take pictures of the whole room for the pixie to study so we can get in there later."

"Guys, there's a problem," I said, pointing to the image. In the glass case wasn't a book at all but a long piece of wood. I squinted to look at the inscription under it—*last remnant from Noah's Ark.*

"Shit!" Pete said. "They must have moved it. Or maybe it's somewhere else in the museum. We need to buzz around some more and find it before—"

A loud crash preceded the camera being jostled around until it fell from the air and hurtled to the ground. A confused angel, dark-skinned with light hair, knelt and picked up the camera. He cocked his head to one side and the other before a red light went off.

"Uh oh," I said. "We've been found."

Below us in the valley, a dozen angels flew into the air, fanning out in every direction.

"We have to move," Pete said, grabbing on to both of us. As he did, Ivan snapped his fingers, and we vanished back to my room.

***

"What makes you think it's there?" Doctor Dankworth asked after I had debriefed him in his lab. I directed Pete there to discuss where we could go now that our mosquito spy had been found in Eden.

"It's there, mate," Pete said. "Trust us."

Doctor Dankworth shrugged. "I mean, I'm not disagreeing with you, but I'm a scientist, and my job is literally tracking down missing artifacts, so maybe I can be of use to you as a sounding board. Think of it as a thought experiment."

"I hate thought experiments," Ivan said.

"Come on, guys," I replied. "Don't be dicks. We're trying to figure this out together."

"I don't know this guy," Pete said, walking toward Doctor Dankworth with a snarl. "And I don't like him."

"That's neither here nor there," Doctor Dankworth said. "I've only had one interaction with your kind before, and they nearly killed me, so I am not fond of you, but at least I'm still trying to help."

"Fine," Pete said, throwing up his hands. "There is a passage in a seminal angelic text that reads, 'where it all began, we shall find the canon.' We tortured four angels to get that much out of them and have them confirm the passage is accurate."

"Well, that's quite vague," Doctor Dankworth said. "And that doesn't mean Eden, necessarily, either, though it's certainly a possibility."

"What else could 'where it all began' mean?"

Doctor Dankworth stroked his chin. "For one, all human life began in Africa, nowhere near the Urals. Or maybe the actual Eden, which is somewhere in the Fertile Crescent. Or even the Catholic church."

My eyes went wide. "That one. Where did the Catholic church start?"

"That's really tough to answer," Doctor Dankworth said. "So many places. However, if I had to pin it down, I'd say the Cenacle is the site of the first church, and I would think, the founding of the church."

"What the hell is a Cenacle?" Pete said.

I spun to him. "The site of the Last Supper. It makes enough sense, I guess. Plus, it's a place demons wouldn't be able to go. Even if they did, nobody would think that it would be the home of a book that contained a spell about death."

"That is a wild-ass theory," Pete said.

"I mean, the other option is we fight our way through a heavily guarded, angelic compound. Hell, if I'm wrong, we can still do that."

"Whatever," Pete said. "What do you think, Ivan?"

Ivan shrugged. "Do I have to go?"

I shook my head. "Nope."

He leaned against his backpack and closed his eyes. "Well then, it sounds perfect."

***

I waited until it was midnight in Jerusalem before flashing into the Cenacle. I needed time to study pictures of the room anyway so that I didn't get lost in the ether when I teleported. Luckily, Doctor Dankworth had several books on it scattered around his office, depicting its simple columns and the pelicans carved into the tops of them, along with the rest of the room, in great detail. The doctor and I decided there were two spots in the room where somebody would potentially hide a book.

The first was the center of the room, on the spot where Jesus was supposed to have sat during the Last Supper. I took a knife and pried up the square tile, revealing only mud underneath. I settled the tile back into place and moved toward the doorway where Jesus revealed himself to his disciples. Dr. Dankworth and I agreed this was the most likely spot for Jesus to have appeared.

Kneeling down, I scraped around the tile to pry it up from the floor. This time, however, it wasn't mud underneath the tile but a hole. I reached inside the hole, hoping there wasn't a trap, and pulled out a small book, no larger than a calculator. Slowly and carefully, I brought it into the light.

El Canon de Bernard of Alzira.

I had found it.

CHAPTER 10

I spent the better part of the next day copying every page of the book. It was written in an old, dead language I didn't recognize, which meant I couldn't read it, but that didn't mean I was just going to give it to Lilith, especially because I was sure that she was setting me up to eventually betray me. It wouldn't be her fault, necessarily. After all, she was only a demon. Trickery was in her blood.

When I had finished copying the book, I hid the pages behind one of the less used books on the bookshelf in Doctor Dankworth's lab. I was returning home again, finally, though I didn't expect to find Pete and Ivan there, asleep on my couch, spooning each other.

"Adorable," I chuckled at them.

Pete rubbed his eyes as he sat up. "Oh, grow up. Physical contact is nothing to laugh at."

I held up my hands. "Love is love, man. I don't care."

Ivan sat up. "You're pretty immature for a college chick."

"I suppose you're here to bring me to Lilith?" I asked.

Pete stood. "You got that right."

"I remember the way. You aren't as stealthy as you think you are, you know."

"That's why Lilith moves every night. She's never in the same place twice." Pete walked to the door and opened it. "Let's go."

I followed them to the car. "You know, there's something I've always wondered. How do you demons walk around looking all red and sporting horns? Don't people freak out?"

Ivan laughed. "We don't look like this to everyone."

Pete waved his hand in front of his face, and he was suddenly a very pretty black man with bronze eyes and a flashy smile. "Glamour, baby."

"Then how can I see you?" I asked. "How come I can always see you?"

"You have magic," Pete said. "Magic cuts through all the bull. Also, we can reveal ourselves to anyone we want. It's a lot of work to keep up the glamour."

"Plus, sometimes it's just nice to be seen, you know?" Ivan said.

I never thought I would agree with a demon on anything. "Boy, you said a mouthful."

Ivan picked several tickets off the windshield of their black sedan and burned them in his hand, then stepped inside the driver's seat. Pete got in on the other side, and I took the backseat.

We hadn't driven long before entering an opulent neighborhood guarded by a security gate.

Ivan pulled up to the gate, and a security guard bent down. "Who are you here to see?"

"Helen Keller," Ivan replied. "No relation to the famous woman."

The security guard looked at his sheet. "Your name?"

"Ivan Drago. No relation to the Rocky character."

"Ah yes, thank you, Mister Drago. Do you know how to get to Ms. Keller's house?"

He nodded. "I do."

The gate was lifted, and when we were through, I let out a laugh. "Wow, could you be any more obvious?"

"It's okay to be obvious when you have Hellfire on your side," Pete said. "Besides, nobody checks because nobody cares."

"And what are you, then? Pete's Dragon?"

"Frampton. I love that guy. Of course, when we move, we change names and faces. It's easier to pick famous names since we shed them so quickly."

"For powerful beings, it must suck to have to live in the shadows, huh?"

Ivan shrugged. "Better than Hell."

"Oh boy is it," Pete added. "They got no TV, not even pornography, and they're stacked ass to ankles down there. Gonna be a reckoning soon, I reckon."

"What does that mean?" I asked. "Is the Apocalypse really coming? You can tell me. I won't say anything to anybody."

Pete shook his head. "Nothing. It doesn't mean nothing. I'm just rambling."

I slumped back in my seat. "Whatever."

After that, Pete turned and stared out the window, like he didn't have anything to say, or he had said too much. I watched the McMansions pass. I couldn't believe somebody would pay to live in something so generic, but the ways people spent their money always seemed stupid to me. They cared more about status than things that actually mattered, leading to stupid choices like keeping up with the Joneses and drowning in debt to buy a house that's not even worth the balsa wood it's made with, just to keep the façade that they were a somebody.

We turned down a short street with an extra-large house at the bottom of it. It was bigger and even more lavish than the others, which were already four times bigger than a standard home. This house towered over every other building around it and rose to the level of the tree line.

Once we'd parked, Ivan stayed in the car while Pete and I exited. He didn't knock on the red double doors. He simply opened them and walked inside, and I followed. On either side of the foyer were more sets of double doors, these ones white instead of red, and in front of us, a winding staircase led to the second floor.

Pete walked through the second set of double doors. Inside, the room was paneled floor to ceiling with wood, and every surface was lined in books. In the center of the room, Molly sat gagged and tied to a leather chair, dirt and soot covering her face.

"Molly!" I screamed as I rushed over to her.

"She's fine," a dulcet voice cooed from behind me. I turned to see Lilith in the doorway. Her long, red dress shimmered in the light. "Just a little frightened, which is to be expected."

Tears streamed down Molly's face, making paths in the dirt of her face. "I'm going to get you out, okay?" Molly nodded and gave a whimper. "I swear to you."

"Well, then I assume you have the book."

I spun to her and pulled the book out of my back pocket. "Yeah, I have it. Now, let her go."

Lilith held out her hand. "Not yet, first the book."

"That wasn't the deal."

"Sure, it was. Perhaps you should learn to negotiate better or listen more astutely in the future."

"You're changing the terms of our agreement. How demonly of you."

"I am not quite a demon," Lilith said. "And I am not quite a human. I am something better than both and comparable to none, even God himself. Now, hand me the book, or I do promise she will suffer greatly and scream your name in hatred before the end."

Demon trickery. Luckily, I had a copy of the book, and I could do my own research if she double-crossed me. For now, I had to protect Molly.

I handed the book to Lilith. "I couldn't read it."

"Of course not," Lilith replied. "It is written in the oldest language, spoken by the gods, and written by few. You would need a codex to comprehend it, silly girl. That is what makes this book so unique. It truly was dictated by the gods, who came to the author in a vision." She flipped through the book until she stopped on one of the pages. "Ah yes, here we are."

"You speak it?"

"I read and speak every language, the advantage of being here since the beginning. It gives you a lot of time to bone up on all sorts of subjects."

"What does it say, then?" I replied.

"I won't tell you that. I will say that I can get most of these myself. However, a few of these items are…problematic for a demon to acquire. I'm afraid I will need your help."

"What do I need to do?"

"Three ingredients, and by the time you get them, I should have the rest of the items that we need to make this happen."

"What are they?"

She smiled. "Just like that? You were so angry only a moment ago."

"I just want to end this."

"You keep surprising me." Her gaze lingered on me for a moment before she looked back to the book. "So, we need the feather from an angel's wing, a halo from one fallen from grace, and three strands of hair from a cherub."

I nodded. "Well, I know where to get the hair and the feather, but I don't know anything about getting a halo."

"Then, I suppose you should get cracking. While you're getting the first one, we'll work on where to find the other two."

CHAPTER 11

Bang. Bang. Bang.

I knocked hard on Clarice's door. Even a fallen cherub was a cherub, right? So, it should count for the sake of the ingredients. It's not like her DNA changed when she was kicked out of Heaven.

When there was no answer, I knocked again until I heard something smash to the ground behind the door. Several minutes later, the door creaked open. Clarice didn't even bother flying or shining her blinding light. After she opened the door, she fell backward onto the ground. The distinct smell of rotten cheese wafted into my nose.

"Ow," she said, lying turtled on the ground.

"You don't look so good."

"I'm fine," she replied. "I'm just hung over. God, am I hung over. Also, screw God."

I leaned down and helped her to her feet. She grabbed onto the edge of an old table and pulled herself to sit on a fuzzy chair next to it. I closed the door as she popped two aspirin and swallowed them without water.

"What do you want?" she said with a hoarse voice.

I sat down across from her on a plastic yoga ball. "I was going to ask you for three strands of hair from your head, but I'm worried about you. You look even worse than the last time I saw you, which was pretty awful."

Her eyes were yellow, and her skin pasty. She had lost two teeth, and those that remained were significantly more rotted than just a few days before. "I told you I'm fine."

She didn't say anything for a second. "Do you know what it's like to feel the warmth of the gods' light?"

I shook my head. "No."

"It's pure bliss, following you around every second of every day. I didn't realize that until it was stripped from me, and now…now I feel nothing. No matter what I try to fill that hole in my heart with, nothing makes me whole. I just want to die, but that's the cruel joke." She placed her head in her hand. "I can't die. Not at least with any of the crap that exists on this planet. Trust me. I tried. I tried so hard, but I just can't."

"That's horrible," I said. "Isn't there anything you can do?"

"I've prayed. I've groveled. I've begged. There's nothing I can do except hate every minute of every day."

"No," I replied. "I don't believe that." I stood up and held out my hand. "Come on. We're going."

"Where?" she replied.

"Honestly," I said, "does it matter?"

I pulled her up and closed my eyes. I thought of the pub in Scotland where angels and demons mingled together, and when it was real in my mind, I vanished there.

"Ugh," Clarice said when she saw the pub in front of her. "I hate it here. Can we please go?"

"No," I replied. "There are angels inside who will help you."

"Turn their back on me is more like it," Clarice grumbled. "I hate them."

I squeezed her hand tightly and led her at a brisk walk through the forcefield. A sharp tingle rushed through my body as I did, but I didn't lose my grip on Clarice. Once we were through the forcefield, she smiled at me slightly, and we walked toward the door.

The bar wasn't as gregarious as I'd seen it on previous visits, but there was a speckling of demons and angels drinking by themselves in different corners of the bar. "You recognize any of these people?"

Clarice pointed her pudgy finger at an angel with slick back hair. "That one is Patricio, I think."

"Perfect." I stomped over to him, a broad-shouldered angel with short hair, staring down at his beer. "Hi, are you Patricio?"

"I am," he said, in a thick Italian accent. His teeth glistened as he smiled at me. "Who are you?"

"I'm Kimberly." I pointed to Clarice. "This is Clarice. She was kicked out of Heaven, and I need your help to get her back in."

"Ha!" Patricio said, downing the rest of his flagon. "Fat chance. Bacchus is an angry cuss, and if he kicked the pudgy cherub out, there's nothing anyone can do about it except the Metatron, and she is the worst."

"How do I find her?"

He shook his head. "You don't find her. She finds you when she has a message to deliver."

"Not good enough."

Patricio leaned in toward me. "All right, you want to know? She sometimes comes in here, stays low-key, doesn't talk to anyone, but we never know when she'll be here, and try to stay away from her when she does. She is a total buzzkill."

"If you see her, you tell me, okay?"

He smiled. "Yeah, sure. I'd love to watch her destroy you."

"Come on, Clarice," I said. "I need a drink."

***

It felt like we were in the bar forever, but ten or fifty beers later, a cloaked shadow wandered through the door. When I looked at Patricio for confirmation, he nodded. That was her: the Metatron. She walked around the long tables and took a seat next to a group of imps, who scattered at the sight of her.

"Come on," I said, brimming with alcohol-induced confidence.

I pushed off from the bar and stumbled over to the Metatron, sliding in across from her. "You the Metatron?"

The woman pulled back her hood, and she radiated light from the middle of her head, which was one large eye surrounded by a glimmering halo. Most of the angels I'd met were beautiful, but this creature was hideous.

"I am." The sound didn't come from her mouth but inside my head, and every word was painful to hear. "I wish to be alone."

"We need your help." I looked over at Clarice, who was turned away from the light. In fact, everyone in the bar was looking away, and the normal din of the bar had fallen into complete silence.

The voice of the Metatron was in my head again, "No."

My head was splitting from the inside. "You haven't even heard what I have to say."

"You wish me to intercede on the cherub's side." The Metatron stayed silent for a moment. "It is impossible."

"Nothing is impossible."

"This is. Ten more words from me, and your head will explode."

"You can't be so obtuse. This woman is suffering, she needs your help."

"No."

"This is bull," I replied. My lip was warm and wet. I felt blood dripping down my nose. "You suck."

She pulled up her hood. "Go now or die painfully."

I grabbed the sides of my head, trying to keep my brain from ripping apart inside of me.

"Come on," Clarice said. She gave my arm a tug.

I slid out of the chair and walked across the bar, bumping Patricio as I passed. "Your boss is a dick."

"She's not my boss, and you should pity her, honestly. She is the voice of the gods, but she cannot speak to anyone for more than fifty words without killing them. It's quite lonely." He looked down at his drink. "I pity her."

"So, there is nobody to help my friend, then?"

He shook his head. "Not an angel, but demons. Some of them fell from the heavens. I know of one who could help her learn to cope, but it won't be easy."

Clarice shook her head. "I don't want to be a demon."

"Why not? At least they'll accept you. It's a far cry better than filling the hole with drugs and booze."

"Why would you do that?" I said. "You're on different sides."

Patricio laughed. "Sides. That's funny. You look world-weary, but you must truly be naïve to believe something so black and white." He slammed his drink and stood up. "If you want to come, cherub, I am about to go."

Clarice nodded and then turned to me. "Thank you for helping me. Nobody has ever done that before." She reached up and yanked a few strands of thinning hair out of her head. "Here. I don't know what you are doing with this, but you earned it."

I nodded as I coiled the hair in my hand. "Thank you."

"I'll be seeing you around, pixie," Patricio grumbled.

I slid in front of him. "Actually, there is one more thing."

"Of course there is." Patricio sighed. "What is it?"

"Could I trouble you for a feather from your wings?"

Patricio furrowed his brow. "A weird request, but I don't see why not. I'm due for a molt, anyway." He shook his wings, and two feathers fell down on the ground. "There you go."

I reached down and picked it up. "Thank you again."

"It was my great displeasure."

CHAPTER 12

After securing both the angel feather and cherub hair, I made my way to Doctor Dankworth's office. He was hard at work deciphering something, and when I entered, he skittered nervously and packed away what he was working on.

"What are you doing?" I asked.

"N-n-n-nothing," he said, lowering his head to avoid my gaze.

I sighed. "You understand I am a bit of a detective, and you are a horrible liar, right?"

He nodded, pulling out a stack of papers from under the bag where he stashed them. I recognized them immediately as the photocopies I made of the book I gave Lilith.

"It didn't take you very long to find them," I said. "Were you looking for them?"

"No, I swear." He shook his head. "I was trying to find a fourteenth-century English manuscript documenting the life of a knight by his own hand, and this came out. Please forgive me. I wasn't searching, but once I found these pages, I couldn't help myself."

"No, it's okay." I placed my hand on his shoulder. "I'm glad you found them. I wanted to show them to you, but I didn't want to set back your work."

It was true. I needed his help. That was why I didn't bring them to Aziolith's to hide in the stacks of books I already had there. I wanted Doctor Dankworth to see them. I wanted to geek out with him about finding a rare book. I had never been able to talk to anybody about my work, my true work, before, aside from Aziolith, who wasn't really geek as much as brood.

"I've never seen a language like it before. It incorporates parts of Chinese, Hebrew, and Latin, along with some Greek and Russian symbols." His eyes were wide as he pored over the script on the page. "Is this what you were looking for inside the Cenacle?"

I nodded. "It was."

"So you found it."

"I did."

"What language is it?"

"It's ancient. The angels spoke it. Or the gods. At least that's what Lilith told me, though I don't believe anything that comes out of her forked tongue. She has me questioning everything."

"I would like to work on this some more."

"Do what you can. I trust you." I stepped over to him and flipped through the pages before stopping on one toward the end of the book. "I got a quick glance at the page she was looking at, and I think this was it. It's supposed to be the ingredient list and spell we need to contact Thanatos."

"The god of death?"

"I need to talk with him."

"Fascinating." Doctor Dankworth glanced at a picture on his desk of a smiling woman, his wife. "I think we all have words for the god of Death. I'll work on this then, for you."

"Thank you." I pulled the feather and hair out of my pocket and handed it to him. "And can you keep these safe?

You don't come across angel feathers and cherub hair often."

Doctor Dankworth nodded. "Of course, I will."

I placed the items in his hand and closed his fingers around them. "I'm serious. Even Lilith doesn't have access to these items. She said she could get everything else we needed except for these and one more thing."

"What's that?"

"A halo from a fallen one."

"What do you think that means?"

"I don't know, and I'm not keen on finding out, but I don't have much of a choice. Remember, keep these safe. Don't lose them."

"I won't." He smiled. "Your secret is safe with me."

***

Pete and Ivan were waiting for me in my apartment when I got back to it. They had gotten quite comfortable there and were eating Chinese food out of the box and watching Scooby-Doo in my room, their nasty feet up on my bed.

"Are you kidding me?" I scoffed. "Get off my bed."

"All right, all right, but it's rude not to have a TV in your living room." Pete stood up. "What choice did we have?"

"To not be in my apartment at all," I snapped. "I have a phone, you know."

"No, thanks. I don't use phones," Pete said, holding up my phone. "That's how they track you."

"Who?"

"Them," Ivan added.

"You ready to go?" Pete said. "You get what we need?"

I nodded. "I got them, and I hid them."

"Lilith's not gonna like that."

"I don't care. She's keeping my friend hostage, and if she wants what I have, she has to let her go."

Pete shrugged. "I mean, you can bring it up with her. It's no skin off my nuts either way."

Pete brushed past me and threw his Chinese food in the trash can behind me. Ivan did the same, and I followed him out the door. This time Ivan drove us to the middle of town to a sushi restaurant that was closed. Ivan slid the door open and walked inside. Lilith stood behind the counter, wrapping a tuna roll delicately.

"Hello," Lilith said. "That didn't take very long. Did you find anything?"

I nodded. "I found the feather and the hair. All that's left is the halo."

"Very nice." She set down the sushi roll and held out her hand. "Give them to me, then."

I didn't move. "I'm not going to do that. Not until you release Molly."

Lilith placed her hands on the counter and set me with a level stare. "You don't have much leverage. You're the one who wants to call forth Thanatos, not me."

"Oh, that can't be true. I see the look in your eyes when you talk about it. You have business with Thanatos as well. Admit it."

Lilith shrugged. "Very well. I have my own business with him, but I have eternity to find him, and you only have the life of one mortal pixie."

"That will be enough, with or without you," I said. "Where is she, anyway? Where is Molly?"

Lilith methodically cut the sushi roll. "She's fine. I'm actually making this for her. Do you want one? I'm a very good chef. I learned it from Hanaya Yohei himself in 1852, right before his death."

"Who?"

"My dear, my dear, my dear. He is the great-grandfather of sushi, or at least the modern concept of sushi. Seriously, what are they filling your head with at that school of yours?"

"I don't really care who you learned it from. I'm not interested in sushi from you or anyone. I just want Molly back."

Lilith came around the counter. "Funny story about that. Did you know that Molly is part pixie? A teeny tiny part, almost too minuscule to detect, but yes, she is, just a bit. It's fascinating. Pixie blood can be used in all sorts of ways. Perhaps I won't give her back at all."

"That wasn't the deal!" I screeched.

"Sorry, she's quite valuable to me now." Lilith placed the sushi into a box and closed it. "Take some advice: if you want to ensure her safety, don't screw with me. I don't care about the little whelp, but you do. I hold all the cards here for both of your friends—Molly and Julia. The only way you get both of them back is through me." She leaned in before adding, "In other words, I suggest you treat me with the level of respect you reserve for your betters."

Julia had taught me well when to fight and when to capitulate. "I'm sorry. You're right." I bowed my head. "Please forgive me."

Lilith smiled. "That's better. Now, the good news is that we have discovered where you can find a halo. However, it is problematic."

"How problematic?"

"Quite," Ivan said. Lilith shot him a look, and he turned away.

"It's so hard to find good help these days. However, our dear demon friend is right. You see, there is a desert in the middle of Africa where man first walked upright. In this desert is the exact place where human souls fall from grace when they are judged wanting from Saint Peter."

"They literally fall from Heaven?" I asked, blinking my surprise. "I thought it was a metaphor."

"Indeed. Not all of them, of course. Most are judged in Hell, especially given that humans are simply the worst. However, those on the cusp are sent to be judged by St. Peter at the Pearly Gates. When they are inevitably judged wanting—" Lilith pointed her finger to the sky, and with a whistle, it sank until it crashed onto the glass counter. "Well, they are sent down, through the desert, to Hell."

"What does that have to do with the halo?"

"Everything, darling. A halo is assigned to everyone waiting at the pearly gates. It's kind of like taking a ticket at a meat counter. You see, as the unworthy fall through the earth, their halos are knocked off of them, and, in the instant before their unused halos are returned to Heaven, they bounce off the ground. A deft individual such as you would be able to snatch one of them up."

"So you want me to grab a halo off a condemned person falling to Earth at thousands of miles an hour?"

"Yes, that's exactly it."

"All right." I shrugged. "Sounds fun."

"That's the spirit," Lilith said before her face shifted to a scowl. "And Kimberly. Let us not lower ourselves to trickery."

***

Pete snapped us onto the top of a large sand dune overlooking a cracked desert beneath us. Twisted trees stood about, gnarled and decaying, with no leaves and only tiny sprouts for branches.

"Where are we?" I asked as Pete looked out over the horizon.

"Don't worry about that," he said. He pulled a pair of sunglasses from his pocket and handed them to me. "Put these on."

I slid the glasses over my nose, and the whole desert went dark except for a thin blue stream of light that connected the sky to the ground. Inside the stream, the light swirled in eddies.

"Do you see it?" Pete asked.

"Do you mean the stream of light? Because if so, then yes."

"Good. Watch for a second, and you should get a pretty good show. Sometimes I come out here just to watch."

"What am I sup—"

But then I saw it, falling almost faster than I could note. It was a man, and his screams filled my ears as he fell through the ground and vanished into the depths of Hell. As he did, I saw something shiny shimmer in the light and then disappear a moment later.

"Did you see it?"

"I saw it. I saw it. That's horrible, and yet somehow also beautiful. What was that?"

"Just another damn damned soul," Ivan replied.

As he spoke, another soul fell from Heaven. This time it was a woman, clawing at the sky, trying to find some way to halt her fate. Just like the man, she fell through the ground. I tried to focus on the ground this time, and I could make out a golden halo. Less than a second after it happened, the halo was gone.

"That's not much time," I said. "It's less than a second."

Pete nodded. "Yeah, and you don't know which way the halo will bounce. On top of that, you can't touch the stream, or your soul will be sucked in just like the damned. You must be quick and precise. Luckily, you have a lot of chances because Heaven sends quite a bit of their people down to us. It's almost like they don't take anybody these days. You all must have done something bad to piss god off."

"Probably killing his son," Ivan grunted.

"Oh yeah," Pete replied. "That would do it." He slapped me on the back. "Anyway, good luck with that."

I growled at him before unfurling my wings and floating down onto the cracked, desert floor. As I made my way to the stream, another scream echoed out, ending when the soul vanished into the ground. I leaped forward and tried to catch the halo, but it bounced out of my reach. I was too close to the stream to maneuver around it safely. No way was I risking my immortal soul.

I sat back to watch the stream up close and determine where the halos most often bounced, then moved my position without having to risk touching the stream. The first halo bounced on the other side of the stream, too far for me to reach. The souls came like water from a sieve. They dropped every minute, and my heart cried out to them. To have been so close to Heaven and then lose it was worse than never being near it at all.

Another five fell to Hell, and I wondered if any who were judged got through the eye of the needle. Finally, one halo bounced close enough that I could reach out and pull it toward me. I expected it to vanish, but it stayed solid in my hand, cool to the touch.

Before I could stand, another soul fell to the earth, and the halo bounced right into my lap. I grabbed it quickly. Now, I had a backup, and if Lilith double-crossed me as I knew she would, I might be able to reconstruct the spell. I tucked the second halo into my pants, then stood up and turned to Pete and Ivan, who were watching me from the top of the dune.

"I got it!" I shouted, waving the halo in the air.

CHAPTER 13

When we returned to the sushi restaurant, it was empty except for a confused-looking kitchen sweep preparing for the day. Pete and Ivan led me outside, and we drove out of town. The halo under my shirt jammed against me, so I sat straighter than I normally did.

"Why are you sitting like that?" Pete said.

I twisted myself side to side. "This seat is really uncomfortable. Why are we even driving when you can snap anywhere?"

"You humans are so impatient," Pete replied. "Everything had to come quickly to you. Maybe we like driving. Did you ever think of that? Helps us think."

"Waste of time."

"When you have all the time in the world, wasting a little bit of it isn't that big a deal. No sense in spending eternity always in a rush everywhere. It's just mortal chumps who have to worry about things like aging and time."

I rolled my eyes. "Whatever."

I stayed silent the rest of our ride to a large lake I'd never been to before. Ivan turned up a rocky path and led us to a boat house in the middle of a forest. It was taller than the tree line and wide, painted blue with a large hangar door, which Ivan led me through. Lilith had created a summoning circle on the floor, surrounded by a pungent incense that smelled like my grandmother's floral potpourri.

"Did you find it?" Lilith asked softly. Behind her, a twenty-foot fishing boat sat in the water, rising and falling with the lapping of the water.

I held up the halo. "I have it. Where's Molly?"

Lilith snapped her fingers, and a fat, slovenly demon ambled out behind a skein of canoes carrying Molly in his disgusting hands. He pushed her forward, and she fell at my feet.

"Are you okay?"

She shook her head.

"I mean, I know you're not okay, given the circumstances, but did they hurt you?"

She shook her head.

"Good. I'm going to get you out of here now."

"I told you that she would be fine," Lilith said. "You need to learn to trust better. Now, give me the halo."

I set my jaw. "Promise me you'll let her go."

"I told you I would."

"Promise me again."

She rolled her eyes. "Fine, I promise. My goodness, you are touchy."

"Promise me you will let her go when I give you the halo."

"I can't do that. What's to stop you from leaving?"

"You said it yourself. I want to meet Death, and you are going to bring him to me. Why would I do anything to jeopardize that?"

Lilith thought for a moment. "Okay. You give me the halo, and I will let her go, and then you will bring me the other ingredients. Deal?"

"That's a deal."

I walked over to her and handed her the halo. She smiled as she felt it, but within three seconds, it started to sizzle, and she was forced to drop it. "Pity. Very well." She waved her hand at me. "Take her."

I turned to Molly and grabbed her in my arms. "Don't vomit on me, okay?"

I closed my eyes and thought of Doctor Dankworth's office, and once it was real in my mind, I vanished. Dankworth screamed as he jumped in his chair at the sight of us.

He pressed his hand to his chest. "Jesus Christ. I will never get used to that."

I went behind Molly's head and unknotted her gag. When it was free, she collapsed into my arms, crying. "Oh my god. Oh my god. What just happened?"

"It's okay," I said, stroking her nappy hair. "You're safe now. I'm so sorry. I'm sorry for putting you through that. I'm so sorry."

"Seriously, what was that?" Molly hiccupped a few times. "What in God's name was that?"

I cupped her face in my hands. "Hey, I swear to you I will tell you everything when this is all done, but I have a date with a demon, so for now, just stay with Doctor Dankworth, okay? Promise me you won't leave here for any reason. It's really, really important."

She nodded, staring off at nothing. "I promise. I won't move."

I stood up. "Good."

"I assume it went well?" Doctor Dankworth said.

I pulled out the halo with a smile. "Yeah, good enough. I need you to hold onto this for me."

"What is it?"

"Insurance, in case Lilith screws me over again. Have you had any success decoding the ingredients?"

Doctor Dankworth shook his head. "No. Not yet, but I'm still trying. It's only been a couple of hours, and we don't have a Rosetta Stone, so it could take years."

"All right, well, keep trying." I held out my hands. "Give me the feather and the hair."

Doctor Dankworth took the items from his bag and handed them to me.

"Good. Keep her safe. I just found out that she has a little bit of pixie in her, so she's going to have a lot to explain when I get back. Until then, try to get her mind off all this."

He looked at Molly, who was still staring into the middle distance. "I'll do what I can."

***

I reappeared in the boathouse. The lights were dim, and except for the lights from the candles, I couldn't see much, especially since my eyes were still adjusting to the dark. Lilith sat in the center of the circle, cross-legged at one end of a five-pointed star she had painted on the floor. The runes for death, grief, love, immortality, hope, and life were marked in blood at each point. Five hooded demons sat on each of the star's five points with a nauseating incense wafting from a glass jar between them. As I walked forward, another demon slid and barricaded the hangar door.

"Are you ready?" she said, weaving a strand of cherub hair around the halo I gave her earlier.

"Absolutely not," I replied, walking forward. "Let's do it anyway."

"That's the spirit." Lilith used another strand of cherub hair to suspend the feather between them. When she was done, she hung the halo above a black cauldron she'd set in the center, then moved back to the fifth point on the circle. "We only have one chance at this. The halo will break the seal, and the other ingredients will call Death, who will be bound to this place until the hair breaks and drops the feather into the brew, sending him back beyond the void for an eternity."

"Let's hope this works."

"We'll know soon enough. The feather and hair call to the halo and power it. It all works together. Let us begin."

Lilith took a breath. "*Azhalyi Vordu Mesvop Iluuu*," she chanted.

After she repeated herself three times, the other demons opened their mouths and chanted along with her. "*Azhalyi Vordu Mesvop Iluuu. Azhalyi Vordu Mesvop Iluuu. Azhalyi Vordu Mesvop Iluuu.*"

The halo began vibrating slightly. Lilith opened her eyes. "Now, my child. Cut yourself and add a drop of your blood to the brew."

"Excuse me?" I said.

"It is the final ingredient. The blood of a pixie. As I told you, it had all sorts of uses, including raising Death itself."

Of course, she would wait until the last minute to tell me when I'd already invested too much to say no. I shook my head. *What did I care about a couple of drops of my blood anyway?*

I stepped into the circle and used a dagger from my belt to prick the side of my wrist. Anybody who cut their palm was stupid. Blood could come from anywhere on your body, and if you used your palm, you would have problems using your hand for weeks.

Wincing, I held my wound over the cauldron while the demons and Lilith chanted around me. The blood sizzled as it dropped into the brew, and the putrid stench of death filled my nostrils.

"Is that enough?" I asked.

"Perfect."

"*Azhalyi Vordu Mesvop Iluuu,*" the group chanted. "*Azhalyi Vordu Mesvop Iluuu. Azhalyi Vordu Mesvop Iluuu. Azhalyi Vordu Mesvop Iluuu.*"

The halo shook and began to glow, but then something happened I didn't expect. It cracked, popped, and sizzled until it fell onto the ground, black and tarred.

I had ripped the bottom of my shirt and was wrapping it around my wrist to stop the bleeding. I looked up when I heard the halo. "What happened?"

Lilith growled. "Somebody has been lying to me."

"Not about the halo, boss," Pete said. "We saw her grab it ourselves."

Lilith stood up. "Then about the others. Where are the real feather and hair?"

"I don't—I don't understand," I said, moving backward as the throng of demons rushed to gather around me. I tried to vanish, but I was unable to do so.

"You're not going anywhere," Lilith said. "I warded this place in case you double-crossed me."

"Why would I double-cross you?" I shouted. "You're the one who's been double-crossing me!"

"Exactly!" Lilith said with a snap. "That's what I do. You are going to pay for this betrayal!"

"Listen, I know what you think—but I didn't do this. It doesn't make any sense…The only person I told was—"

And then it flooded back to me—the reason why Doctor Dankworth never stopped working. I'd never known his wife because I came to the school after she had died from cancer, but I heard that Doctor Dankworth used to be a funny man, full of life. I never knew that person. I only knew the shell of a man. If the stories were true, I'd given him the perfect way to save his wife—and the materials.

"Don't do anything stupid…" I said, but it was too late. The demons lunged at me. I leaped into the air to avoid them. This would be a perfect time to have pixie dust, but I had left it at home, lulled into comfort by the idiots Pete and Ivan, though perhaps they were closet geniuses in disguise.

With the wards on the boathouse, I couldn't teleport at all, which meant I needed to get outside, but the doors were locked and boarded. Pete lunged toward me, and I dug a dagger into his brain. He wasn't dead, but he would wake up in Hell with a splitting headache.

"My baby!" Lilith screamed. "You will pay for that."

"I don't want to fight you," I said. "Just let me go, and I can make this right."

"Yeah, right," Lilith growled. "Ivan, attack!"

Ivan was more plodding than Pete and oafishly uncoordinated, but his long arms allowed him to grab at me without getting into any danger of my daggers. The other two demons flanked him. I couldn't let them circle me. I kicked off the ground and flew above them.

Lilith shot fire from her mouth, and I weaved through the air to dodge it. The whole place was heating up something fierce. I had to get out. When her fire died down, I saw my opening. There was a bit of light coming in from under the water in the middle of the boathouse. I could get out through the water.

I dove under the water and swam to the other side, just as the demons pushed through the boathouse door and spotted me. It didn't matter because I was free of the wards. Before they could react, I closed my eyes, imagined Doctor Dankworth's office, and vanished.

CHAPTER 14

I reappeared in Doctor Dankworth's office, which was empty. *Of course, he was gone.* I searched the desk and came across a note on Dankworth's desk.

Kimberly,

I'm sorry. If you survive, just know that I'm sorry. I know you understand the pain of loss and how it makes you do crazy things.

This is my crazy thing.

-Dr. D

That son of a bitch. I crumpled up the note and threw it in the wastepaper basket. Not only did he betray my trust, but he stole my one chance to save Julia.

Wait. *Where was Molly?*

Shit. He knew she had pixie blood coursing through her veins. He wouldn't bring an innocent into all of this, would he? *Of course, he would.*

If Molly were anywhere, she would be sleeping off her confinement. I flashed and reappeared in our apartment. Every inch of the place looked like it had gone through a wood chipper. I heard the growls from my bedroom, and when I spun to address them, Ivan lumbered toward me.

"Wait!" I said, holding out my arms. "I'm not the enemy here."

"You killed my Pete!" he roared. "Far as I'm concerned, you will always be my enemy."

I spun out of the way and pulled out my daggers as he barreled right past me. "You don't have to do this."

"I know I don't have to," Ivan said with a toothless grin. "I get to."

He rushed me again. As he closed in, I ducked and slid, ramming my dagger deep into his gut and spinning around to lodge the other one deep into his neck. When I pulled the second dagger out, it was covered in green blood, and Ivan was stumbling mightily, but he wouldn't fall.

"It's over," I said.

"Never!"

He staggered toward me, and I leaped aside, lodging my dagger deep into his eye. He fell to the ground, dead. I pulled the daggers out and sighed, grabbing a dirty rag from the kitchen to wipe them clean.

"You definitely won't get your security deposit back now," Lilith grumbled, walking into the apartment as if she owned the place.

"I can fix this," I said.

She nodded. "I know. I'm afraid I might have been a bit hasty with you before. I am a bit hot-headed. Side effect of being part demon. I've had time to think about it, and I believe you are correct. You would have never jeopardized your chance to save your mentor. You have an outmoded sense of loyalty to her that both fascinates and confuses me."

"I owe her my life, many times over," I replied. "It is the least I could do."

Lilith raised a finger to make her point. "That's not true. The least you could do is nothing. I know because I come across it every day. People who want something for nothing, who are willing to sell their immortal soul to take the easy way out of something, and yet, here you are, doing the hard thing."

"Does this mean you aren't going to kill me?"

"I'm thinking about it," Lilith said, looking around. "It would be so easy to burn this whole place to the ground with you in it, to make it my life's mission that you never sleep until I hunted you down." She stopped. "And yet, I find myself drawn to you in an odd way. If I had a dozen like you, I could take over the world. Of course, then I would have to run the world, and where's the fun in that? So…no. I think, for now, I will keep you alive, as long as you tell me who has my ingredients."

"My professor, Doctor Dankworth. He's trying to save his wife. It's kind of sweet—no, it's not. He's terrible, and the worst thing is I don't know where he is, or where he's going to go, just what he plans to do."

"Hrm. Well, magic leaves a trail, and great magic leaves a signature. The minute he tries to use it, then we will know where he is."

"What is it?" I asked. "What could you possibly want?"

Lilith sighed. "I want to die. I want the choice to die. Not be sent to Hell or Heaven. Just…die and vanish from the universe. It's not fair that I have to sit and watch it all go by, to watch those I care about wither away. I just want to be done with the ceaseless agony of existence."

"I'm sorry. I never thought…"

"That immortality was a curse? Oh, it is. I have long ago passed the interesting part of a long life and the boring part, and now, nothing interests me. Utter banality at every turn. This was the first time I was excited for something in a century…or even more. It's hard to tell, the years all blend together, and all I have are demons for company."

I placed my hand on hers. "That must be hard."

She looked at me, tears welling in her eyes. "It really is. You know I was in love once, maybe twice, but they died like mortals do, and I was left to carry on with only their memories. You can only take so much pain until you completely shut it off, you know."

I shook my head. "I don't know. I would love to shut off the pain for even a second, but it is there, waiting for me, when I sleep, when I wake, when I move. It is there, the ache."

She smiled at me. "We are both cursed, it would seem."

"We've got to end this before Doctor Dankworth ruins it for both of us."

"I have an idea," Lilith said. "Though it's a bit crazy."

"I don't think we have many other options than crazy right now," I replied with a dry chuckle. "Unless we want to wait until the portal is open."

"No. We certainly don't want that." Lilith sniffed. "My idea is pretty simple. Do you remember when Pete and Ivan taught you how to manipulate objects with your powers?"

"Yes." I nodded. "Of course."

"Theoretically, if you can imagine the item you are trying to find, you should be able to see where it is, just as easily as you could send something to another location. You can't bring it back, but perhaps we would be able to see where the halo is right now, and that would give us some idea of where he's headed."

"It's as good as any stupid plan we have."

"I assume you have your pixie dust?" Lilith asked.

I patted the pouch on my hip. "I am never dealing with you again without having it."

Lilith laughed, her teeth showing. "I have been alive long enough never to say the word never."

The two of us flashed out of my apartment and reappeared in Doctor Dankworth's office.

"Where were you when you handed him the halo?" Lilith asked.

I pointed to the stool where Doctor Dankworth had been sitting.

"And what did he do with it?"

I thought backward. "He spun on his chair and placed the halo down on the desk." I walked toward the desk and placed my hand on it. "Right here."

"Okay," she nodded, staring at the spot. "This is all you. Use the dust."

I pulled out a pinch of the dust and rubbed it on my gums. The tingling came immediately, and my hands shook as the dust began coursing through my whole body.

"Ready," I said.

Lilith took a deep breath. "Look inside yourself and feel the remnants of the halo. Envision it in your brain and reach out to it with your essence."

I tried to reconstruct the halo from memory, but for something so simple, it was impossible to recall in my memory.

"Why can't I picture it?" I asked.

"Angelic trickery," Lilith said. "Try harder. It's in there, just shrouded."

I stared at the spot where the halo once was, imagined myself spinning my fingers around it. When neither of those things worked, I searched my memory for anywhere else I might have had the halo. I touched my hand to a dozen different places on the table and even into the air around it, but I felt nothing.

"I'm sorry," I finally said. "This is not working."

Lilith's eyes narrowed, and she bit her lip. "Perhaps we need to take a less magical route to this. Do you know where Doctor Dankworth lives?"

I had only been to Doctor Dankworth's house twice before, both times to deliver some papers for grading, but I remembered it well. It was a gray house with white shutters and columns on either side of the yellow door. Aside from the door, it was completely non-descript. Doctor Dankworth once told me his wife had chosen the color because she knew it would piss off his uptight neighbors.

I flashed us to the front of Doctor Dankworth's house, and after trying the locked door, I went to the window and studied the inside. I grabbed Lilith's hand before flashing into the living room.

The house was dingy and dusty, as if nobody had been there in months. I walked from the living room to the kitchen, where the smell of rotten food was palpable.

"Um, Kimberly, my love. If you could come this way," Lilith said from the other room.

I found her in a room across the hall, which seemed to act as Doctor Dankworth's study. There were books strewn around the floor and papers piled high on every surface. Unlike the rest of the house, this room looked lived in. There was a pillow and blanket on the floor.

Lilith was pointing to a framed picture on the wall. It was Doctor Dankworth, much younger, holding a blushing, brown-haired bride around the waist. Behind them had a sign that read First Episcopal Church of Albuquerque. They both looked so happy.

"That has to be it. Let's go."

I took Lilith's hand, and we vanished. Being hopped up on dust was incredible. I barely looked at the photo for five seconds before it appeared in my brain. I liked not having to think too hard before constructing the church in my mind.

The building was small and white, nothing interesting or auspicious about it at all. Still, it had a charm all its own. If I wanted to bring my wife back, I could see doing worse than that church.

I pulled out my daggers and held them at my sides. "Be ready for anything," I said, walking to the front door.

"Darling, I always am."

I kicked open the front door…and found nothing—no Doctor Dankworth. No spells. No ingredients. Nothing.

"No!" I said. "He has to be here. He has to—" And then an idea flashed in front of my eyes. "No. Of course, he wouldn't go here. His wife isn't here. She's—"

"Buried somewhere else. We have to find out where."

CHAPTER 15

I flashed inside the local library and found the wife's obituary in the public records. It was after hours, but 24/7 access was one of the advantages of having magical powers.

Doctor Dankworth's wife was buried in a cemetery two miles from the school. Lilith and I flashed there once we had the address, and I had studied a few pictures of the cemetery. The minute we appeared, a magical chill in the air cut up and down my spine.

Lilith breathed deeply. "Yes, there is great magic here."

As we stood gathering our bearings, a blue light shot into the air like a beacon on the other side of the cemetery. Its source was hidden by the funeral parlor, but I knew it was Doctor Dankworth, and he had begun the spell. "Oh, no."

Lilith rushed forward, and I leaped into the air after her. On the other side of the funeral parlor, I saw the nexus of the bright light and a familiar, squat man sitting cross-legged next to the summoning circle, surrounded by gravestones.

"He doesn't have any help!" Lilith said. "He can't hope to contain Death by himself."

I fluttered my wings as fast as I could until I caught up with Doctor Dankworth. "Hey! What do you think you're doing?"

Doctor Dankworth broke his concentration and turned to me. "Go away, child!"

"How did you even decode this?"

"The cipher!" he said, his eyes flashing. "I had it the whole time."

"You lied to me."

"You did the same, all these years. Now, go away. It's too late to stop me!"

"I'll say!" Lilith said. "You're going to let Death free from his prison to wreak havoc on the universe!"

"No!" he snapped. "You're wrong! The text says—"

"I know what the goddamn text says!" Lilith screamed. "As the only person here who has read the text in its original form, I can tell you that at least four are needed to contain the god of Death from breaking the circle. Why do you think cults work together? Only their combined power can contain what they hope to summon."

"No," Doctor Dankworth said. "It can't be. I was so careful!"

"How careful could you be rushing through the translation in an afternoon?" I asked. "You got careless and sloppy! If you had just waited, I could have helped you."

"I couldn't wait. Every minute without Evelyn is torture."

"That's so selfish, you pathetic asshole!" I grabbed my hair at the temples.

"It's too late to yell about this now," Lilith said. "Sit down, and we will try to contain Death as best we can."

I craned my neck past the graves and saw Molly lying on the ground. "Molly! What have you done to her?"

"Nothing!" Doctor Dankworth shrugged. "I only needed a drop of her blood. I'm not a monster."

I flew over to Molly and knelt next to her. "Molly…Molly. Are you okay?"

She blinked her eyes and looked up at me. "I think so. I just want to go home. Can we please go home?"

I pulled her to her feet. "Soon, but we need your help."

"What do you need me to do?" she asked, then stopped when she saw Lilith. "YOU!"

"I know you hate me, girl," Lilith said. "But we need your help, or the universe is screwed."

"I can't—"

I grabbed Molly's face and turned it toward me. "We need you. Please, just trust me and say okay."

"I shouldn't trust you, but I do." She nodded. "Okay."

I brought her over to the summoning circle and sat her down. "Just sit here and repeat after me." I turned to Lilith. "What is the thing we're saying?"

"*Azhalyi Vordu Mesvop Iluuu,*" Lilith said.

I inched closer to the point of the star. "Just say *Azhalyi Vordu Mesvop Iluuu.* Close your eyes and your ears. Act like you're not here, okay?"

"And then this will be over?" Molly asked.

"I promise," I said, though I was unsure how I could enforce such a statement. "I promise."

"*Azhalyi Vordu Mesvop Iluuu,*" Molly said.

I shot daggers from my eyes as I stared at the doctor. "Now you."

"*Azhalyi Vordu Mesvop Iluuu,*" Doctor Dankworth said.

"*Azhalyi Vordu Mesvop Iluuu*," Lilith added her voice. "When Death appears, I will handle it. Does everyone understand?"

I nodded. "Yes."

"I can't—" Doctor Dankworth started.

Lilith reached out and grabbed him by the throat. "You should be dead. You only still live because you need to help us fix your monumental screwup, so if you want to keep living, then I suggest the next words out of your mouth are *Azhalyi Vordu Mesvop Iluuu* and nothing else. Got it?"

Doctor Dankworth gulped. "*Azhalyi Vordu Mesvop Iluuu*."

"That's better."

"*Azhalyi Vordu Mesvop Iluuu*," I added my voice to the chorus of the others. "*Azhalyi Vordu Mesvop Iluuu*."

The blue light shooting into the air contorted, widening into an oblong oval as the power of the spell collapsed upon itself over the black cauldron feeding it. The light from the halo glowed brightly and shook.

There was a crackling from the portal, and a shadow appeared in the blue light. A cloaked figure pushed its way out of the oval and appeared in front of us. Two glowing yellow eyes were all that emanated from under the sackcloth robe. "Who dares summon Death?" The voice was hoarse and dry.

Lilith held herself straight and powerful, shoulders back and eyes forward. "It is I, Lilith, mother of demons, who calls to you."

"Hrm, Lilith. Of course, you would be so bold as to contact me. I had hoped it was my father or mother, breaking my confinement and allowing me to return once again back into the universe, but now that I see that it was nothing of the sort, I assume you want something, then, Mother of Demons."

"We all do!" Doctor Dankworth shouted.

"Shut up!" Lilith said, but it was too late. Death turned to Doctor Dankworth, his tattered robes sliding across the ground. "And what is it that you desire, human, so bold as to call forth a god?"

Doctor Dankworth looked over at Lilith and then to me for validation but found none in either of us. "I wish for you to raise my wife from the grave and bring her back to me."

"Interesting," Death posited. "And we sit above her grave, yes?"

Doctor Dankworth nodded. "Yes, we do."

"I feel her under me, her body slowly decaying, and her soul in the underworld, waiting for judgment. If I brought her to you, it would cause a rift that could never be repaired between the living and the dead, and even then, she would live a life much worse than death."

"Then what good are you?" Doctor Dankworth said through his tears. "What good are you if you can't reunite me with the one I love?"

Thanatos shook his hood. "I did not say I could not reunite you. I cannot bring her to you. However, if you wish, I can send you to her."

Doctor Dankworth thought for a moment and then nodded. "Yes, I wish that, then."

"Are you sure?" Thanatos asked. "You will be tortured for your sins, and there is no guarantee you will wind up together in the pits of Hell."

Doctor Dankworth was blubbering. "I am tortured for as long as I am here. So yes, send me to her."

"No, Doctor! That's stupid. Don't—"

Doctor Dankworth held up his hand. "You have never been in love, so you will not understand." He looked up at Death. "Do it."

Coward.

Thanatos picked up his rail-thin fingers and touched Doctor Dankworth. The doctor fell back, eyes open, dead. "It is done."

I couldn't cry. I couldn't move. All I could do was watch as Thanatos turned to Lilith.

"He will remain contained as long as we do not break the circle," she said.

Thanatos inched closer to Lilith, stopping inches from her face. "And what of you, Mother of Demons? What do you wish from Death?"

Lilith's eyes were blazing. "I wish for you to grant me the same as you gave to him. Kill me. Let me die. I have lived too long and have dealt with too much tragedy."

Death sighed. "I cannot, and more, I will not do that, not for you. The gods are cruel, and I cannot go against Bacchus's wish to see you suffer for taking sides against him. The only one who can kill you is him. I am powerless."

"You aren't powerless. You are spineless, just like every other god I've ever met. What do you care about the rule of the gods?" Lilith barked. "Their divine wisdom brought you to this place and trapped you for all eternity."

"Not all eternity," Thanatos replied. "Just for a while longer now. Soon there will be a reckoning, and I promise you will want to be on this side of the divide when it happens."

"Shouldn't that be my choice!" Lilith threw her hands in the air. "Shouldn't I be able to choose the manner and time of my demise?"

"Wouldn't it be nice if it were so?" Death turned from Lilith to me. "And what of you? Do you want as childish a wish as the others?"

"I fear with what I have heard, you will not be able to help me. It's my mentor, Julia Freeman. She was sent to Hell. I wish for her to come back as a ghost, here, and to stop her torment."

Death chuckled, which I hadn't expected. "Yes, I see her. I could do this for you, but your friend is happy now, or at least as happy as one can be in Hell. She is surrounded by family and has work and a full belly. Do you wish her to feel the emptiness of being a ghost instead of allowing her an ounce of happiness?"

"It can't be!" I said. "She's in Hell. She can't be happy."

"I do not speak falsehoods, little one. I swear what I say is true. Are you the one who determines what is Hell for another? The underworld is not good or bad. It has a function, one which you will see in time, should you live long enough."

"What does that mean?"

Death breathed deeply. "I smell a great destiny in you, should you live long enough to see it. You will survive a great many things and become a vessel for—I have said too much. I will not give you this gift you seek. However, I can do you a favor."

"What other favor would I want from you?"

"I promise that if you live long enough, you will find your beloved friend again. I can tell you that without my kiss, you will be dead in a year, and then you will have to deal with your own version of Hell. However, if you accept my kiss, you will live forever, and in that time, you will see a great many things, including your friend."

"How can you be so sure?" I said.

"Death is the end of everything. As such, I have a great many powers. I see my own end in your eyes, and I am intrigued. I also see your friend in your eyes, but down a path only you could take. If you choose to die, then I see nothing but pain for you and the universe. Of this, I swear, you will see her again if and only if you accept my kiss. As my blessed, you will live longer than Lilith until the end of all time."

"Don't do it," Lilith said. "It's a trick. A dirty trick."

"I do not play at tricks," Thanatos said softly. "There is no need. Death always wins in the end." The blue light flickered above him as the halo vibrated louder, the angel's hair loosening. "Make your choice. I fear you have little time."

"I accept."

Death pulled back his hood to reveal a gaunt, pale white face, and his yellow eyes spiraled and swirled. He pressed his lips against mine, and I felt a jolt of power surge through me. When he was finished, he turned to Molly. "And what of you? What do you wish of Death?"

Molly shook her head. "I just want to go home."

Death laughed an uproarious laugh. "That is rich. I appreciate you."

The hair that protected the feather snapped, and the halo fell to Earth. A moment later, the feather fell into the cauldron, and the portal fizzed and popped.

"I look forward to our next encounter. You have given me much to discuss with my brothers and sisters."

Death pulled back into the portal, and a second later, it imploded on itself, vanishing. We were alone in the darkness.

"You made a mistake," Lilith said, looking at me with traces of anger and sadness on her face.

"It was mine to make," I replied, taking Molly by the hand.

"What should we do with him?" Molly pointed to Doctor Dankworth.

"I say leave him," Lilith said. "He's already in a cemetery. What better place to deal with him?"

"Are we good?" I said to Lilith. "Or should I always be looking over my shoulder?"

Lilith smiled. "We are…square, as they say. This life is long and now longer for you. It will be nice to have somebody else to talk with about it. If you ever need me…well, you know how to find me."

I frowned. "No, I don't."

Lilith smiled. "Well, I will have to be on the lookout, then." She snapped her fingers, and she was gone.

"This has been a weird couple of days," Molly said. "Can you please tell me what just happened?"

I smiled. "Yes, I suppose I should, huh? How about we get some food in you, first? When was the last time you ate?"

Molly thought. "I can't even remember. Lilith brought me some sushi. It was pretty good."

"I was thinking pie."

"Pie is good."

EPILOGUE

"How will I be able to tell the kelpie?" Molly asked as we flew over Tilago Lake. She had been working with me every night for six months until she could use her wings on command. She still needed pixie dust to disappear, but she was making great progress.

"Look at their feet. They retain their horse-like feet even when they turn into human form."

"And you really think it's a kelpie that's been terrorizing campers up here?"

"It's not terrorizing," I said. "This is her home, and the campers are trashing it. If anything, she's defending it, and a 200-year-old water spirit isn't going to react with civility. They prefer quiet lakes for a reason. They aren't good with people."

Molly looked out at the lake. "There!"

She flew down impulsively. I had to chuckle because it was exactly what I would have done in my youth and did when I first learned of my powers. I thought I was invincible, then. Working with Molly gave me a new respect for Julia to train a new pixie with attitude and confidence in spades.

"Wait for me!" I called out.

I dove faster than Molly, who was still only flying at sixty percent of her capacity. By the time I was down on the ground, I saw a naked woman, gaunt, pale, and naked, walking seductively up to two young men who couldn't have been much older than Molly and me.

"Stop!" I shouted at the kelpie. She turned, and I got a good look at her hooved feet. "You don't have to do this."

"I don't do it out of obligation but out of enjoyment."

She lunged at the boys, but Molly slammed into her at full speed, knocking her into a large rock.

"What is going on here?" one of the men said.

"Just stay there and look pretty, okay?" I pulled out my daggers. "There is a better way."

"These two creatures are leeches," the Kelpie hissed. "They threw a can of used motor oil into my beautiful lake. They deserve everything they get!"

"Hey!" the second man said. "We're not hurting anyone! It's just oil."

"Shut up!" Molly screamed, blocking the kelpie from the campers. "Or I will let this one tear you apart."

"As if you could stop me," the kelpie said.

"What's your name?" I asked.

"I know better than that," the kelpie said, regarding me with a cool look. "If I tell you my name, you have power over me."

"Fine," I said. "Don't tell me, but I can't let you hurt these people."

"If you stop me, pixie, then you betray your own kind."

"No, I'm not betraying you. I wouldn't be here if I weren't trying to help you. They are sending a military unit to find you and capture you. We're doing you a favor. If you go now and stay out of sight and stop killing people, they won't find you. If you don't give it up, we can't protect you, and you can't protect any lakes at all. You cannot kill these two."

"Fine," the kelpie said. "You're no fun. They still need to be taught a lesson, though."

"I like that idea," Molly said. "What if we just scare the piss out of them so bad, they never come back?"

The kelpie sighed. "It's not ideal, but I suppose I can pull back…a bit."

"A wise decision." I nodded at Molly, who moved out of the way. "Go have your fun with those two."

The kelpie lunged forward, and the two men screamed as they tried to escape. Molly turned to me. "How long do we let her go like this?"

"Five minutes?" I replied.

She looked down at her watch. "This should be fun."

It was nice to have somebody else to share my travels with and all my secrets. I felt a duty to impart as much to Molly as possible, so she could help train the next generation and the generation after that. I grabbed her hand and intertwined her fingers with mine while the kelpie scared the piss out of those two college kids. For a moment, all was right with the world. I knew it wouldn't stay that way, but I wanted to enjoy every stupid minute of it while it lasted.

BOOK 2

"Death's Return"

CHAPTER 1

London was one of my favorite cities on the planet, especially at night. I could sit high atop Big Ben and watch the cars drive across Westminster Bridge, looking out over the Thames, forever. Since I'd become immortal, I literally could…if there wasn't work to do that needed my immediate attention.

"It's time," Molly said as she floated down and sat next to me. She was still as beautiful at 51 as she was at 21. Her skin sagged around her eyes, and deep bags formed under them, grooved by time and experience. I loved her face. Fighting demons and saving fairy folk kept her in good shape, but I didn't care much about her physique. Her soft heart still beat for me and mine for her, which was all that really mattered.

I took one last look at the shimmering lights across the Thames. The clock struck one in the morning, and Big Ben sent out a vibrant exaltation to the city below. I turned to Molly with a smile.

"I'm ready."

She searched my face. "Are you okay?"

"I'm fine." It was a lie. The world weighed heavily on me, and though fairy folk lived longer than humans, it was becoming abundantly clear that I would outlive Molly, and looking at her filled me with as much sadness as love. In the best of all possible worlds, I still had decades with her, but how much longer could she keep working with me before she lost too many steps?

The bruise on her left cheek was just the latest example of Molly not having the same reflexes she did when we first started fighting for pixie-kind so many decades ago. It was only because I stabbed the ghoul Molly was tussling with through the eye that she didn't die.

What would have happened if I wasn't there? It was hard enough to do the work and stay sharp for myself. If I had to look after her too, how long before I missed an attack and fell into the great beyond…if I could even die.

So far, despite being shot a half dozen times and stabbed more often than I cared to remember, nothing was fatal, and I usually bounded back in a couple of hours, even from the most horrific attacks. When I became immortal, Thanatos told me that if I didn't accept his gift, I would be dead within a year. Sure enough, ten months later, while tracking a human who was pimping underage pixies, I was shot directly in the heart by one of his enforcers. I didn't die. That was the moment that it really sunk in I truly was immortal.

When I didn't age for the next thirty years, people just thought it was because "black don't crack," but it was so much more than I could explain to them. Soon, if Molly wanted to stay with me, we would have to move to conceal my immortality, and it pained me to force her to choose between her family and me.

"You're lying," Molly grumbled. "But we don't have time for a psychology session now. Let's go."

She clasped my hand, and we vanished together. We reappeared in front of a fishmonger building, and the stench of dead salmon, cod, and mackerel wafted into my nostrils. Usually, the facility was filled with dozens of demons cutting through fish, trying to make an honest living. It used to be uncommon to find demons on Earth, but more of them were coming, seeking a normal life.

I was confused as to why I didn't want to stab them and surprised that some of them I even very much liked, as long as I kept them at arm's distance. I don't know how they escaped the pits of Hell, as it didn't seem like summonings were on the rise, but Lilith took them all in all the same and helped them acclimate to Earth.

In fact, she was the one leading the raid tonight. Tall and majestic, standing in the center of the building with her head shaved and two small horns poking out. She wasn't quite a demon, but she wasn't quite a human, either. When she was banished from the Garden of Eden, she became something wholly her own.

"All right," Lilith grumbled to the four low-level demons who knelt around her. "Your brothers and sisters are being butchered by the Cult of Lilith, an abomination to my name. Demons come to Earth looking for me, and this cult takes them in and makes them feel whole, right before they are slaughtered and sold for scraps."

It was a horrible fate, and I didn't usually feel anything for demons. The Cult of Lilith also trafficked pixie children and used them for gruesome rituals, which is what convinced me to help Lilith free her people. She agreed to help me and Molly free ours in turn.

"These horrible beasts are only human, which means we should cut through them like butter," Lilith said. "They have a lot of firepower, but they are spongy and frail. We have the advantage. The plan is to hit hard and hit fast before they can defend themselves. You have your assignments. Show no mercy." Lilith clapped her hands, and the demons broke from her and began talking amongst themselves.

"Good to see you, Lilith," Molly said.

Lilith scoffed as she walked toward us, her hips swaying like an oversexualized cartoon character. "No, it isn't."

Molly had never forgotten being Lilith's prisoner or forgiven her in the subsequent thirty years, even though Lilith had helped us save hundreds of fairy folk over the years. "I know. That's just a thing you say to be polite."

Lilith shook her head. "Americans have never been known to be polite."

Molly smirked. "We're not in America."

"All right, you two," I said, stepping between them. "You don't have to like each other to work together." I turned to Lilith. "Are your demons ready?"

Lilith nodded. "They are. Are you, though?" She stared at the bruise on Molly's cheek. "This isn't some little mission to save one pixie. This is the big leagues. We've been planning this for months, and we can't have a human mucking it up."

I narrowed my eyes. "I'm not a human."

"You have human plasma contaminating your blood. You are a human. Both of you."

The left side of my lip rose instinctively in contempt. "How many times do I have to tell you; I am not contaminated. Molly is not—"

Lilith held up her hand. "I don't care. If you help me save my people, none of that matters. However, if you fail, then I will take it out on your half-breed hide." Her head swiveled between us. "Both of you."

I went to slug her, but Molly pulled me back. "It's not worth it. Let's just get this over with."

I shook her off and gave Lilith a cool stare. "Fine. Are you ready? Are your demons ready?"

"To torture and flay a bunch of evil humans? We were born ready."

CHAPTER 2

The headquarters of the Cult of Lilith was just a couple of blocks from the Thames, about a ten-minute walk. The building was as old as the rest of the city, and I often wondered who lived in those buildings two hundred years before, back when demons mostly stayed in Hell. Then, I wondered who would be living in the tenements in another two hundred years. Would I even be able to remember this raid or Molly, or would they swirl in the muddy waters of my memory, like the fog of my childhood?

No, I couldn't believe that I wouldn't remember Molly, no matter how long we were apart. Thirty years didn't just disappear, and with any luck, we would be together for thirty more at least. That kind of time has a lasting memory on the soul, no matter how old the soul became.

Lilith and the others had their mission. They were going through the front of the building and drawing the fire of the cult head-on. Meanwhile, Molly and I would jump to the roof and infiltrate the third floor where the majority of the prison cells were. Once there, we needed to find the key and unlock the demon prisoners, who would join us on the march downstairs to take out the cult and free the last of the prisoners in the basement. Molly would stay with the young pixies and make sure they were protected. Any cultist we found was to be slaughtered.

It was the biggest raid I had ever been part of, and there were close to a hundred members of the cult. They were protected by the police and politicians, along with a cohort of influential Londoners who cared more about power than compassion. They didn't even think demons and monsters warranted protection since they weren't human. Much like Lilith, they didn't afford half-breeds any standing.

I peeked around the corner of a building across the street from the well-preserved historical relic that the cultists used as a base. In the US, it would have been one of, if not the oldest building in the city, but here it was just another one of several holdovers from the Renaissance. Lilith looked back at me for a moment as she crossed the street with her demons. Then she raised her hand into the air and screamed, "GO!"

The demons didn't waste a moment crashing through the windows on the ground floor and smashing through the front door. Gunfire broke out as fire raged through the windows. "That's our cue."

I grabbed Molly's hand, and we disappeared, rematerializing at the top of the building guarded by three cultists with machine guns and full battle fatigues. I pulled the daggers out of my belt and stabbed one of them through the chest before he could fire his gun. He wore a bullet-proof vest, so I had to angle the attack to come in through his underarm.

I spun the man through the air and flung him at another cultist just as Molly was finishing hers off by snapping his neck. She rushed to the door and kicked it open. She nodded at me and descended into the building as I stabbed the final cultist through the neck and left her to bleed out.

I flashed away from the carnage and into an office on the fifth floor. Part of my preparation for that attack was studying the building for hours by staking it out and scouring through photos. I needed to make sure I could recall anywhere in the building from memory at a moment's notice.

I ended up on top of an oak desk. A freckled man with glasses was sitting there when I appeared. He screamed and scrambled for a gun on his paper-strewn table. I stabbed him through the hand with a dagger and grabbed his other arm. "Where is the key for the cells?"

"I d-d-don't know. I'm just an accountant."

I sliced him across the neck with my remaining dagger and leaped off the desk before pulling my other dagger from his hand. He might have only been an accountant, but he wasn't an innocent. "What good are you, then?"

When I opened the door, I saw Molly enter the hallway. She acknowledged me and turned, her berettas ready, knocking open a door and shooting two cultists before they could defend themselves. She was more comfortable with guns than I was and relied on them as her primary weapon. I preferred being where I could hear my enemy's heart stop beating.

The sound attracted two more guards to open a door on the other side of the hallway. *Another reason I hated guns.* They were noisy. I pulled two throwing knives from my boot and flung them through the encroaching cultist's necks.

"Were there stairs down in that corridor?" I asked, pointing to the door Molly had just exited.

She shook her head.

I walked forward, checking every door as I passed but finding no other cultists inside the rooms. I checked for a key on the two who'd attacked us. Nothing. I removed my daggers from their necks and wiped them off on my pants.

Molly followed behind me, and we found the stairs at the end of the hallway. The crackling from the fire and screams from the bloody massacre below echoed up the stairwell. We were passing the fourth floor when the door opened, and four cultists unloaded their machine guns on us. *Stupid.*

I vanished and appeared behind them, sticking two in the back with my daggers before dislodging one and ramming it through the third's jaw. The last one got a throwing dagger into the gut which sent his intestines spewing out onto the ground. I pushed them all down the stairs and they fell in a heap on the landing.

The guards stopped to reload, and Molly let loose with her berettas. I followed closely behind her as she emptied her cartridges. When she was out, I flashed in front of her and threw daggers at the two remaining guards. Once they were gone, there was silence on the floor.

Molly and I searched the rooms and the guards for keys but found nothing. When the floor was clear, we walked down the stairs to the third, checking the dead guards on the landing for keys. I kicked open the door, expecting to see a dozen guards. There was only one, holding up his hands. He dropped to his knees.

"Don't kill me," he said, crying.

"Open these doors, now!" I screamed.

"I—can't—they'll kill me."

Molly pointed her gun at the cultist's head. "And what do you think we're going to do?"

"You can still do the right thing," I said. "Open these doors, and I'll flash you across the street. You will survive this."

"O-okay," the guard said. He reached toward his back but instead of pulling out keys, he pulled out a pistol. Before he could lift it to attack, Molly fired a bullet through his head. As he fell, I heard the jingle of keys. I rushed over and found a thick key ring dangling from his belt loop.

I walked to one of the cells and looked inside. It was a small imp with only one leg and a tall demon with only one horn. "When I let you out, you'll come with me to Lilith."

"Lilith!" the small imp cried. "No! Please!"

"It's okay," Molly said. "You've been lied to. Lilith is here to help you."

"I swear she is here to save you," I said.

"Really?" the imp said with what resembled a smile. "The mother of demons came for us?"

"Absolutely," Molly said. "When we let you out, take the stairs down to find her, okay?"

"Okay," the imp said.

I opened the door and the demon hobbled out and down the stairs. I continued opening all the cells around the floor until I had freed ten demons and four pixies around me.

"All right," I said. "Demons, with me. Pixies, stay with Molly. She'll take you across the street and to safety." I gave Molly a quick kiss. "Good luck."

"You too," she said with a flash of a smile.

Twisting my daggers in my hands, I led the demons down the stairwell into the second floor. There were already demons there battling the cultists, and the fire was raging everywhere. I knew there was another group of cells in the basement, and I had to get there before the building went up in flames. Leave it to demons to fall to their baser impulses and destroy the place.

I let the demons loose to attack the cultists as I pushed through the fighting and flashed to the first floor, which was engulfed with flames. Lilith stood in the middle of it, smiling at the crisp bonfire that her demons created.

"This floor is clear," Lilith said. "I have sent the dishonorable Lord Bishop to Hell where he belongs."

"Great," I replied. "Then let's free the rest of the prisoners and get out of here."

We ran down the stairs to the basement. The basement was made of stone, and the fire hadn't reached it yet. There were four cells, and I fiddled with the keys until I found the right ones.

"This whole place is coming down," Lilith said. "Hurry."

"If your demons would have been a little less rowdy and not started a hundred fires in an old building, maybe we would have more time." I unlocked the third door, and demons flooded out to Lilith, who welcomed them with open arms. The last cell had a small pixie, no more than eight years old, with dark skin, big blue eyes, and a sad smile.

"I'm gonna get you out of here, baby girl," I said. "Don't worry." I found the key and opened the cell. "Come on."

She wouldn't budge. I walked into the cell and knelt next to her. "It's okay. My name is Kimberly. I'm a friend."

"You helped the bad demons." Her voice was meek.

I shook my head. "Demons aren't bad, or good, really. Nothing is black or white like that. Come on. I'm here to help you. I swear."

I held out my hand, and the little girl placed her tiny hand into mine. "You promise."

"I promise, and I promise I won't leave you until we find your family."

She smiled and pushed herself into my gut, hugging me tightly. Lilith came into the cell. "You ready?"

I nodded. "Let's go."

"It's warded like crazy in here, so we can't flash. We need to get out before the building collapses."

The roof was moaning, ready to collapse on itself. I followed Lilith, pulling the little girl with me as I weaved through the burning building. Finally, we reached the front door, and I knocked it open. Smoke plumed out behind us when we ran into the street. I stared across the street until I found Molly and waved at her. She waved back happily. We had done it.

And that's when the Earth opened up and swallowed London.

CHAPTER 3

One moment I was smiling at Molly, and the next, the ground started to quake under me, twisting like a wet rag being wrung dry. I had experienced my fair share of earthquakes, but this was like nothing I had ever felt before, and it made no geological sense.

The building we had just evacuated collapsed with a groan, knocking into the building next to it and setting it ablaze. I pulled the little girl I had just saved up to my hip and spun back to Molly. The street had cracked open, leaving nothing but a gaping hole where she and the children had been standing.

"Molly!" I screamed. I turned to Lilith, who was surprisingly calm in all the chaos. "What should—"

"Go to the safe house," Lilith said. "I can't believe it's really happening."

"What's happening?" I said. "Tell me!"

"The big one," Lilith said. "Lucifer's been complaining about the overcrowding in Hell for years, and now, looks like he finally had the balls to pull the trigger."

"You're saying—"

"That's right, my beloved." She took a deep breath of air, extending her arms out in front of her in a broad gesture. "This is the Apocalypse."

I couldn't believe her. I didn't believe her. "There's no way."

Lilith pointed into the air. "Fly up and see for yourself. Six-hundred-and-sixty-six Hell rifts will open around the world, and the demons will pour out onto Earth. Imagine this destruction everywhere on the planet."

Lilith was talking giddy gibberish. The little girl looked up at me. "What is the mean lady talking about?"

"Nothing, sweetie," I said. "Just hold on, okay?"

We rose into the sky together. Hundreds of Londoners flooded out into the street, screaming bloody murder. I couldn't believe what I was seeing. Buildings all over the city, reduced to rubble. A massive hole cracked through the middle of the Thames and stretched from London Bridge to Big Ben. The mighty river drained into the gaping crater, and I watched as Big Ben crumpled and fell in, along with the Westminster Bridge and dozens of cars.

"No!" I screamed. "It can't be."

The red hands of demons grasped onto the edges of the gaping hole in the earth. I flew higher above the city and beheld a truly horrifying sight. Thousands of bodies latched onto the edges of the crevice from every inch of the cavern, climbing toward Earth at once. I had never seen so many in one place before. *Was Lilith right?*

Only one thought flashed through my mind. "Molly."

I closed my eyes and thought of the house where we'd planned to meet, then paused. Odds were that it had been destroyed. It was not far off the Thames, and if I made it appear whole in my mind and it had been destroyed, I would be lost in the ether forever.

I had to fly. The little girl was heavy in my arms, but I had to find Molly.

"Hold tight, okay?" I said to her. "And don't look down."

I took off across the river, or what was once a river. By the time I reached the other side, a wave of demons had already risen onto land and was marauding across the streets, ripping people in half and destroying storefronts with gleeful abandon.

A big, meaty demon with fiery eyes and four arms picked a woman up with one arm and her child in another, ready to either kill or eat them. I couldn't allow that. I swung my dagger and cut the demon across the chest. It howled and dropped the woman. I couldn't let go of my charge, so I had to do my fighting with only one hand.

"Run!" I screamed at her.

"Not without my baby!" She pointed into the huge, clawed hand of the demon.

I growled and turned back, avoiding the demon's hands that flew at me. I cut open the closed fist that held the baby, and it fell to the ground. The mother slid and grabbed it, pushed herself up, and disappeared into an alley, and I kicked back into the air above the fray.

The demons swarmed over what remained of Westminster Abbey and rushed through the streets like a typhoon, swallowing the city like locusts. I covered the little girls' ears to shield her from bloodcurdling screams coming from every direction.

Finally, I reached the townhome, where we agreed to meet after the raid. A standard yellow affair, not uncommon for the inner rings of London. I set down the little girl and walked forward. It hadn't been spared, but it was still standing. I pushed my way inside the house.

"Molly!" I screamed. "Molly!"

The TV was blaring, and when I walked into the living room, I saw the scratchy BBC broadcast, fuzzy and pixelated. An older, harried-looking woman stood on the side of the road, shaking, covered in blood and dirt. Behind her, a collapsed building smoked and plumed dust into the air.

"This is the remnants of the BBC broadcasting center in Central London. We will stay on the air as long as possible to make sure you receive updates."

The screen changed to an even older man with white hair and a suit, but he was in a studio this time. "Thank you, Kathryn. Stay safe if you can. We are receiving reports from all over the world that these craters have opened everywhere, in cities and countries from France to the Congo. Marseilles, Moscow, Chicago, Reno, Cairo, and small cities all over the globe. In every case, there seem to be demons rising from the craters as if they were coming from Hell itself. This truly is the end of times, ladies and gentlemen. I suggest you repent." The man held a finger to his ear for a moment. "We're getting another report from Newcastle. Theresa Biggby, over to you."

A woman in a blue blazer appeared on the screen, standing next to a thin young man wearing a red baseball cap. "Thank you, Reginald. Young man, can you please tell the people of England what you told me before we came onto the air?"

He nodded. "Well, I got two mates, Bobby and Kendall. We was talking and having a laugh, and then there was a blue light, and they were gone, like poof. Damnedest thing. Like they vanished into thin air." Theresa turned to the camera. "There you have it, Reginald." She walked a couple of feet until an old priest stood next to her. "Father, could you tell us what you think happened here?"

"Absolutely," the priest said. "It would seem possible that these two were raptured, and those of us remaining are left behind to deal with the demons."

"And if that's true, father, then why are you still here? Shouldn't you have been raptured? What do you think this means for your immortal soul?"

"I…don't…know." The priest began to cry.

The screen cut to Reginald. "Oh, my god. I don't understand. I led a good life. I was proper. I was kind." He looked into the air. "God, why have you forsaken me?"

I felt a rumble under me and ran outside with the little girl to see a horde of goblins, orcs, and demons thundering toward me. "Oh, no."

If Molly were smart, she would have gone to Aziolith's cave. It was high in the Swiss Alps and protected from all of this madness, at least for a time. I turned to the little girl.

"What's happening?" she asked.

"I don't know," I said. "But I need you to be brave, okay? It's all going to be okay."

"Are you going to leave me?"

I shook my head and grabbed on to her, looking her in the eyes. "Of course not. Not until we find your momma. You have to be brave for me, though, okay?"

She nodded. "Okay."

"Good girl."

I closed my eyes and thought of Aziolith's cave, vanishing just as the horde of Hellspawn rushed over the house.

CHAPTER 4

We reappeared inside Aziolith's cave. I thought about the first time I took Molly there to meet Aziolith. He had heard me talk about Molly for long enough and didn't think anybody could make me laugh or fill the part of me so desperate for belonging. Yes, in a world full of dragons, demons, and all manner of monsters, the only thing Aziolith didn't believe was that I could be happy. After being in her presence for five minutes, he changed his tune. He loved Molly as much as I did or more, if that was even possible.

I dragged the little girl through the cave, her eyes boggling at all the astonishing treasure around her. We passed valuables ranging from gold bullion to crowns, weapons, armor, and everything in between. The Queen of England was relatively poor by billionaire standards—but Jeff Bezos would be dwarfed by Aziolith's fortunes. I had access to it all. Not that it mattered, what with the end of the world and all, but I was quite wealthy.

"Molly!" I screamed. "MOLLY!"

"My gods, woman!" a rough voice replied. "Are you trying to wake the dead?"

A prescient turn of phrase. Aziolith rose up, coins and miscellaneous treasure rolling off his back as he stretched into the air. The little girl screamed.

I bent down to comfort her. "It's okay, sweetheart. He's not going to hurt you."

"Perish the thought. I would never eat a child," Aziolith said, his front legs slamming on the ground. "They are mostly fat. A fully grown human, perhaps—"

"Aziolith!" I shouted. "Stop scaring her."

"I'm sorry," Aziolith cooed, his head dropping to my level. "It's okay, little one. I am a friend to Kimberly, and any friend of Kimberly's is a friend of mine."

The little girl turned her head toward the great dragon, her eyes bulging. "Really?"

Aziolith nodded slowly. "Of course, child. What is your name?"

"S-S-Sabine," she said, smiling slightly.

"That is a lovely name. My name is Aziolith."

"Azzazalith?" she said.

Aziolith chuckled. "Close enough, but you can call me Az."

I scoffed. "You hate when I call you that!"

"Yes, well, you are not nearly as cute as this little one."

"Fair enough," I said, not trying to hide my smile. "Have you heard from Molly? Please tell me you heard from Molly."

He didn't answer, but he didn't have to. His face dropped, and his eyes turned away from me, and mine dropped as well.

"Sabine, dear," Aziolith said, "would you like to play with my toys?"

Sabine nodded.

"Well, go for it, then, my friend. I believe there is a music box somewhere in the pile on the left."

"Can I?" Sabine said excitedly, hopping up and down. "Can I?"

I nodded. "Of course."

She let out an excited squeal as if she hadn't witnessed the end of the world moments before and ran off through the coins.

"What is going on, my dear?" Aziolith said, concerned.

"I think it's the Apocalypse."

"Hogwash. They've been predicting them for years, and every time they have been wrong."

"Yeah, well, a lot of times that's because Molly and I stopped them. Right now, as we speak, world rifts are opening all over the world. People are getting raptured or something."

"I don't believe it."

"Well, I don't know if it's an actual rapture-rapture, but people are disappearing in a ball of blue light, vanishing right in front of their friends. I read about so many Apocalypse scenarios in your books and my studies. I thought I would be prepared but it's completely different when you're living through one."

"And where is Molly in all this?"

I shook my head. "I don't know. We had a raid. When it was over, the ground opened. Molly was there, then she wasn't. She wasn't at the safe house. She isn't here. I don't know where she could be."

"You have to find her, Kimberly."

I rubbed my forehead with dirty palms. "I know. Can you watch the kid while I—"

"Of course. Does she know how to use her powers?"

I shook my head. "I don't think so. I have to find her parents, too, but first, I have to find Molly."

"Then what are you still doing here?" Aziolith said. "Go."

He didn't have to tell me twice. I closed my eyes and vanished, fingers crossed that I could find Molly before she died, or worse, became enslaved by the demons that now walked the Earth.

CHAPTER 5

The only place I could safely assume hadn't been destroyed was Buckingham Palace since they had an army of guards to protect it. I had to hope it could withstand an attack, even from demons, at least for a little while. Luckily, the palace was a straight shot to Big Ben, and then across the Thames to where I hoped I could find a clue, or even better, run into Molly searching for me.

At Buckingham Palace, my worst fears were realized. The wave of demons had crashed upon the walls surrounding the palace and was in armed conflict with the guards throughout the courtyard. The guards might have been formidable against humans, but against demons, they were woefully outmatched. I didn't have time to help them.

I took a moment to mourn the death of Great Britain, which after today would surely be ruled by whichever demon could claim the throne. Just as I was beginning to soar above the city again, I heard a screech cut through the sky. An enormous black dragon descended on me like a hawk to a rabbit, hooking me in its claws. I struggled to break free as we rose into the clouds, but it was no use. Instead, I closed my eyes and disappeared, winding up outside of the dragon's talons.

It took a second for the dragon to realize I was gone, and by the time it did, I was flying as fast as I could in the opposite direction, heading into the treelined park that connected to the palace. I used to walk through it often, stopping to watch the joggers and admire the ducks swimming through the lake in St. James Park, but now there was nothing but carnage. Dozens of bodies were strewn about, bloody and mangled. Several demons crouched above them, munching on the entrails of the dead humans.

I wanted to push the monsters away from the bodies, but any such inkling vanished when the heat of the dragon's breath scalded my feet. I headed for the lake, then turned back toward the Thames, zig-zagging every few feet, trying to confuse my pursuer. The dragon was fast but lumbering, and I could turn on a dime. My advantage was unpredictability.

I weaved left and right through the park and back into the streets. I snaked through the buildings until I ducked into the third floor of an old bank and rolled to a stop. The dragon flew overhead and continued on its way, unaware of my deception. I looked out of the window to make sure it was gone, hoping it would follow my path for a long time before it realized I was no longer there.

"Are you a d-d-d-d-demon?"

I spun to see an old woman, white-haired and shaking, curled up in the corner of the sparse room, knees curled into her chin. "No, I'm not a demon," I said with a smile.

"Are you here to eat me?"

"No, and if I were here to eat you, I doubt that speaking politely to me would have stopped me."

"Are you here to help me?" she asked, hopefully.

I took a deep breath. "No. I'm sorry. I'm looking for somebody. I'm afraid you're on your own." I reached into my boot and pulled out a throwing knife. I spun it around, so the handle was away from me, and handed it to her. She took it sheepishly. It would be little comfort when the demons came, but at least it was something. "Stick them with this. It's been enchanted to kill a demon, so maybe it will save your life."

"I don't much want to save my life. I just want it to end quickly. They took my Edgar, and…it was not a dignified end for him."

"I'm sorry."

"We had a long life together. I feel bad for my grandchildren, so young and full of life. I…" she trailed off, not finishing her thought.

"Perhaps they were raptured."

The old woman nodded, a faint smile rising on her face. "That's what I hope, too. I thought I led a good moral life. My Susan brought them to church every week…I didn't go…I hope that was enough…they're good kids."

"I will keep them in my thoughts," I replied, before taking a moment in silence, with nothing but the chaos to fill the space between us. "I have to go."

"I understand."

"Good luck to you." I nodded, making my way through the door. As I did, I smiled. Perhaps Molly was raptured. It was something I hadn't thought of until that moment. Maybe she wasn't in London because she was in Heaven. That would be something. My heart sank, thinking that we would never be together again. There was no way I was going to Heaven. I might only hunt demons, but murder was murder, no matter what or who you killed.

The truth of that statement hit me at once. I remembered that Molly had killed with me, sometimes in greater numbers and with greater relish.

No, she was not in Heaven. She was either on Earth, or she was in Hell, and I would find her if it took the rest of my days.

CHAPTER 6

When I stepped out of the building, I could hear the dragon screeching high overhead. I decided to try and navigate London on the ground. I hadn't taken more than a stride when a demon raised its club and swung it at me. I disappeared and rematerialized behind it, stabbing the beast through the neck.

Another demon leaped at me with a sword before I'd had a chance to take a breath. I vanished a second time and reappeared on the side of a building. The demon clanged its sword onto the ground where I had just been. The vibration of the metal against the concrete caused the sword to fall out of the demon's hands. I kicked off the building and grabbed the sword in midair, and shoved it through the demon's stomach, listening to it gurgle and fall over itself.

Directly in front of me were the remnants of Big Ben, its beautiful face cracked and moaning a loud death knell, its body broken into a million pieces like the rest of the city, along with the hopes and dreams of its citizens. Right behind it lay the chasm that separated one side of the Thames from the other. The rest of Westminster Abby had fallen into the pit, and I rose back into the air to cross the great divide. As I did, I watched thousands of demons, zombies, ghosts, and other monsters pouring out and crawling onto land.

I heard the familiar shriek and looked up to see the dragon rush for me again. Before I could react, a shadow flew over the top of me, and an enormous griffin uncurled its four paws and smashed into the dragon. I didn't wait for the conclusion of their battle before I took off toward the gorge.

The hot air sizzled from the lava pits below. The gusts of heat knocked the wind from my lungs and caused me to drop precipitously toward the chasm below. I closed my eyes and flashed forward slightly and repeated that maneuver until I tumbled out onto the other side of the chasm, inches from falling to my doom into Hell.

A horde of zombies crested over the edge of Hell and shambled toward me. I rushed toward them, daggers at the ready. I stabbed the first two in the chin and used my momentum to kick into the third, sending him flying back over the chasm. By the time I was done yanking the daggers out of the zombies' brains, another cohort had risen over the edge of the crater.

I couldn't waste my time killing every monster that came out of Hell, or I would never rest. I flew away, turning back for a moment to see the griffin and dragon crash into the park below. I smirked in satisfaction then fluttered away above the streets as fast as I could toward the fire in the distance.

What the chasm hadn't eaten was engulfed in the fire which had raged across the city with no end in sight. The building we'd infiltrated just a few hours before was burned to a crisp, as were the ones to either side of it.

I caught a glimpse of something I barely recognized in the wavy air through the fire: A bald woman with two little horns protruding out of her head—Lilith. She snapped her fingers and disappeared, reappearing in a red cloud on the top of a building that was teetering on collapse. She pointed to her right and snapped again, appearing in a flash several buildings away.

She continued vanishing and reappearing on a different rooftop every time I got close, and I kept following until she was safely on the top of a building where I could land without fear of the fire consuming me, and when she pointed to the ground, I floated down onto the top of a flat top building next to her.

When I landed, she wrapped her arms around me. "Oh, thank the gods you're okay."

I couldn't help but chuckle. "This is weird. Also, of course, I'm okay. I'm immortal."

She pulled back and grabbed me around the shoulders. "Immortality means very little right now. Up is down. Left is right. Everything is going up in smoke, and I worried about you, especially after—well, after Molly."

"Molly?" I said. "Do you know what happened to her?"

She shook her head. "No, just that she was here one minute and gone the next. I've been trying to use my whisper network…which I suppose is now a shouting network…to find either one of you."

"That's good, in a way, I guess. It means she hasn't been captured."

"It's not been long enough for me to know anything for sure. Everything is chaos. I don't know if that means she's been captured, or that she's fine…or that the worst has happened."

"I think it's clear the worst has happened." I narrowed my eyes. "But why do you care? This should be like paradise to you. All of your demons are coming home."

"Oh, grow up. I don't like this," she said, crossing her arms. "I was the point person for Lucifer when demons coming to Earth was uncommon. Demons needed me then, but now…now the world has opened for them, and…well, look at this." She swept her arms around the city. "It's undignified."

I stared at her for a few moments before I said, "That's not the response I was expecting. Honestly."

"We aren't savages, at least not all of us…and yet…right now..." She stopped. "You can't do any more here, love. I'll keep working my network and try to find news. How is your family?"

My family. I hadn't even thought of them. Not for this whole time. I felt guilt, and then shame, and then fear. "Mom. I have to go find her."

She nodded. "Of course. I'll be here for you." She handed me a burner phone. "This phone has my number on it. It's the only way to get in contact with me."

"What if the phones go down?"

She sighed. "Then I assume you know how to summon me."

"I do."

"It's so gauche, but if you must. You must."

CHAPTER 7

Damnit. Why didn't I think about my mother earlier? I had my head so far up my own ass that—no, that wasn't it. My mother still lived in a small town in Colorado, while Molly was in the epicenter of an Apocalyptic event.

And oh god, what about Molly's parents? They needed—okay, one thing at a time. First, save my mother. Then, save Molly's parents. Then save Molly. I hoped that Aziolith didn't mind more company. He was quite secretive. Now, he would have a whole group of pixies who knew where he lived and could come knocking at any time.

My mother had lived in the same house for the past two decades. It was nicer than what she could afford, in a nicer area of Boulder than she ever thought she would live, but having access to a substantial amount of money meant I could give my mother the finer things. The house was the only thing she ever let me buy her, though. She didn't approve of my life choices—no, not because I was gay. She was super supportive of my sexuality, and she loved Molly. She hated that I hunted demons.

I often wondered why she didn't want to travel more or ask for a vacation house in Mallorca. All she wanted was a little place to call her own, along with some peace and quiet. She still flew coach when she took a vacation, and even though she had the same pixie powers I did, she never asked me to teach her. She wanted to be normal in every way. That left her ill-equipped to fight demons.

I flashed to her house and breathed a sigh of relief. I was right. There were no zombies or monsters on her street, even if that would surely change soon enough. The demons in London had already fanned out through the whole city and would soon be tearing across the countryside. The same would happen in the USA. I didn't know where the closest chasm would open, but eventually, demons would reach Boulder, and I had to make sure my mother was far away when they did.

I had a key to the place, but mom never locked her door, so I pushed my way inside. "Mom!" I shouted, stomping through the house. "MOM!"

"In here!" she replied, and I rushed toward the sound. I found her in the living room, staring at the TV, and when she saw me, she jumped up from the couch and wrapped me in a strong hug. "My god, it's good to see you."

"Good to see you, too," I said, squeezing her tightly. "I'm glad you're okay."

She pulled back from me. "I'm fine. The nearest one of those things is out by Chicago. It's going to be a long time 'til they get here."

"And we have to make it far away from here before they do. Get your stuff."

"I am not going anywhere," Mom said. "I am too old to go off to some damned safehouse."

"Better than being damned!" I said. "Having demons rip you to shreds. I've seen what those demons do to humans, and it's brutal."

She sat back down and patted the seat next to her. "Sit down with me for a minute. Catch your breath. Have you been watching the news?"

I shook my head as I sat down next to her. "No. I've been living the news."

"Best people can figure out, the churchgoing people were raptured up to Heaven. Not all of 'em, mind you. That horrible Pat Robertson is still around, but a lot of 'em.

Seems that the only way to get through the needle's eye was through the church. Kind of shitty backdoor, huh?" She sighed. "Guess I did you wrong not taking you to Sunday school. Did myself wrong, too. I gotta admit, I was thankful you came through that door, but I hoped you wouldn't come. I hoped you got out of this mess."

I patted her leg. "I'm glad I'm here, Mama."

"Me too, child. I know that makes me a bad mother, but if I were a good one, then I would've been raptured, I guess."

"You were a great mom. You are a great mom."

She began to cry but choked back her tears. "Since then, these demons have been pouring out all over the world. All sorts of monsters. I ain't never seen nothing like it."

Mom was frail. I knew she was old. I knew it, but I couldn't let her die, not when I could help her. "Please, Mom. I won't be able to do what I gotta do if I know you're here. I need you safe. Please."

"Look at you, a complete wreck." She turned to me. "All right, child. I'll go. It doesn't matter none, though. Whether I die here or I die out there, when I go, I'm going to Hell, and there's nothing I can do about that."

I squeezed her frail hands as she collapsed into me, crying. I could hope for a better world if this somehow all got fixed, but someday my mother and everyone else left on Earth would die, and they would all go to Hell. That was a guarantee. For the first time in a long time, I saw my immortality as a blessing.

I helped Mom pack a suitcase and a duffel and then teleported us both to Aziolith's cave. If the monsters ever found us there, then they would have destroyed the rest of the world, and there would be nothing else for us to care about.

"What a dreadful place," Mom said as I guided her through the stacks of money. "So much opulence, and yet not a bit of comfort anywhere."

"I don't need comfort, Adelaide," Aziolith grumbled as his head poked out atop a pile of gold. "But thank you for insulting my home. It's nice to know you haven't changed one bit."

"You either, Az," my mother said. "Still the same old dragon, I see."

They hated each other more than Molly and Lilith. Aziolith represented everything dangerous about my life, while my mother represented everything yoking me to humanity and the world.

"Please don't call me that," Aziolith grumbled. "I expect respect when in my house, even if you can't show an ounce of it otherwise."

Mom shook her head as she turned to me. "This ain't gonna work, child."

"Make it work, okay?" I hissed. "I have to find Molly."

"Molly?" she said. "What happened to Molly?"

Damn. I was trying to keep her from worrying. My mother lived to worry, about me, about Molly, about the world. In fact, the Apocalypse was the calmest I had ever seen her. Probably because she was always waiting for the other shoe to drop, and now it had.

"She's gone," I said. "I can't find her."

"And you're worried about an old woman?" She slapped me in the arm. "Get out of here and go find that girl, and don't come back 'til you do."

"I'm going. I have to save her parents, too. They're in Philly, which means they're much closer to danger." *Come to think of it. I probably should have saved them first.* I looked up at Aziolith. "Don't kill each other."

"No promises," Aziolith murmured. "But I will try."

"I can behave if he can," my mother said, shooting the dragon a look.

The sound of coins jingling and rattling preceded Sabine running out from behind the stacks and latching on to my leg. "Kimmy!"

"Hi, munchkin!" I replied. "Having fun?"

She smiled, pulling a coin out of her pants pocket. "Aziolith said this one is four thousand years old. That's so many years it's blowing my mind."

I laughed. "Yeah, he's got a lot of cool stuff around here."

"He sure does!" Sabine screamed, her round eyes studying the piles of loot. "Can I show you some of it?"

I shook my head. "I have to keep looking for your parents." I pointed to my mother. "But this is my mom. I'm sure she'd love to hear all about it."

Mom nodded slowly and smiled wider than I had seen in years. "I sure would, sweet pea. Where did you find this coin, precious?"

Mom held out her hand, and Sabine switched from gripping my leg to squeezing my mom's hand. "I'll show you!"

Mom gave me a light nod as she disappeared behind the stacks. "Be good."

"I will." I looked up at Aziolith. "That goes for you, too."

"What?" he said with a sheepish grin. "I'm always good."

CHAPTER 8

One family down, and one more to go. Maybe Molly was waiting for me at her parent's house. I would walk in, and she would be there to wrap me in a big hug, and we could find a way to get through the Apocalypse together.

It was wishful thinking, and while I wasn't one for that sort of thing, in the moments where all hope was lost, you had to hope the most. I'd had my share of hopeless times but nothing like what I was going through now—what the world was going through. Not only were demons taking over the world, but everybody left on Earth knew for sure they were not good enough for Heaven. That was a one-two punch.

After we learned that Molly had pixie blood all those years back, we secretly tested both of her parents and found they both had a pixie lineage in them, even if only a hint. It allowed both of them to survive well into their nineties with relatively good health and energy.

I knocked on the door of their Philly brownstone like a polite child, still wanting to make a good impression. Even after thirty years, I worried about them liking me. For a moment, there was no noise behind the door, and I hoped that maybe they'd been raptured. They were both lovely people, though loveliness did not seem to be enough to get beamed up to the mothership. After a few seconds of hope, something moved behind the door.

"Who's there?" a gruff voice called. "You a criminal?"

"Oh, Horace," a more delicate voice said. "Why would a criminal knock?"

"I don't know, Lydia," the man's voice said. "Why would anybody knock? This is the Apocalypse, for goodness sakes, woman."

Footsteps clomped toward the door. A hand yanked the curtain hiding the window inset in the door, and a woman's face glared through the glass. When she saw me, she smiled. "It's Kimberly! Hi, Kimberly!"

"Hi, Mrs. Brown," I said with a little wave. "May I come in?"

"Of course," Lydia opened the door and stepped aside. "My, you haven't aged a day."

"Thank you, ma'am," I said, exchanging hugs with both of them. "Is Molly here by any chance?"

They looked at each other before Horace spoke. "She was here. She left something with us. Something rather precious. Four somethings, actually."

Before I could ask, four little children rushed into the room, squealing and playing like they didn't have a care in the world. "You're it!" the tallest one said after touching one of the little girls on the head.

"Okay!" The girl closed her eyes and began counting to ten. The rest of the children rushed out of the room. "Ready or not, here I come!"

"How are they doing?" I asked after the girl had left the room.

"Okay," Horace said. "We're trying to keep their spirits up. It's not easy, but you know children. Easily distracted."

"What are you doing here, child?" Lydia said. "Molly said you would be in London trying to help."

I looked at her. "I was there." Tears welled in my eyes. "Then I was...I've been damned near everywhere looking for her, and now you're telling me that she's back in London?"

"Last we heard," Horace said. "Though that was a while ago. Oh god, you don't think something happened, do you?"

"I hate to tell you this, Mr. Brown, but this is literally the worst thing that could ever happen."

Lydia grabbed Horace's hand and squeezed. "No, my love. It's not. We still have each other."

I nodded. "I need to get you to safety. It won't be long before the demons are at your door."

"We've been in this house fifty years," Horace said. "How are we supposed to say goodbye to it?"

"And what happens if Molly comes back?" Lydia added.

"We'll write a note, but I'm sure she'll want you safe," I said. "I know it. Besides, we have four other little ones to take care of, and my mother can't take care of them all by herself."

"Your mother?" Lydia's eyes brightened. "So, she's safe?"

"Oh yes," I replied. "She's as safe as she could possibly be. And I need to take the children there, and I'd like to take you as well, though I won't force you, even if Molly would want me to."

They looked at each other, and then Lydia spoke. "All right, Kimberly, we'll go with you. Let me get some things together."

Once they were ready, I gathered them all in a circle. It was difficult to bring them all with me in one jump, but I didn't want to leave a single person behind. Using all of my remaining energy and concentration, I was able to jump everyone at one time. When we landed at Aziolith's cave, I collapsed on the ground, coughing blood.

"Kimberly!" Lydia screamed.

I held up my arm. "I'm okay. I'm okay. It just took a lot out of me."

My mother popped her head from behind a shelf filled with ancient goblets. "Oh, hello, Lydia, Horace! You brought new visitors."

Lydia pushed the children forward. "Go say hello."

The children sheepishly walked forward. As they did, Aziolith rose from behind the stacks and shot a small puff of fire.

"Ahhh!" they all screamed together.

"We're gonna save the princess!" Sabine shouted, and when Aziolith spun, I saw Sabine riding on his back, latched on to one of his dragon scales. "Huzzah!"

Aziolith stopped short when he heard the screams. He turned abruptly and spoke. "Oh, my. I'm so sorry, children. I didn't mean to scare you. Welcome to my cave." They were stunned into silence. "It's okay. I'm very friendly, for a dragon."

"Do you guys wanna play dragons and princesses?" Sabine said. "It's super fun, and with you guys, it will be even more fun."

"Yeah!" they all shouted.

"Then come on!" Sabine said, beckoning them forward. They ran toward Aziolith.

I looked up at him. "I didn't ask you if this was okay."

Aziolith shrugged. "This is what family does. Go save your girl."

"I need something first."

I walked through the piles and stacks all around me until I reached my bed on the far end of the cave. Reaching into the top drawer of my dresser, I pulled out a pouch of pixie dust—the blue one with stars and moons on it, which used to belong to my mentor. I would need it if I were to save Molly. I could feel my energy fading, and I needed to stay alert.

"You should rest," my mother said behind me.

"I'll rest when I find Molly."

"And what if you don't?"

I shot a glare at her. "Don't even talk like that!"

"I'm sorry," she said, walking toward me. "But it's true. You're no good to her dead."

I opened my mouth to speak, but only a whimper came out. She wrapped me in her arms and squeezed me tight, and I began to cry. "I—can't—lose—her."

"*Shhhh*," Mom said, stroking my hair. "It'll be okay, girl."

But it would not be okay. Not now. Not ever. Not unless I could find Molly.

CHAPTER 9

All eyes were on me when I finally left my mother's embrace. I wiped my eyes and the snot from my nose with the sleeve of my shirt. "Was it a good show?" I asked.

Everybody had gathered around me, and there was silence throughout the cave, save for the crackling of the fires Aziolith constantly kept ablaze to keep himself warm. I felt no shame in crying. I often broke down in my quiet moments, but I had never done so in front of so many people.

Horace dropped his eyes. "We know how hard this is for you."

"It's hard for all of us," Lydia added.

"But you saved us," Sabine added. The rest of the children nodded in agreement. I needed to find their families, too, but none of them brought that up.

I spent the next hour sharpening my blades and scouring the cave's artifacts for any that could help me. There was a set of golden pauldrons I was never comfortable wearing because they were gaudy and a piece of light chain mail armor that fell over my chest and felt as light as an old cardigan. I found some golden bracers to match my pauldrons and a pair of black leather boots rumored to make their wearer silent, even though they were wholly uncomfortable.

When I was dressed, I hung the bag of pixie dust from my leather belt along with my two daggers. I placed throwing daggers inside the notches of the belt and added a few more to my leg and bracers. I wasn't a huge fan of swords, but I knew they'd be a help against a horde of demons. A black metal katana, forged in Hell itself and used by one of the greatest monster hunters to ever roam the world, Albrecht the Deceiver, slid into a sheath on my back, where I also kept a quiver of arrows and a bow.

I walked to the other side of the bed, where Molly had often curled up next to me, and pulled two Desert Eagle .50 caliber guns out of the cabinet I built for her. I holstered them around my shoulders and slid several extra clips into the notches built for them.

"I thought you didn't like guns," Aziolith said, watching me.

"I don't," I replied. "But I need more firepower if I'm going to be facing down thousands of monsters."

"Makes sense to me."

We had melted down dozens of demon-killer swords, collected over the years, in order to make the bullets for Molly's weapons. She made them herself, usually while I was busy poring over old texts. It became a ritual that I looked forward to every week.

I looked up at Aziolith. "I need your help."

"I'm here whenever you are ready."

I walked over to my mother. "You have to look after these kids like they were your own."

She smiled. "I never did that good a job of looking after my own. Look at you, about to go face down a horde of monsters like a damned fool. I'll look after them like I wish I looked after you."

"Good." I turned to Horace and Lydia. "I swear I will get your daughter back if it's the last thing I do."

Horace smiled. "She's lucky to have you."

I shook my head. "I don't know about that. If she wasn't with me, she might have been with you, and then you could have figured out how to survive together, instead of being stuck God knows where."

"She knows how to survive because of you," Lydia said. "That's how we know she's okay."

I gave them a hug and walked over to Aziolith. Sabine still sat on his neck. "Oh, man. Do I have to get off now?"

I nodded, and she slid down. When she was on the ground, I hugged her. "I'm sorry you have to live through this. You don't deserve it."

She hugged me back. "Don't die, okay?"

I winked at her. "I can pretty much guarantee I won't." I didn't know how deep my immortality ran, but I had been stabbed, shot, and maimed more times than I could count, and in every instance, I was fine. It still hurt, though. And I had never been up against so many demons so adept at eternal torture. I didn't need to be dead to be tortured, and that's what I feared more than anything.

Aziolith bent down, and I hopped onto his back. I had never been able to work with Aziolith in his traditional dragon form before, but for the first time, he didn't have to hide. He could be as majestic, as beautiful, as terrifying, and as deadly as he once was considered before dragons were hunted to extinction.

"Are you ready?" I asked him.

"I've been ready for this my whole life."

I closed my eyes and thought of England, and then we were gone, ready for battle and anything the Apocalypse could throw at us. Of course, that was just another lie that I told myself.

CHAPTER 10

I didn't want to take my chances flashing into the center of London to maneuver down tight corridors, especially with a companion as big as Aziolith. It was impossible to know what parts of the city would not be destroyed, but I took my chances that demons wouldn't have destroyed the Joy of Life fountain in Hyde Park. It was just a bunch of metal people running and playing in the water, after all. There wasn't anything to topple or crush, and while you could tip them over or burn them, I figured that would be less appealing than finding real humans and gutting them.

I was right and breathed a sigh of relief when we reappeared into the middle of Hyde Park, near the fountain, which had been shut off in the chaos. The boys and girls frolicked on the cold concrete, out of place in the city falling apart around them. It was only about five seconds before Aziolith drew the attention of a half dozen demons and imps that festooned the park.

"Let's get out of here!" I shouted as Aziolith rose. He shot a thick stream of fire at the demons, but they only seemed reinvigorated by the flame and started throwing their lances and pitchforks at us.

"Little help!" Aziolith shouted to me.

I fired arrows down at the demons as they leaped toward us. A lithe one leaped onto a fatter one's back and latched onto Aziolith's leg. The others jumped up and grabbed on, creating a chain of demons.

"Enough of this." I pulled out Molly's guns and fired down at them. I clipped it in the leg, and it howled out in pain. Clearly, the demon didn't think that I was any sort of threat, but two more bullets into its chest proved me deadly.

The demon fell off and crashed upon his friends, allowing Aziolith to rise into the air.

I realized too late that I hadn't gotten rid of the first demon to crawl up Aziolith's leg and only caught sight of him as he charged at me, war hammer in hand. I spun around and unsheathed my katana. I dodged the hammer blow, but it cracked down right on Aziolith's back, causing the great dragon to howl and thrash. I kicked away from him to avoid being shaken off.

The demon latched onto the scales on Aziolith's back, off-balance, and I saw an opening. I swung my sword up into the air and brought it down on the demon's head, which split open like an apple. I kicked the carcass, and it fell back to the ground.

"Are you okay?" I asked Aziolith.

"Just a wee sting. I've not been in a fight for a long time. It gets the old blood pumping."

"Let's hope we can avoid any more fighting. I have no interest in getting maimed by demons on this day."

"I don't think you'll have much of a choice. Look down."

From our vantage point high above London proper, we could see every street covered with demons, zombies, and imps, looting stores and destroying storefronts with reckless abandon; thousands of years of civilization torn apart in a matter of hours.

"Let's find Molly and get out of here."

"Isn't there anything we can do to help these people?"

"Probably," I replied, pulling out the burner phone that Lilith gave me. "But every minute we waste is another one where Molly could be in serious trouble."

"A pity," Aziolith said, soaring over the city. "You'll tell me where I am going, yes?"

"Yes," I said. "I should probably figure that out, shouldn't I?"

I dialed the only number on the phone and waited for someone to pick up. After two rings, I heard Lilith's dulcet voice. "Took you long enough."

"It's good to hear your voice, Lilith," I replied. "Where are you?"

"I'll drop a pin," Lilith said. "Though it's kind of hard to miss it."

She hung up the phone, and a second later, it vibrated. I opened the text I received, and it showed me a map of London. True to form, Lilith had placed her pin directly in the center of Buckingham Palace.

My phone buzzed again with another text from Lilith: *Land directly in the quadrangle in the center of the castle. Don't worry about the demons. They won't hurt you on my order.* I barely trusted Lilith when she wasn't commanding an army of demons, and her reassurance made me suspicious. However, her next text made me reconsider. *And don't dawdle. We found Molly. She is in grave danger.*

It didn't matter if I believed her or not. She claimed to have a lead, which was more than I'd managed thus far. I either had to trust Lilith, the demon queen with a forked tongue, or take my chances on my own in a city filled with demons looking to rip me apart. It was an easy choice to make.

"Head northeast," I said.

"Into the belly of the beast?" Aziolith said.

"That's where we're going," I sighed. "Let's hope it doesn't swallow us whole."

CHAPTER 11

I didn't know what a quadrangle was, but when we finally reached Buckingham Palace, I noticed the big courtyard formed by the four buildings that surrounded it. I didn't know why they would have called it a quadrangle when it was clearly just a square. Leave it to royalty to make a simple thing more complicated just to sound better. Pompous.

"Are you sure about this?" Aziolith asked, hovering high above the castle. Demons and imps walked along the roof of the palace and milled around the square. They had taken up posts along the fence line outside and the gardens behind the castle.

"No," I said. "But I'll walk through Hell for Molly. The least I could do is brave this bullshit." I fluttered beside him. "Wait here in case I need you."

"I don't like the idea of you going in there alone."

"If I get in trouble, I need you to come in swinging, and I don't want to risk you being surrounded, either." I started away and then turned back. "Watch out, though. So far, I've seen a dragon and a griffin up in the air, so I don't know how safe it is."

"Thanks for the warning," Aziolith grumbled.

I floated down slowly, guns drawn. The demons guarding the castle hissed at me, but they did not draw their weapons or fire. When I finally landed, a group of goblins surrounded me with spears. They kept their distance as I pointed two very large guns at their faces.

"Oh, put those away," Lilith said behind me. "How uncivil. This is a palace."

"Tell your goblins to stand down."

Lilith raised her hands in the air. She now had a head full of long, black hair and wore a burgundy dress that sparkled in the light. "Enough. She's a friend, no matter how uncivilized she is." Lilith walked across the quadrangle toward me. "It's good to see you're not dead."

"Does it even matter anymore? The dead have risen, or haven't you heard?"

Lilith chuckled. "You have always had a rapier wit. Come with me." She stalked across the grounds, oozing regal authority. A demon wearing a tux opened the door for her, and she turned to beckon me with her finger before she entered.

I had never been inside Buckingham Palace before. It looked like somebody vomited blood on the floor and painted gold everywhere else with a firehose. There were stairs all over the place, along with columns and exquisite details I couldn't possibly appreciate, not if I had a hundred years to do so. It was baked in the history of oppression, and it sent shivers down my spine.

Lilith walked across the floor toward a set of stairs on the left of the foyer. She walked straight up the middle, splitting the stairway in two with her steps. "Come now," she said with a smile.

Upstairs, there was even more red carpet, along with dozens of paintings, any of which was easily worth more than my life. Aside from Hieronymus Bosch, I didn't appreciate classical art. Most of it was self-portraits commissioned by a self-righteous, pompous asshole. Of course, I stood in the royal palace, so a large amount of pomp was expected.

"We're expecting you," Lilith said.

"We?" I said. "Who's we?"

"Thomas, the demon prince." Lilith smiled. "The Devil's son has taken control of this palace and made me his regent so that we might restore order."

"Order…to the Apocalypse. That's rich."

"Somebody has to do it. Stand up straight. You're about to meet royalty."

Lilith turned down another hallway. This red carpet had yellow circles on it, which…okay, it looked nice. I just didn't know why rich people must be so elegant about everything. Every pillar was covered in intricate, crisscrossed pattern designs, with mirrors all over the place. Who wanted to look at themselves that much?

Lilith stopped in front of a door, and I turned to see myself in the mirror. I was dirty, and nothing about me matched. My golden pauldrons and bracers clashed with my black boots, and my black shirt clashed with my faded brown belt and gun holsters. Compared to Lilith, who looked like every hair on her head was meticulously placed with hours of thought, I was a wreck.

She pushed open the doors and entered the throne room. The demon prince blended into the red of the walls and floor. It made sense why a pasty white king and queen would choose red. It looked great against the white of the hallway, but it was silly, frankly, for a red-faced demon to be in the room, and I wondered how soon until he would redecorate if he intended to stay.

"Enter," Lilith said. She walked forward and took a seat on the red throne at the demon's left hand. Behind them on four panels were golden, intricately designed…things that had all sorts of berries and twigs and leaves on them. I honestly couldn't believe something like that could adorn a throne room, but good for the artist pulling one over on the queen and hopefully getting paid handsomely for it.

I walked into the room, my silent boots muffled by the plush carpet under my feet.

"And who have you brought in front of me, my dear love," the male demon said, stroking his beard slowly. "She is a trifle, is she not?"

"Thomas," Lilith said with a smile. "This is Kimberly. You remember the pixie girl I told you about who lost her lover. You said you knew where the other one was."

"Ah yes," Thomas said, rising from his throne. He was tall and broad, easily the prettiest and best-dressed demon I had ever seen. "Funny. I thought you would be taller."

"Funny," I said. "I've never thought of you at all."

He stepped down the stairs slowly and met me in the center of the room. "No need to sheer venom on me. I am not your enemy."

"All demons are my enemy."

"Even Lilith?" he said, cocking his head toward her.

"We have an uneasy alliance, and it took years to build even the semblance of trust."

Thomas circled me slowly, and I turned to keep him in front of me. "If even half the stories about you are a quarter true, you are the greatest fighter in the western hemisphere, maybe the world."

"I've killed my fair share of demons."

"Yes, you would be perfect to help me," he said, taking the steps back to his throne.

"I'm not interested in helping you."

"Really?" Thomas said as he sat down. "I thought we could be friends."

"I don't make friends with demons."

"A pity," he replied. "I only help my friends. And if we aren't friends, then we are enemies. Guards!"

"Wait!" Lilith said as four burly demons ran into the throne room hoisting machine guns. "Kimmy, if you want his help, you need to play the game. You scratch his back, and then he'll scratch yours."

"Or, we can scratch each other's," Thomas said, holding up his hand to stay his guards. "That's always fun."

"Why would I help you take over the world?"

"Oh, my dear. I don't need your help with that. I need your help to help bring order back to the world. I need you to help me kill the Devil."

"Why would you want to do that?"

"As I mentioned, not all demons are bad. I'm not sure any of them are. They are mostly…just misguided. Still, many of us don't like what my dear old dad has done, and we are working to return to Hell. Until we can do that, we must retain order on the surface, and that's where you come in."

"I'm not a mercenary."

"No," Thomas said. "But I have heard you are very interested in helping fairy folk, and what would be more helpful than ending this dreaded Apocalypse quickly?"

I frowned. "I don't believe you."

He shrugged. "You don't have to believe me. You just have to work for me."

"There's only one thing I'm interested in doing, and that is finding Molly."

"I can help. We can kill two birds with one stone, I believe is the expression. It just so happens that your paramour is being held by one of the biggest thorns in my side."

"And who is that?"

"An imp named Charlie. Not much of a fighter, but he's a manipulative little cuss."

Why is it always him? I chuckled. "Yeah, I know him."

"Perfect," Thomas said.

Lilith shook her head. "It's a pity. I took such good care of that boy, only to have him turn against me…and to capture your beloved. That's a low blow, even for him."

"So, you bring Charlie to me, and you get your paramour back. It's win-win, as they say."

"If you're messing with me, I have all sorts of ways to kill you."

He held up his hands. "Let us hope it doesn't come to that. Do I have your support?"

I nodded. "For now."

He clapped his hands together. "Perfect! This is going to be so much fun."

CHAPTER 12

Thomas and Lilith walked me back outside the castle, and I called for Aziolith, who flew down into the quadrangle. His eyes darted back and forth between the demons and imps that surrounded him. He didn't like to be caged in, but I knew a little piece of him was eager for them to start something.

"Thomas," I said. "This is Aziolith."

"Oh, good," Thomas said, rubbing his hands together. "A dragon. That will be helpful."

"In doing what, exactly?"

"Storming the Tower of London. Those wishing to see the Apocalypse continue in chaos forever, like Charlie and his ilk, have taken up residence there, using it as a base while they raid and pillage the surrounding land and bringing back their ill-gotten treasures and hostages to the prisons within its walls. It's truly despicable."

"That's funny," I said. "Since you basically stole this place and killed the queen."

"The queen is not dead, I assure you," Lilith said. "She's quite safe in her residence and will be reinstated once we get this whole thing sorted."

"Oh, I'm sure," I replied with a smile. "You'll both willingly give back that power?"

"Of course," Lilith said. "Once I have what I really want, which is the throne of Hell."

"And you shall have it, my love," Thomas said, kissing Lilith's cheek. "We will rule Hell together and hold the power of the gods in our hands." He turned back to me.

"Before then, we need to defeat those who resist our rule, which means breaking their stronghold and driving them to kneel before me, willingly, or by force."

"I prefer by force," I interjected.

"Which is why I like you," Thomas said. "Once inside, there is something I need you to obtain for me...call it my price for your Molly's soul."

"What is it?"

"Charlie has a dagger stolen from Lucifer himself. It will lead to the Devil's downfall."

"What does it look like?"

"Long, twisted and black, with a red jewel encrusted in its hilt."

"I know the weapon," Aziolith said, looking startled. "The Dagger of Obsolescence."

Thomas nodded. "The very one."

"It was offered as a trade for my help from a treacherous pixie." He turned to me. "Akta, your ancestor. It is precious to me."

"Then you will bring it to me?" Thomas asked.

"It should be mine." Aziolith gave a solemn nod. "But I love Kimberly as if she were my own, and she loves the girl more than her own life, so if we get Molly, then yes, I will relinquish my claim on it to you. Why do you need it?"

"The weapon is one of the few in the galaxy that can kill a Devil," Thomas said.

Lilith clenched her fists. "If we want to end the Apocalypse, we must kill Lucifer and take his throne."

I nodded. "Then I will bring it to you. Better to end this sooner than later."

"Good," Thomas said. "You will have a battalion of my best men. The Tower is heavily guarded, and Charlie keeps his most precious prisoners in the highest tower. It is likely he will be keeping your Molly there."

"You'll storm the castle by force," Lilith said. "They have the numbers, but we have the superior strategy."

"Bull rushing the Tower is the best strategy, really?" I grumbled. "It seems like a suicide mission."

Thomas shook his head. "It's not. I have many moles inside the Tower, and they will turn on Charlie and his ilk at the first opportunity. However, as you know, he is a tricky one and will disappear given a moment's chance. Unless we time this perfectly, he will slip out of your hands."

"Then, we'll make sure to time it perfectly."

"My men will be wearing black shirts emblazoned with a red dagger." Thomas waited until I nodded. "We'll wait on your signal. Aziolith here will land you on the roof so you can make your way to the floor below as we attack the front. You must be quick and deadly. Find Charlie before he has a chance to snap away."

I leaped onto Aziolith's back. "When will your men be ready?"

Thomas grinned. "They are already in position. I started the chess match after you called Lilith. They await you to fly over them before they launch their attack."

"Let's get going."

Charlie. The dastardly little imp. I hadn't run across him in years, but I knew him to be among the most devious demons I had ever met. He wouldn't slip through my fingers, not again. If he really did have Molly, I would cut him up into a million pieces and make sure he could never resurrect. Hell, I would probably do it either way, for the sheer fun of it, after everything he'd put me through in my life.

Aziolith flew northeast, over the chasm that had opened over London. Water from the Thames poured into it, though the remains of Big Ben and Westminster Abbey were still visible. The demon flood had slowed to a trickle. They had spread out around the city, ready to infect all of England and cover the world with their stench.

"There it is!" I shouted, pointing toward a tall fortress in the distance.

The Tower of London was really four towers with a big fortress between them. Surrounded by an enormous stone wall, the Tower itself was as big as four city blocks. The world had modernized around it, and now a thoroughfare and what was left of a busy bridge rested high above the castle. The place had become a tourist trap, but it was still as formidable as ever to an opposing force.

As we passed over the surrounding woods, I heard rustling under me. I recognized the limbs of demons through the trees, and as we crested over the wall, hundreds of demons climbed the walls to attack. On the other side of the tower, squads of demons wearing Thomas's red dagger leaped off the highway onto the wall, beginning their assault on the tower.

I didn't worry about them, though. I was focused on one thing—Charlie. Aziolith landed on the roof of the building and lumbered forward to meet the dozen demons posted there.

"Go!" he shouted. "I have them!"

I didn't wait for him to tell me a second time. I beelined toward the door. When four more demons rushed out to greet us, I pulled out my guns and opened fire. Two of them fell over the side. I holstered my gun and pulled my sword, slashing the other two in a single, fluid motion. I stepped over their bodies on my way to the door.

On my way down the stairs to the next floor, I heard the demon battle far under me. It wasn't clear who was winning, but it was sure to be a bloody mess. Demons loved a spectacle, and the more blood, the better. I reloaded and made my way down the stairs until I stepped foot on the top floor, beretta drawn.

The Dagger laid atop a stack of papers on a small desk in the middle of the room. I was walking toward it when I heard the jingling of chains. I slid one of my berettas into its holster so that I could pick up the Dagger. Charlie hobbled through the archway, adorned in gold chains and baubles. It was the mark of a being that desperately wanted power but had no idea how to wield it, so they turned to gaudiness. The difference between Thomas's innate regal power and Charlie playing at it was palpable.

"Charlie!" I shouted. "Don't move! Where is Molly?"

"Holy shit!" Charlie said. "Kimmy? Is that you? What the hell are you attacking me for? Why are you partnering with demons?"

"I know what you're doing. I know you don't want this nightmare to end, but I'm here to end it, Charlie."

"Are you kidding me? Why would I want this Apocalypse to keep going? It ruins everything for me. I'm a civilized being, used to the finer things, and these demons…they are not. No, kiddo. There is nothing I want more than the Apocalypse to end, but I ain't gonna let Thomas end it. That guy is a madman. You think Lucifer is bad? That kid is psychopathic. He wants to take on Heaven itself. I was already part of one idiot's attack on Heaven. I ain't gonna do it again, so yeah. I want this to end, but I would not trust anything that guy says."

"That's rich, coming from you."

He stepped forward, his jewels tinkling against each other. "It's exactly cuz it's coming from me that you should take it seriously. You ever seen me scared of another demon before?"

"No."

"That's cuz he's a friggin' nutjob. This whole thing is bonkers, but I would rather it go on forever than give Thomas the Dagger."

"Enough of your lies." I was sick of hearing him talk. "Where's Molly?"

"All right, I'll be honest with you. I have her here. She was in bad shape, and I thought it would be safer here than out on the streets. But she ain't a prisoner. She's my guest."

"Give her to me," I said.

I shook my head. "Not if you're gonna give the Dagger to Thomas. Give me the Dagger, and I'll show you the girl."

"No deal. You bring me to the girl, and then we'll talk about the Dagger."

"You drive a hard bargain, but deal." Charlie hobbled across the room to another set of stairs. The jewels were weighing him down something fierce. "Come on."

He led me down the stairs to the next level down. "Get off of her!" I heard Charlie scream when we got to the next floor. I rushed out and saw a tall, lanky demon pulling a girl by the hair.

No. It wasn't a girl. It was her. It was Molly.

"Molly!"

"Kim!" she screamed back, her voice cracking and her face lined with dirt. "Help me!"

"Shut up!" the lanky demon squeaked before turning back to Charlie. "I knew we should have killed this pixie when we had the chance! Now, she is mine!"

"Let her go!" Charlie said.

"You have no power here, little one. You were just a convenient mouthpiece, and now your usefulness has come to an end." The lanky demon snapped his fingers, and he was gone, Molly along with him.

Charlie looked at me, scared, and then his hand jerked to vanish himself. I dropped my gun to the ground and whipped out my sword. With one upward strike, I cut off Charlie's hand before spinning around and taking out the other.

"Dammit!" Charlie screamed. "Again! Do you have any idea how long it takes to grow these back?"

"Where did Molly go?" I shouted.

"I don't know! I don't know! I don't—know."

"I believe you." I sneered, grabbing him by the gaudy jewels. "Let's go. You're going to tell me everything you know, but first, we're bringing you to Thomas. He can figure out what to do with you."

CHAPTER 13

In the six months after Molly's disappearance, I never stopped searching for her. I looked everywhere that I heard a fairy tale that she might be close. I didn't sleep for a month straight, using a mixture of pixie dust and caffeine to stay awake until I literally collapsed from exhaustion. It didn't matter how many cities I visited. Nobody had seen Molly.

Meanwhile, I had been able to find the parents of all the children who were captured by the cultists and reunited them at Aziolith's cavern...all except for Sabine's father, who was still at large and likely dead.

I looted beds, and chairs, and food at every opportunity and made something of a thriving community in the piles of gold that adorned Aziolith's cave. Each member of the colony was now a billionaire many times over, not that it mattered since money didn't matter anymore, but it was a fun thing to joke about in the moments when levity invaded our thoughts.

It felt like we were somewhat of a family. Lydia had been a schoolteacher, and so she taught the children what she could, and the other parents did their part to keep them happy and healthy. I had trained a few of them with fairy blood the rudimentary basics of their powers and brought them with me on raids when we needed medicine and food.

Sabine tried to keep a stiff upper lip. I looked for her father for a long time before reaching the conclusion that he was either raptured or murdered. I never found his mangled corpse in my travels, so I hoped for the former. I didn't want to imagine a world where he had been captured or what would happen to him if demons took him for a plaything.

"Good morning," Lilith said as I flashed into the top floor of the Tower of London. "Back again?"

I nodded. "Is he up?"

She shrugged. "He never sleeps. Whether he'll talk to you is another thing."

Every day I made sure to visit Charlie, hoping he would break and tell me something I didn't already know about his demon friends. He had been on Earth longer than anybody except for Lilith, and his spy network was legendary,

"I could help you, you know," Lilith said. "For a price."

I shook my head. "It's a price I'm not willing to pay."

The price was the Dagger of Obsolescence. I kept it hidden in Aziolith's cave. We had a deal. The Dagger for Molly, and without Molly, our deal was null and void. Lilith and Thomas didn't see it that way, so we struck up an uneasy alliance that allowed me to question Charlie and search for my beloved, but without their help.

"You know," I said. "If you helped me find Molly, then you would get the Dagger much quicker."

Lilith furrowed her brow. "And if you gave me the Dagger, then you would have Molly much sooner."

"That assumes you know where she is," I grumbled.

"Who's to say I don't?"

I stepped closer. "Do you know something? Do you have even an inkling of a clue?"

She shrugged. "Possible. I have a legendary whisper network, as does Thomas. With things settling down around the globe, we're starting to get a clearer picture of the world and where things stand."

The demon marauding had largely settled down. Demons infiltrated every inch of the globe and had grown bored of the constant murder and torture. They had found television, electric guitars, and all manner of those things that made us a soft and weak civilized society. Demons fought each other for power, and the strongest had won, taking control of the biggest cities, with the rest falling in line under them.

"Do you know where she is, or don't you?" I asked more forcefully.

"Give me the Dagger, and you'll know."

It wasn't worth arguing with Lilith. Our heels were dug in, and neither of us would see it from a different perspective. I turned away from her and walked into Charlie's cell. He was curled up in the corner, the nubs of his arms wrapped around his greasy knees.

"Why do you keep showing up and ruining my good time," Charlie said. "I was just thinking about Charlize Theron. Did you know she was a succubus? That's why she stays looking so young. Most movie stars are, you know? Or sirens…or demigods."

"I don't care." I pulled a piece of chalk out of my belt and knelt on the ground to draw a circle on the floor. The cell was heavily warded to prevent anyone from jumping in or jumping out, but they didn't account for a summoning circle, which circumvented all other demon laws.

"What are you doing?" Charlie asked.

"I'm getting you out of here," I said. "Do you want to be stuck in this tower for the rest of eternity?"

"That depends where you are taking me."

I shook my head. "That's not important, Charlie. Just know that you are a popular fellow, and there's some information I need, and the demon who has it is very interested in talking to you."

"You're going to risk war against Lilith and Thomas to get some information? Why wouldn't you just give them the Dagger, then?"

"Because I don't trust them," I said, drawing the words around the circle from memory. "I guess you got into my head."

"And you trust this demon?" Charlie scoffed.

"I don't trust any of you, but I trust her enough that I'll risk your measly life for it."

I finished the circle and grabbed Charlie by the collar of the dirty potato sack he wore. "Let's go."

"No!" he said. "HELP!"

"Shut up!" I shouted, opening my phone. "NOW, Aziolith!"

Lilith opened the door just as the blue of the summoning circle washed over me.

"Hey! What are you—"

Charlie and I vanished. There would be a reckoning later, but for now, all that mattered was Molly.

CHAPTER 14

We reappeared atop the summit of Mount Nemrut in southern Turkey. Below us were dozens of broken statues, their heads lopped from their bodies. Once the burial grounds of a proud civilization, it laid in ruin, a sacrifice to time and neglect.

"It seems your crazy plan worked," Aziolith said, sitting on the edge of the circle. "How pissed was Lilith?"

I shook my head as Charlie wriggled under me. "I have no idea. I only got a glimpse of her face before we vanished. I couldn't tell if she was more confused, surprised, or furious."

"Get off me!" Charlie kicked and screamed.

I reached down and grabbed a metal collar in front of Aziolith's feet. I clasped it around Charlie's neck and then shackled his legs with another set of bracers that I'd found in the many piles of Aziolith's treasures.

"You aren't going to save yourself," I said. "Not this time, I'm afraid. These bracers are enchanted to prevent you from using any magic, and you can't wriggle out of them."

"I'm very squirmy," Charlie replied. "You have no idea."

I pushed him down to the ground. "You could have helped me find Molly, and maybe I would have even helped you escape, but you couldn't do that, could you? I had to get creative."

"What are you going to do to me?"

"There's a demon who is very interested in making your acquaintance again, Charlie. You know him as Ril'vir, I believe." Charlie's face dropped in horror. "He said you screwed him over pretty good, and for the price of your hide, he would find my beloved and bring her to me on this mountain." I grabbed Charlie by the chain around his neck. "A fair trade. Something I hate for something I love."

"You can't do this!" Charlie said, scraping across the ground with his feet as I pulled him forward. "I'll do anything. You want to find your girl? I can help you do that. I know people, places, things, and ideas that would be very interested in helping me help you. But please, do not give me to Ril'vir. He's a psychopath. And for demons, that's saying something."

"Is everybody a psychopath, Charlie?" I pushed him forward. "First Thomas, now Ril'vir. I'm starting to think you use that word too often. When you do that, it loses all meaning."

I dragged Charlie down the dirt path, circuitously slinking down the mountain. We passed great columns and the heads of ancient statues as we passed. At the bottom of the hill, four beings materialized in front of me. The biggest, with long, spiraled horns, was Ril'vir, broader than the other two demons, who I had never met. Ril'vir's massive paws gripped a dark woman wearing a burlap sack on her head.

"Welcome, pixie," Ril'vir snarled. "I thought you wouldn't show."

"A promise is a promise." I pulled Charlie forward. "I have delivered on my end. Have you brought Molly?"

Ril'vir lifted the girl in the air. "Right here. Push him over, and I will push her to you."

I shook my head. "Not gonna be that easy. Take off the sack. Let me see her, and then we'll exchange at the same time."

"You're not in a position to make demands," Ril'vir said. "I could rip her in half right now, and then where would you be."

"I would still have Charlie, and I would kill you."

Ril'vir laughed. "I like you. You have spunk. Very well."

He pulled the burlap sack off the girl. My heart leaped for a minute, hoping to come face to face with my beloved. However, it wasn't Molly. The girls' face was thinner, lighter, and her eyes a dull black with none of the vibrance of my Molly. She was also far too young. My heart sank back to my feet, lower than it had been for a long time, as my best lead withered on the vine. It was nothing but a fool's errand.

"That's not her."

"Of course it is!" Ril'vir yelled. "This is Molly. How could you say otherwise?"

"I know the love of my life." I turned away. "No deal."

"NO!" the girl screamed out. "Please, please. PL—"

Ril'vir slashed the girl across the face with his giant claw, and she dropped to the ground, bleeding out of her neck, face, and chest, dead. "Now, look what you made me do."

"That won't make me give you Charlie," I growled. "Find my girlfriend, and then we'll talk."

"He won't, and he can't!" Charlie said. "He's a coward. Nobody likes him. He's all bluster!"

"Why, you little!" Ril'vir leaped forward, and Aziolith's tail swung into the air, smashing into him and sending him backward into the rocky statues.

"I suggest we leave," Aziolith said.

I nodded. "I agree." I turned to the other demons. "Don't follow us, and don't try to contact me again, or I swear to god I will kill each and every one of you and salt your corpses to make sure you never wake up in Hell again, either."

I hopped onto Aziolith's back and pulled Charlie up to join me. Aziolith laid down a swath of cover fire as he rose into the air. When we were safely airborne, I turned to Charlie.

"You said you can help me. So, you have two choices. Either you help me get Molly back, or I'll bring you back to Ril'vir, or worse…I'll bring you back to Thomas and Lilith."

"And if I find her for you?"

"Then I'll conveniently lose you."

"Thomas won't like that."

"No, he won't like it, but he'll accept it. He's a politician, and he's got bigger things to deal with than your scrawny ass."

"If he gets that Dagger, all Hell will break loose."

"If I don't find Molly, all Hell will break loose." I glared at him. "Worry about that right now."

"Very well," Charlie said. "Then it's a good thing we're in Turkey. Tell your dragon slave to take us to Constantinople."

"Watch it, Charlie," Aziolith said. "I don't like you either. I would rather drop you from 30,000 feet. You are only here because Kimberly requests it."

"Fine," Charlie said, wrapping his arms around his chest. "You know, some people like me."

"Who?"

"Some demons!" Charlie shouted. "And I'll prove it to you when we get to Constantinople."

"What's there?" I asked.

"Your girl and my ex-partner. Unless I'm wrong."

"Well, then, Aziolith. You heard the demon. Take us to Istanbul."

"It will always be Constantinople to me," Charlie grumbled.

CHAPTER 15

Embarrassingly, the only thing I knew about Istanbul was that it was once Constantinople, and I only learned that from the They Might Be Giants song "Istanbul (not Constantinople)." It had been on my list of places to visit, but even with a nearly boundless ability to travel around the world, there were still places that I had yet to visit. The world was fascinating, and I had still seen so little of it, even after 50 years.

The Istanbul I knew was from pictures taken before the Apocalypse, so I was uncomfortable teleporting us there. It was too easy to get lost in the ether. That meant we had a lot of flying to do. We passed over Kayseri, Ankara, and Bursa before turning toward the Sea of Marmara, toward Istanbul. Everywhere we traveled, we found cities that looked as if they had been embroiled in armed conflict, buildings demolished, fires still ablaze, and little sign of any people left.

A Hell rift had opened right in the middle of the country, and as we passed over it, the hot air gushed into my face. A few demons hobbled out of it, but it was mostly the dead that made their way to the surface now, zombies and other humanoids who fanned out into the world. It was amazing how quickly the new world order had become the new normal. Six months ago, demons escaping Hell to terrorize the Earth was unique, novel even, and yet now it was an everyday occurrence. The weird and magical thing about humanity was that we could acclimate to just about anything, for better or for worse.

"You see that big building?" Charlie said, pointing ahead. Over the water, five blue and white minarets surrounded a massive domed building set against the

Istanbul skyline. "That's the Blue Mosque. That's where Tal'gen and I were supposed to meet if everything went to pot for us in London."

"How can demons make a base in a mosque? Isn't it as holy as a church?"

Charlie chuckled. "Nothing's sanctified anymore, toots. We got demons playing in the Vatican and banging in every temple in Jerusalem."

"Weird."

Charlie pounded his chest. "I mean, Apocalypse, baby. The rules are out the window. God abandoned you, and his powers are useless now."

"Wonderful."

Aziolith landed in front of the mosque. I expected to see hundreds of demons guarding the place, but it looked empty. If there was a demon base inside the mosque, it must have been long abandoned.

"Where is everyone?" I asked.

"Let's get inside," Charlie said. "Maybe there's an orgy."

My stomach tightened. "I don't like this, Charlie. Not one bit."

"Yeah, well, you're not the one in chains. If you don't like it, assume I hate it, all of it." He slid off of Aziolith's back and hobbled toward the front door. "I'm still going. Let's go."

"I'll just wait here," Aziolith said. "Since I don't fit through the door."

I slid off to join Charlie, grabbing his chain as I followed him toward the gate embedded in the wall surrounding the mosque. He pushed open the door, and it gave with a low groan. When I walked through, I saw the majesty of the mosque close up. It wasn't one dome but dozens stacked on top of each other. I turned right and saw that one of the minarets laid across the square, cracked into a hundred pieces.

"Keep walking," Charlie said. I realized my feet hadn't moved in a few minutes as I soaked up the majesty of the building and regretted not seeing it in better times. I shook off my awe and continued through the square.

Inside the high-walled mosque was an intricately detailed pattern of columns and arches that worked their way up to the heavens, but I wasn't looking upward. I was studying the mats spread across the floor. Hundreds of demon bodies, heads separated from their necks, lay on the ground, their green blood mixing with the original red along the floor, creating a muddy brown.

"What happened here?" I asked.

"Tar-gen!" Charlie screamed, hobbling forward and pulling me with him. He stopped in front of a gaunt demon, the red drained from its body. They were not newly dead. It looked like they had been lying there for a month or more. "What have they done to you?"

Charlie was crying, actually crying. I didn't know demons could do that. "Isn't that the demon that betrayed you and stole my Molly?"

He nodded. "The same. He was my best friend."

"I hated him."

"So did I!" he wailed, kneeling into the dried blood on top of the body. I let him have his moment. I didn't know what else to do. I had never seen a demon cry, and I was not built for sympathy, especially not for a demon, and especially not for one who had done so much to hurt me and my kind over the decades.

I stood there, behind him, until the tears dried up. Finally, after some time, the imp wiped his nose with his nub and stood up. "I'm going to find these guys."

"Me too," I said. "I'll be sure to throw them a party."

"Not funny."

"No, not funny. Just the truth." I pulled on Charlie's chain. "Come on. This was clearly a dead end." We moved solemnly outside of the massacre. When we walked outside the wall, we heard Aziolith wailing. He had been covered in a chain, and no less than fifty humans, filthy and angry, stood around in a semi-circle pointing guns at him, as another stood on his back, pointing a black sword at his neck. A few of them trained their guns on us.

The short, slim woman with long black hair tied up behind her leaped off the top of Aziolith and walked in front of me.

"Who are you?" she asked me.

"Who are you?" I replied without missing a beat. "And why have you tied up my dragon?"

"This is your dragon?" she said. "I didn't know. We don't take kindly to monsters here."

"He's not a monster. He's my friend."

The woman held her sword to my neck. "Well, any friend of a monster is an enemy of ours."

I pointed back to the mosque. "Is that your handy work?"

She nodded. "Istanbul is a free city or at least mostly free." She pointed to Charlie. "Is that your prisoner?"

"He's my guide. I'm looking for a woman, a pixie named Molly. Have you seen her?"

She stared at me for a moment. "I don't know. We captured several demons and found a bunch of prisoners during the raid. It's possible she was one of them, but I'm sorry to say there were no pixies in the bunch."

My eyes lit up. "Is there any way I can check for myself?"

"Sure," the woman said. "You'll have to leave your dragon here and allow us to take your imp as our prisoner."

I yanked Charlie close. "I can't do that, but I can let you keep him while I'm here."

"Hey!" Charlie shouted. "That's not—"

I slapped him across the face. "Not one more word out of you." I turned to her. "Sorry. He's helpful in a pinch, but he's got a mouth on him."

"Very well," she said. "You'll have to put him in a holding cell. We don't let demons around Istanbul, and for his own safety, we'll cage him. If he's found by anybody else, he'll be slaughtered on sight."

I handed the chain to the woman. "Fair enough. And you'll let my dragon go? He's a precious friend to me. I'll make sure he waits here, as long as you promise not to treat him like a prisoner."

"Very well," she said. "I can make that happen."

"Then we have a deal."

"I'm Emiri." She smiled. "Welcome to the Free City of Istanbul."

CHAPTER 16

"How did you kill so many of them?" I asked, walking next to Emiri. Her hair smelled like a mix of sweat and cardamom. "Humans usually can't kill even one."

"Are you not a human?" Emiri asked.

I hesitated for a minute. "I am a pixie, like the one I search for, but I am not the enemy."

She nodded. "I know. There are good monsters and bad ones. Pixies are one of the few good ones, as long as you don't make a deal with them."

I chuckled. "I'm not that kind of pixie. I'm afraid I don't have anything to offer you unless you like gold."

"Oh, gold." She chuckled wistfully. "Do you remember when that was important? What can shiny metal do for us now?" She pulled a long, jagged, black sword out of its sheath. "Dark, soulless metal is all that matters now."

"So you found demon weapons?" I asked.

She nodded. "Demons are big and bulky, which make them effective killers and hard to take down, but they are sloppy. We quickly learned how to hide from them and use their own weapons to kill them. Once we had the metal, we melted it down for bullets."

"Nice. I had the same idea. Works like a charm."

"Absolutely," Emiri said. "They are so dumb and confident. They assume we will roll over for them. When we don't, it knocks them back—and at that moment, we strike."

"Smart," I said. "And the Blue Mosque?"

"I'm quite proud of that one." A smile flashed across her face. "The result of a month's planning. We leave it to send a message to other demons: If they come for us, we will defend ourselves."

"And do they still come?"

"We have driven them out to one tiny area of the city, and soon, we will force them out completely."

She ducked under an archway, and I followed her. What I saw on the other side nearly made me break down in tears. It was the Great Bazaar, as I had always imagined it, with hundreds of stalls stretching as far as I could see. Hundreds, thousands of humans walked through the tight corridors gathering food as if the Apocalypse had never happened.

"It's beautiful, no?" Emiri said.

I clasped my hand over my mouth. "So beautiful."

"Come, there is somebody I would like you to meet." She pushed up a piece of fabric and walked past a vendor selling figs. "She is the person who taught us all of this. Be prepared. She is a cherub."

"A…cherub?"

"A fallen angel, to be more accurate," she said, weaving through the throngs of people in the market. I had not seen a crowd in nearly a year, and I smiled for a moment before a man with a basket on his head smacked into my shoulder and spun me into two women rushing in the other direction. "She hates demons more than anyone I've ever met."

Emiri ducked into a side alley, and I hopped out of the crowd to follow her. She stopped in front of a thin wooden door and knocked. "Yes, my child?" a voice cooed from behind it.

"Open up. It's Emiri. No need for theatrics."

I recognized the voice, or at least I thought I did, but it couldn't possibly be…. When I stepped through the door, it was unmistakably Clarice, sitting behind a long wooden table, staring down at a map of Constantinople. She looked better than she had the last time we met, having fixed both her teeth and hair, but she was still short, stumpy, and pudgy, barely bigger than a toddler. Two people wearing red hoods knelt on either side of her. "Take them out here and here," she said, pointing to the map with the cigarette in her stubby, fat fingers.

The two soldiers nodded and brushed past us. Emiri walked up and kissed Clarice on her chubby cheek. "Good to see you."

Clarice chuckled when she saw me. "Well, about time you joined the Resistance. I was wondering when I would see you."

"The Resistance?" I said. "I never heard of it."

"Well, you're looking at it, buddy," she said, taking a drag of her cigarette. "We've nearly cleared this city, and we have cells all over Europe and Asia working in the shadows, waiting to take our lead. By this time next year, we'll have at least a dozen cities free, with this one as the shining example."

"Won't Satan be pissed that you're messing with his Apocalypse?"

"Probably, but screw him, for one, and screw demons, for two. He's welcome to come take me on. I have about ten thousand bullets ready for Old Scratch."

I knelt on a red satin pillow across from her. "How did you—"

"Figure it all out? When you left me with Patricio, he took me to a group of demons, and they taught me all sorts of tricks about how to survive on Earth. They would have been nice if they didn't have a habit of raping women and killing people. They were all I knew, so I stayed. They had great blow, and they were great lays. I'm not proud of it but being around them taught me two things: the only good demon is a dead demon, and we weren't going to be able to beat them back by playing nice. When the Apocalypse came, I started a little militant militia group, and here we are. Demons are big, but they're stupid and cocky."

"That's amazing," I replied. "I feel a little bad not doing this myself."

"You should be. If I had your skills, I could take over half of Europe." She looked at me. "But you're not really here to join me, are you?"

I shook my head. "I'm not. I'm looking for Molly."

"Jesus Christ." She pinched the bridge of her nose. "The world's gone tits up, and all you can do is think of a girl. You're hopeless."

"Have you seen her?"

"No," she said. "And I would have, too. I actually liked her. She helped me out of a jam once many years ago."

"I didn't know—"

"Why would you?" Clarice said. "I asked her not to tell you. Nice to see she didn't. Shows class. She ain't here, but the demons have one stronghold left, across the river in Anadoluhisarı. If she's still in this city, she's in that complex."

"I have to get there."

Clarice smiled. "Well then, you're just in time, cuz we're about to take it down tomorrow morning."

"Perfect," I replied. "I am so in."

CHAPTER 17

Emiri led Clarice and me through the bazaar until we reached a large, metal door. Dull, black metal, bulky, ugly, it broke up the flow of the street and seemed out of place.

"This is where we're keeping him," Emiri said, knocking. A slit in the metal slid open, and I saw two eyes scanning the three of us. Then, the slit was slammed closed, and the door clicked open.

"I can't believe you brought him here," Clarice said. "I haven't seen him in thirty years. How is my hair?"

"It's fine," I said. "You know he ruined your life."

"Yeah," Clarice said, running her fingers through her hair. It had grown in thick since the last time I had seen her, and she had a faint glow to her that warmed my heart. She had spent twenty minutes making sure her makeup was perfect. "I want him to see what he missed."

I followed Emiri into a large square room filled with black metal cages. She stomped toward the far wall. "We warded the whole place so demons can't escape."

Two bearded men, with eyes that pierced my soul like daggers, stood on guard. They closed the door behind us. The jail was empty, except for one cell in the far side of the room, where Charlie sat, rocking back and forth.

"Oh, Christ," the imp said when he got a look at Clarice. "Hi, baby. Long time no see."

"No shit, jackass," Clarice said. "You look terrible." She took a long beat. "Good."

"Don't be like that, sweetness," Charlie cooed, and it made me want to wretch. "How was I supposed to know you would go and get pregnant?"

"You couldn't, and that's not why I'm mad. I'm mad cuz you left me to deal with it myself. You know I got excommunicated from Heaven? I had to live with demons!" She grabbed onto the bars. "If it were up to me, I would cut you into a million pieces. Unfortunately, you're not my prisoner, and Kimberly is more gracious than I am."

"Well, thank you for that, then," Charlie said, his eyebrows raised.

"Don't thank me." I shook my head. "You're gonna get way worse from Thomas after this."

"Thomas!" Charlie shouted. "You promised."

"No!" I hissed. "I said you would go free if you helped me. You didn't help me. Clarice did."

"You are a cheating sneak!" Charlie said.

"Takes one to know one," I said. "I'll see you again after the raid."

"What raid?"

I looked over at Clarice, who nodded. "What is he going to do from in here, without hands? Go ahead and tell him."

"We're going to rid Istanbul of demons once and for all."

"Yeah, well, be careful with that," Charlie said. "You never know what you're walking into."

I chuckled. "I've handled enough demons to know what to expect from them."

He pushed his face through the bars. "Let's hope so, for your sake."

Clarice balled up her fist and punched him in the face, sending him flailing backward. "God, that felt good."

Once we were done with Charlie, Emiri led me down to Aziolith, who was burying his face in a pile of fish and swallowing them whole, straight down his gullet.

"Doing okay, buddy?"

"Better than okay," Aziolith said. "This is the best meal I've had in ages. My compliments to the chef."

"Least we could do for an honored guest," Emiri said.

"Is it time to go?" Aziolith said. "Your lack of Charlie makes me think there is still more work to do here."

I nodded. "There's a raid at sunup to destroy the last of the demons in the city. They might still have Molly. I have to help them."

Aziolith stood. "Count me in."

"You sure?" I said. "It's gonna be dangerous."

"I am with you to the end."

I broke bread with the rebellion that evening, and the next morning, before the crack of dawn, I hopped onto Aziolith's back, ready to take to the air. Our job was to come in fast and hot, giving the others time to scale the walls of the fortress. The castle was on the water, surrounded by residential houses, so it took the whole night for the fighters to get into position.

"You ready, buddy?" I asked.

"Of course," he said. "It's just…didn't we just do this? It feels like déjà vu."

I couldn't deny that it felt like we had just raided the Tower of London, even though six months had passed since then. We were following the same playbook, but it worked so well before—why mess with success?

Anadoluhisarı sat across the river from the Blue Mosque, an ancient fortress surrounded by white-washed homes. I wondered, as we made our final descent toward the castle, why demons liked ancient fortresses so much. Perhaps because that was all they knew. I would have taken over an Apple Store, or maybe a whole mall.

I looked down as we passed from the sea and flew over the land again and saw a flash of light underneath us flash G-O in morse code. "That's our cue. Light them up!"

Aziolith swooped down and laid a round of cover fire into the fortress wall. And then another in the courtyard, and finally a third that broke the wall and caused a large section of it to crumble to the ground. No demons came running out to fight us, even as we decimated their hideout.

The rebellion fighters made their way through and over the fortress walls with no problem, and when I landed on the top of the tower, I wasn't met with any resistance. I slid down off Aziolith and walked to the door. The minute I opened it, I heard a "click."

"Bomb!" I screamed. A huge fireball rushed toward me and shot out from the doorframe. It melted the roof under us. I floated into the air while the ground yawed, cracked, and gave way beneath my feet. I rushed toward Aziolith and put my hands on his scaly skin. Closing my eyes, in my terror, I thought of the only place I could, his cave. We vanished as the fire engulfed everything around us.

CHAPTER 18

We reappeared in the center of Aziolith's cavern, my heart pounding hard in my chest. The refugees ducked out of the way as Aziolith smashed onto the ground with a loud thud that rippled across the floor and caused the piles around him to shake. Gold scattered in every direction.

"Holy shit," I said, trying to catch my breath. "Holy shit."

"What happened?" Aziolith asked.

"Are you okay?" Sabine asked, running up to me.

I nodded. "I'm fine. I'm fine." I looked at Aziolith. "It was a trap, and I stepped right into it. My god. All of those people. All of those soldiers. All of—Molly." I wanted to scream and cry all at once. "I have to go back. I have to see if I can help."

"I'll go with you," Aziolith said.

"Are you sure? I have no idea what's going to happen if we go back."

He lowered his wing, and I crawled up onto his back. "That's why I insist on coming."

I couldn't flash back to the castle, so I chose the Blue Mosque, which was just across the water from the fortress. When we appeared, the city was under attack by demons. Hundreds of them crawled over every inch of the streets, and more flashed in with every passing second. Demons clearly didn't like that the free city existed and were doing everything in their power to make it an example.

"Help the citizens if you can!" I shouted, kicking off and flying into the air. "I'm going to see if there's anybody left at the fortress."

I flew as fast as I could, rubbing a pinch of pixie dust on my gums. I felt a surge of power immediately as the dust's electric tingle traveled through my body. It helped me flash faster and further until I was right over the fortress, or at least its smoking remains. Hundreds of human bodies lay inside the rubble, and those that were left alive battled demons in one-on-one combat.

It was a trap. Why didn't I see that it was a trap? Because I was too focused on finding Molly at any cost. *Stupid.*

I pulled the bow from my back and fired two arrows into an attacking demon before it could strike a hapless soldier. I loosed my remaining arrows into a half-dozen demons as I floated through the wreckage, then replaced my bow with a gun and fired into a dozen more until I had created a pocket of safety around the survivors, who had hobbled into a circle around me.

"Have you seen Emiri?" I shouted at them, but they all shook their heads. "What about Clarice?" They all looked at each other blankly. None of them had seen her, either. I reloaded my handguns and handed them to one of the soldiers. "I have to look for them. Hold off any demons for as long as you can."

I fanned out away from the group, looking for Emiri and Clarice. It wasn't long before I saw the charred remains of Emiri lying on the rubble of the fortress wall. I dipped down and cradled her in my arms, trying to find a pulse, but there was nothing. She deserved better than this fate.

"Get offa me!" I heard screaming from the other side of the rubble. It sounded like Clarice.

I sped toward the sounds of struggle, swinging through the streets with my sword until I came upon a pot-bellied demon who had Clarice flung over his back. She was covered in soot and bleeding from a gash in her face, but she was alive.

"Hey!" I screamed. The demon turned, and I sliced off its arm before the monster could go for its weapon. Green blood flowed onto the ground as it screamed, dropping Clarice, who fell into my arms. I kept one arm wrapped around her as I held the sword to the demon's throat.

"What happened to the prisoners you had in this fortress?" I growled.

"They were taken away," the demon replied.

"Where?"

The demon howled with laughter. "Wouldn't you like to know?"

"Yeah, asshole!" Clarice said. "That's why she said it."

Four more demons came out of the woods and encircled us, and while I could have taken them easily, I heard gunfire in the distance. The survivors were under attack, and I needed to get back to them. I chose to simply lop off the head of the demon who had captured Clarice before leaving the other demons to their devices.

"Thanks, doll," Clarice said as we rushed through the air.

"What the hell happened?"

"Sabotage and I think I know just the little imp who could pull off something like this."

"Charlie," I sneered. *He'll pay for this.* I dropped down into the group of soldiers just as another wave of demons streamed toward our position. "Everybody gather around. Grab onto me."

I felt a bevy of hands touch me, and after a moment, I closed my eyes. "Everybody ready?" When I didn't hear a no, I flashed to the Grand Bazaar. High on dust, it was easy to jump everyone at once.

We reappeared inside the room where I had reunited with Clarice. This time, there were screams coming from every direction. The denizens of the bazaar weren't fighters, and they weren't ready for an onslaught like this. Attacks often came when you least expected them, unfortunately.

"Protect as many people as possible," Clarice said to two women before turning to the rest of the group. "Get to the weapons cache and start distributing weapons. Let's prevent a bloodbath and show these bastards what humanity can do."

"What about me?" I asked her.

"We are going to see a coward about betraying us," she fumed. "Too bad we warded the prison, so we'll have to do this the hard way."

CHAPTER 19

"You'll need this," I said, pulling one of my daggers from its sheath and handing it to Clarice.

She had to use both hands for her tiny fingers to wrap around the hilt. "I'm not much of a fighter," she said. "I usually just play dead."

"Didn't you free this whole city?"

"Well, yeah, but I was more the brains of the organization."

"There's always a first time."

We turned right down the main thoroughfare and came face to face with two demons gnashing on the entrails of a dead woman.

"Get off her!" I shouted, slashing wildly through the air, cutting the first demon in half and then the second. I picked up the pace as we continued through the streets. We had reached the next entrance to the bazaar when I heard Aziolith's screams. From the other side of the entrance, he rose on his hind legs and smashed two demons under his feet, ripping off one of their heads.

"Doing okay, buddy?" I asked him.

"No," he replied. "But I am having a whole lot of fun. Does that make me a monster?"

I chuckled. "Lots of things make you a monster, but taking joy in killing demons isn't one of them."

"Oh, good." He ripped the other demon in half at the torso and threw the top half into his mouth. "Cuz I really do love it."

A thin, tall demon made it past Aziolith, and before I could slice him, Clarice flew forward and stabbed it through the nose, dropping it to the ground.

"Good job," I said.

"Let's go." She floated ahead of me as we zigged and zagged through the Great Bazaar. She turned left up a small inset alleyway, but when I went to follow, I felt a jerk on my hair. A mean-looking orc with a nasty overbite was swinging a club at me. I vanished in a flash and reappeared behind him to slice off his head.

"Come on," Clarice called as she disappeared around the corner again.

I followed her through tighter and tighter corridors until we reached one that I couldn't fit through. She shimmied through easily, and when she popped out the other side, I flashed forward to meet her in the middle of a giant food court overrun with battling demons and humans. Hundreds of demons fought a now-armed militia, who were finally holding their own against the monsters. I couldn't follow Clarice as she fluttered through the crowd toward an alley on the other side. I had to do my part to help the overwhelmed human resistance.

I rushed to the side of a burly man and sliced his attacker in half as it went to strike a death blow. I stuck my dagger deep into another demon's neck, kicking it off of my weapon and turning just in time to catch an imp running after a human child. I ran my sword through the demon's mouth, lopped off his head, and flung it at a charging berserker. Bullseye, right between the eyes. With it stunned, I grabbed the longsword out of its hand and stabbed it through the chest.

It wasn't until I saw Clarice dodging a pair of zombies that I decided it was time to chase after her. Luckily, zombies were dumb and plodding, and one swipe of my sword took them both down.

"Done playing?" Clarice said.

"I'm not playing," I replied. "These are your people I'm trying to help."

"They can handle themselves. We've been fighting demons for months now."

"And I've been doing it for generations." I looked back at the humans. I helped even their odds, but she was right. They had to fight their own battles. "Let's go before Charlie escapes."

"That's what I'm saying," Clarice said. "We're almost there. It's just at the end of this alley."

She pulled back a sheet and floated down a hallway. At the end of it, I recognized the large metal door that separated and guarded the prison from the rest of the bazaar. A dozen demons, imps, and zombies worked to force it open.

"Hey!" I screamed, and the group of monsters turned to me. I reached into my boot and pulled out my last remaining throwing daggers. As the first wave of demons ambled toward me, I flung the daggers at them, felling three of them and sending their lifeless bodies hurtling backward into their friends.

I took out the two zombies next because while they were dumb, their bites were deadly. Then, I took on the biggest demon, who charged me with all four of its arms swinging maces. It was a poor choice of weapon in a tight corridor, as the maces kept hitting the sides of the walls. Every time they did, he would have to stop for a second and free his weapon. I used that time to cut off each of his arms until there were none left, and then I made quick work slicing him down into smaller pieces.

With the biggest demon out of the way, that left only six remaining in the alley. I flashed into the middle of them and swung my sword in a circle, cutting four of them down in an instant. Before they could counterattack, I flashed again. One of the remaining imps charged at Clarice, who stabbed it through the chin with her dagger just as I stabbed the other one through the stomach and ripped it up from the naval to the mouth.

By the time we were done, we were covered in green goo and panting heavily, but all twelve of the demons were down.

"You're not so bad in a fight," I said breathlessly.

"You either."

Clarice floated forward and knocked on the door. "It's me."

I heard screaming behind the door. *That's not good.* After a moment, the door slid open, and a guard fell behind it, caked in her own blood and dead. She used her last act to let us inside the room. I stepped over her, and another soldier lay dead on the ground next to a bloody Charlie, heaving hard.

"You son of a bitch!" Clarice shouted. "Why would you betray us like that? These are innocent people!"

Charlie chuckled. "I don't know what you are talking about. I had nothing to do with this attack." He turned to me. "Well, except for these two. I'd look to your buddy Thomas for the rest."

"You shut your mouth," I growled, pointing my katana at him.

He raised his nubs, and chalk fell from them. When I looked down, I realized he stood atop a summoning circle, just like the one I had made in the Tower of London.

"Thanks for the idea, by the way. I could never have escaped without it." He flipped open a phone. "Now!"

He smiled and then muttered under his breath. I rushed over to grab him, but it was too late. My hands only found air. He was gone.

"We have to get out of here," I said to Clarice.

"You go. I'm not leaving while my people are in trouble."

"There are too many of them. You'll die."

"God, wouldn't that be amazing." Clarice smiled. "But no. I'm not going to die here, unfortunately." She handed my dagger back to me. "You have work to do."

I nodded. "I'll get help as quickly as I can."

I thought of Aziolith and flashed to him. He was in the middle of laying down a big swath of fire. When he was finished, I rose into the air in front of him.

"Ready to go?"

"Must we?" Aziolith said. "I haven't felt so alive in eons."

"You don't, but I have to go. I need to find help for these people, somehow, and I have to get to Thomas. Otherwise, this will never end."

"You go. I'm staying," Aziolith said. "I'll be the help, for now. I'll meet you when the cavalry arrives."

"Since when do you care about people?"

"Since I met you and Julia, of course."

I didn't want to argue anymore. "Just be careful, okay?"

"As careful as I can be in the middle of an attack."

I closed my eyes yet again and flashed back to the cavern. There was something there that I needed if I was going to get Thomas's help. I hated to give up the Dagger of Obsolescence, but I didn't see any other choice. It was a betrayal of my promise to Aziolith, but I couldn't let my own feelings get in the way of saving the world. I felt raw about it…but then, I felt raw about a lot of things.

CHAPTER 20

I reappeared inside the cavern and stomped over to the bed Julia had set up decades ago. I reached into my armory and pulled two Glocks out of my drawer to replace the guns I'd given the freedom fighters and filled my pockets with ammo. I replenished my quiver with arrows and found eight more throwing daggers, and placed them in my boots, legs, and arms.

I reached into the bottom drawer looking for the Dagger of Obsolescence…but it wasn't there.

"Are you sure about this?" I spun to see my mother holding the Dagger close to her breast. "You told me to keep it safe in case something happened to you. Remember?"

"Give that to me," I said, holding out my hand.

"I don't know what you are going to do with this, but you told me to protect it once, and that includes protecting it from you."

"You don't know what you're talking about," I spat.

"I know," she said. "You've been very secretive about all of this, which is why I have to ask. Are you sure what you're doing is right?"

"No," I said, shaking my head. "I don't know anything anymore, okay? But I have always followed my gut, and my gut is burning fire right now that the only option to save—" She didn't know about Istanbul, and she didn't have to know. I looked at her, eyes narrow and body steeled. "This is the only way, even if it's not the right way. I don't think there is any right way anymore."

She held out the Dagger. "Then I trust you."

"You shouldn't," I said, grabbing it. "Bad things happen to people who trust me."

She shrugged. "I'm your mother. I will always trust you. That's one of the joys and terrors of having children."

I was about to give one of the most powerful weapons in the world to one of the most powerful demons in the world. No good could come out of that. I was desperate, though. Not just to find Molly but to save everybody in Istanbul and keep the Resistance alive.

"I love you," I said.

"I love you, too," she replied, placing her hand on top of mine.

It took me a minute to gather my thoughts, courage, and fortitude before flashing to the quadrangle at Buckingham Palace. I was greeted by a dozen imps pointing pitchforks at me and another half dozen demons pointing crossbows at me from the roof of the castle.

I held up my hands, still holding the Dagger. "Can you please tell your mistress that I am here for her, and I have something she wants?"

"Well," Lilith said, walking out of the palace into the courtyard a few seconds later as if she was waiting for me. "You certainly do get around." Her eyes fell on the Dagger. "And I see you've come to your senses."

"Can you please tell your imps to stand down before I get angry and slaughter them all? I'm not here to hurt you."

"I know you aren't, darling." Lilith snapped her fingers, and the imps lowered their pitchforks and returned to their work, milling around the yard. "That would be suicide, even for you."

"I need to see Thomas," I said.

"You certainly do," Lilith replied. "He put a price on your head, you know?"

"I'm not surprised," I said. "I'm hoping this gift will make that go away."

She smirked. "We'll see what we can do."

I followed her into the castle. The original red carpet had been pulled up and replaced with black as dark and deep as anything I had ever seen in the murky abyss. The portraits in the foyer were not the dead, white people I remembered, but depictions of gothic horror and demons, which I appreciated much more. The motif continued upstairs and into the throne room. Thomas looked more regal and gallant wearing a black metal crown, sitting atop his twisted and gnarled throne in the center of the raised platform that used to hold two thrones. Lilith's chair was nowhere to be seen.

"What happened to your throne?" I said.

"Sacrifices must be made." She lowered her eyes. "And punishments for trusting the wrong people."

"Oh shit," I said. "Did Thomas demote you for what happened with Charlie?"

Lilith nodded. There was a desperate look in her eyes I had never seen before. "He was wary to trust a human half-blood, but I vouched for you. It's quite all right, though. I knew you would come to your senses. And look at you, the prodigal daughter returned to genuflect before the throne."

"I'm not genuflecting."

"You will if you want to be heard." She walked into the throne room, and I followed her. "My love, the pixie Kimberly has returned with a gift for you."

"Ah," Thomas said with a smirk. "I didn't believe she would, and yet here she is before me, and with the Dagger." He leaned forward and spoke in a faux whisper. "It seems things really have gotten desperate for you."

Against every fiber of my being, I knelt in front of him. "Yes, your grace. I apologize for my impetuousness. I thought I could find Molly on my own, and I denied your glory." Julia had taught me how to grovel well, even if it meant swallowing my dignity. I wondered where she was in all of this. "I come to ask you two favors. The first, you know, help in finding my beloved, but also help for the people of Istanbul, who even now fight demons for control of their city."

Thomas cackled. "Yes, I heard of their pitiful uprising. I loved it. Imagine humans thinking they could beat back demons."

"It worked for a time."

"Yes, but demons just keep coming back, don't they? If you kill them, they rise again, and again, and again. The only way to stop this is to cut the head off the viper, and for that, I need the Dagger."

"And the people of Istanbul—"

"Yes," Thomas said. "I will put them under my protection, as long as they agree to bow to me as their savior."

"I cannot speak for them," I replied after thinking for a moment. "But if you find the cherub Clarice and the dragon Aziolith, and tell them I sent you, then they will hear you out."

"Very well," Thomas said. "Your terms are acceptable. Now, give me the Dagger."

I stood and handed him the weapon.

"Yes," He said, closing his eyes as he clasped it in his clawed hand. "I can feel the power inside of it. The good you and I will do with this instrument of righteousness."

"Not interested," I said. "All I want is to save Molly and get her to safety. I'm not here to kill the Devil."

"I have faith you will change your mind. You are strong-willed and arrogant, and human blood flows through your veins." Thomas looked at me. "But you have upheld your end of the bargain, and thus I will not force you to help me. A pity, but I need you to trust me, willingly."

"Will not happen," I snapped.

"We'll see," Thomas said. "In the meantime, you are free to go."

"And of course," Lilith said, "the price on your head will be forfeited with your kind gesture."

Thomas smirked. "Of course. All is forgiven with this generous offer."

"Thank you," I replied. "Now, where is Molly?"

"She was traded to a demon enclave that's taken up residence in Christiania in Copenhagen. We have kept tabs on her. As of last night, that's where she remains, a slave to the demons there."

"Thank you," I said. Now was the time to get my beloved back.

I started to walk out, but Lilith grabbed me. "I hope you don't think you're going on your own. I'm coming, too."

"I don't need your help."

"Really?" She sneered. "Have you ever parlayed with a demon before that didn't lead to you getting into a fight?"

I considered this. "No."

"And trust me, the first thing that they'll do is slit the throats of all their slaves. Classic demon positioning. Without me, your Molly will die."

"Oh, my beloved," Thomas said, smiling. "I really do think you should stay here. We have much to discuss."

Lilith looked up at him. "It can wait. Just get the help that the humans need in Istanbul. When I get back, we'll figure out how to destroy Lucifer."

I broke away from Lilith. "It's your funeral. If you want to come, be my guest."

"Why, thank you, my dear."

CHAPTER 21

Christiania was a place I knew well, as was anywhere drugs were legal, and the demons I hunted tended to congregate in cities where they had easy access to them. Right-wing Christians were right about that. However, they were wrong as to the purpose. It seemed, at least to me, that demons preferred hanging out near drugs because it chilled them out. Demons were hot-headed, always ready to pop off at a moment's notice, and drugs gave them a modicum of peace. Thus, it became much easier to capture them in a place like Amsterdam or Christiania, where their reflexes were slightly dulled.

Freetown Christiania was famous for being an autonomous district inside of a very not autonomous city. It was a part of Copenhagen, where weed was illegal, but they claimed it was legal within their walls. It was raided often. In a situation like that, it was good to have a big bruising demon around who didn't mind going toe to toe with the cops, which meant they were uneasy allies with the city.

We flashed into one of the entrances to Christiania. Its graffitied walls still rose as high as ever, even if they looked like they could crumble at any moment. I could see why it was a covetable base of operations. It was a highly defensible position.

"Let me do the talking," Lilith said. "I know the demon who runs things in Christiania, though we've never met in the flesh."

"Fine," I said. "Why are they holed up in such a small area of the city, though?"

"Demons are very territorial, my dear," Lilith said, walking slowly toward two demons with machine guns that guarded the entrance to the city. "There are hundreds of enclaves fighting for superiority, being pushed back, and gaining control of different pockets throughout Copenhagen and the world. In Hell, these demons had a purpose, a mission, and millions of years of structural order that doesn't exist on Earth. They were forced to work together in too small a space, and now that they've been set free, they want their own forty acres, so to speak. Of course, some have more ambition than others."

"STOP!" one of the demons screamed. "Don't move."

"Oh, F'tyi," she said, disappointed. "Go and tell B'v'xol that Mother is here, will you?"

F'tyi looked over at the other demon, who nodded, and he ran off beyond the walls. Several boring minutes later, the demon returned.

"Follow me," F'tyi said.

F'tyi led us through the camp. Everywhere we walked, the eyes of demons followed us, snarling and grunting. Every once in a while, some demon or imp recognized Lilith and ran up to kiss her ring, which she accepted gracefully. There was nothing Lilith enjoyed more than adulation.

Most of the demons kept to themselves, dressed in their best Mad Max attire, sharpening their weapons over roaring fires, smoking their joints and bongs, and tracking us skeptically, if not aggressively.

Eventually, we reached a large shack in the middle of a grassy area. Grass had grown to obscene levels everywhere, and Christiania was no different. There were no gardeners in the Apocalypse.

"Wait here," F'tyi grunted before disappearing into the shack. I had been to Christiania many times before, and while it was quaint, it certainly wasn't a third-rate hovel city. It didn't make sense that B'v'xol would need a shack.

I understood when I watched the demon waddling toward us. B'v'xol could barely fit through the wide entrance, and even moving a couple of feet made him suck wind hard. He ducked out of the shack, and when he stood to his full height, he was twenty feet tall and wide as a Mack truck, if not wider. He resembled a pig, with a nose ring the size of a door knocker flapping in the middle of his face. He was dressed in a poorly fitting leather coat and wore sunglasses too small to hide the bulbous, bloodshot eyes offset too wide for his fat head.

"Mother," B'v'xol grunted. "What do you want?"

"Can't a mother come to check on her children?" Lilith said quietly. "How are you, B'v'xol?"

He snorted. "Not that you care, but things have been wonderful since we escaped Hell. No thanks to you."

"What is he talking about?" I whispered.

"Didn't you hear?" B'v'xol said. "Mother dearest had been working for years to prevent an Apocalypse. She and her band of demons, relieving pressure at every chance and trying her best to sabotage the Almighty's vision."

My eyes widened. "Is that true?"

She shrugged. "I really did not like Hell. I like Earth, and it suited me to make sure things did not change." She stepped toward B'v'xol. "That does not mean I did not care about you."

"I don't care," B'v'xol said. "We are here now, and this is a glorious revolution."

"Are you eating enough?" Her words dripped with concern. No matter how monstrous the demon, Lilith cared about each and every one. "Have you lost many demons in the fray?"

"Enough!" B'v'xol shouted. "I know you are here for something. You would never come unless you needed something. Isn't that true, mother?"

"I would like to think that it isn't, but I suppose it does nothing to alleviate your statement to confirm that I do, very much need something."

B'v'xol sneered. "And what is that?"

"This pixie is searching for one of your slaves, an older black woman named Molly. She would have been brought in here four months ago."

"Four months!" I screamed. "You knew where she was for that long and didn't tell me?"

"You refused to help us. We had no choice but not to help you."

"That's not how friendships work," I said.

"Boy, you said a mouthful." B'v'xol let out a croaking laugh. "Mother has never made a friend in her whole accursed life. Have you, mother?"

Lilith ignored him. "Have you seen her, this Molly?"

B'v'xol nodded. "I know her. Pixie blood is very powerful. If we were to give her up, then we would need something even more powerful in return."

Lilith opened her arms. "You will have me."

"What?" I asked. "You don't have to do that. We could just kill them all."

"Oh, I know, my dear." Lilith turned to me. "Now that I am free of him, I can tell you the truth. Thomas is an evil demon. He has no plans to stop—he wishes to kill his father and take over his power and then turn it against Heaven itself. Then, he will control Hell, Earth, and Heaven. He's mad. You must get the Dagger back from him and hide it where he will never find it."

"No," I said. "If that's true, he's not going to help the people of Istanbul, either."

"He absolutely does not care about them. I wouldn't be surprised if it were his people who attacked them in the first place. He believes humans and angels are inferior to demons and should cower before him."

"He's right, there," B'v'xol chuckled.

"Quite, my child," Lilith said. "But why should he lead an uprising in Hell when you could?"

B'v'xol thought for a moment. "Huh. You make a good point. Very well. If you agree to stay here as my prisoner, then I will release the fairy."

"I agree," Lilith said, turning to me. "Don't say I never did anything for you."

I watched her walk toward B'v'xol, who snapped his pudgy fingers. A thin demon rushed in from the shack with a metal collar lined with runes and snapped it around Lilith's neck.

"Now," B'v'xol said, "you are mine." He turned to the demon. "Get the pixie. Bring her here. Set her free."

I wanted to feel sorry for Lilith, but I couldn't help the butterflies from fluttering in my stomach, and a broad smile crossed my face the minute when Molly came into view from around the shack. She was thinner than I remembered and filthy. Her right eye was bruised, and her lip fat on the same side. Scars and bandages covered her arms.

"She was my favorite," B'v'xol said. "Her blood brought many demons to my cause."

Molly's face was hard, but when she saw me, it softened, and the smile I loved came through every crack on her face. When the demon removed the collar around her neck, we crashed into each other and held each other close.

"I knew you would come for me," Molly whispered.

"Sorry it took so long," I replied, squeezing her tightly. "I'll never let you go again."

And I meant it. I could have stood there holding her for the rest of time, and it wouldn't have been enough. Even the sweat in her hair smelt sweet, like honeysuckle, and my heart leaped out of my throat. I cried, loudly and fully, out of sorrow and joy all at once.

I pulled back from her hug and kissed her, softly at first and then deeply. She pushed her lips into mine, and for a moment, nothing in the world mattered. For a moment, the world made sense, and everything else fell away.

CHAPTER 22

I held Molly for longer than was appropriate for a public place surrounded by demons, but I didn't care. Even covered in muck and grime, she smelled like home, and for the first time in months, I could be still.

"Come on," I said, sliding my hand into hers. "Let's go."

She squeezed my hand tightly. "No, we can't."

"Molly, I did a lot to get you out of here." I pointed to Lilith, who was still bound in a metal collar. "She gave up her freedom for you."

"Kim, they have other fairies. They're collecting them, experimenting. Using our blood…" She shuddered. "I can't leave them here."

"Something wrong?" B'v'xol grumbled unhappily. "Cuz it's about time you pissed off."

"One second," I said, holding up my hand as politely as possible before turning back to Molly. "Are you sure?"

"Of course, I'm sure! Where do you think I was being held?" Her face lost all of its softness. "They keep us in a cage not far from here. We can't…we can't go…not without them."

"All right, all right." I sighed, understanding what it meant to deny B'v'xol's hospitality. It was tantamount to declaring war. "Slide your hands over my shoulders. Take the gun holsters. Do it smoothly and get ready."

"What about you?" she said, sliding her hands down around my chest and softly unclipping the holsters until they hung loosely around me.

"I have a sword and arrows. I prefer them anyway. Guns are kind of your thing."

She slipped her hands under the holsters. "Got it."

"You ladies should really take that into private," Lilith said. "I know you're excited to see your paramour, but please don't mount each other in public. It's uncouth."

My holsters slipped from my shoulders, and I spun to B'v'xol. "I wish that were what we were doing, but it seems like we can't do that yet. Are you holding more fairies like Molly?"

B'v'xol scoffed. "That's none of your business, pixie."

I slid my sword out of its sheath around my back. "I'm afraid that's not true. I wish I could just walk away, but I can't. I made a promise long ago to protect fairies, and if you are keeping them prisoner, that puts us at odds."

"Typical pixie," B'v'xol grunted. "The mother of demons sacrificed herself for you, and this is how you repay her? By declaring war on me?"

"Oh, darling," Lilith said, touching the collar on her neck softly until it snapped open and fell to the floor. "I'm afraid I've tricked you, B'v'xol. I'm sorry, I am, but my work is too important to be bound to any one demon. And you are simply not powerful enough to satisfy me. I mean that in every possible way."

Lilith walked away from B'v'xol, and from the look on the demon's face, he had never been insulted so much before in one instant. A combination of hatred, sadness, and venom washed across his face.

"I had my suspicions," I said.

"I like you, Kimberly," Lilith replied, sidling up next to me. "But not enough to be chained to a demon for all eternity…especially that demon. Now, let's go get your friends."

"Why are you helping us again?" Molly said. "You hate pixies."

"No," Lilith said. "I hate humans. I don't really care about pixies but having more allies on my side is never a bad thing if we're ever going to stop this Apocalypse."

"GUARDS!" B'v'xol shouted. "Kill all three of these miserable whores!"

My jaw clenched. "You definitely should not have called us that."

Molly pulled up her guns and fired ten bullets into B'v'xol's head and chest. He was so massive he was impossible to miss, and by the time she was done, B'v'xol let out a gasp and fell over without another word, dead.

"A terrible end," Lilith said. "But necessary."

"Lead the way, baby," I said to Molly as she reloaded. She floated into the air and led us past B'v'xol's shed just as a squad of demons and imps rushed to greet us, holding a mix of guns and swords.

Molly took out the machine gun toting demons while I jumped forward and cut open the chests of the imps that came at me with pitchforks. When I turned back to look at Lilith, her face had turned from angelic to one twisted by demonic possession, blood-red eyes, and fangs, with long, taloned claws protruding from the ends of four arms. She leaped forward, her dress torn to bits, and sliced open the faces of another squad of orcs.

Behind them, a bevy of goblins shot at us, and Molly rose into the air to take them out with her guns. I pulled out my bow and shot at them, too, hitting three in the chest and one in the throat. Molly cleaned up the others.

"This way!" she screamed, laying down cover fire as another squadron of demons with machine guns took position on our left flank.

Molly turned right and led us down a hill. At the bottom of it, a dozen pixies of varying heights, genders, and ethnicities mulled inside a cage that was much too small for them. They were guarded by a squad of ogres, gorgons, and imps. The fact that any fairy would have to suffer such humiliation made my blood boil but knowing it was where they kept Molly sent me into a psychotic rage.

I leaped forward and sliced the throat of an ogre guard, and spun around to rip the throat out of a gorgon. I ripped out the monster's eyes and threw them on the ground. Then, I pulled out my sword again and ripped through the horde of soldiers surrounding the cage.

Molly and Lilith joined in on the carnage, and when we were done, green blood oozed everywhere and covered our faces. Lilith turned back into her human form and wiped the blood from her cheek.

"That was fun. I haven't had so much excitement in a long time," she said, smiling.

"I'm sorry you had to kill your own people."

"Please," Lilith said. "I killed nothing that didn't deserve it, and besides, they will all rematerialize in Hell, a little worse for wear, and hopefully having learned a valuable lesson."

I searched through the muck and found a set of keys in a pool of green blood. I tried fitting them inside the lock at the front of the cage, one by one.

"Don't be scared," I said to the frightened prisoners. "You're okay now. You're going to be safe. We're going to get you safe."

"Yes, child," Lilith said. "Bring these ones to safety, and then meet me at the castle. I need a shower, and I will attempt to keep Thomas busy until you arrive. Then we can take him out."

Thomas. I'd forgotten about him in all the ruckus. "Sounds good. Actually, it sounds terrible, but it's not like we have a lot of other options. I'll see you there."

Lilith snapped her fingers and vanished just as the door to the cell clicked open, and the pixies rushed out into the yard.

"We don't have much time," Molly said, with her guns pointing at the top of the hill. "There will be more squads coming for us. We have to get out of here now."

I nodded. "Everybody gather around. Grab onto either Molly or me, and we'll take you to safety." I looked over at Molly and smiled. "Just like old times."

"Unfortunately. Where are we going?"

"Aziolith's cavern. Let me know when you have it."

She was silent for a couple of seconds. I heard the storm of footprints stomping toward us. "Got it."

"Everybody on?" I didn't wait for the answer. "Now!"

The bullets began to spray as we disappeared to safety. For the first time since the Apocalypse began, I let the weight of the universe fall from my back.

CHAPTER 23

We reappeared inside Aziolith's cavern, and when she looked around at the safety of the cave, Molly dropped down to her knees and began to cry. I knelt next to her and wrapped her in an embrace. She was wheezing as she sobbed big, wet tears.

"It's okay," I said. "It's okay. You're safe now."

"You have no idea," she said through her choked breaths. "You have no idea what I went through."

"I don't," I said. "But when you are ready, I will be here to listen."

Lydia and Horace crested around a pile, and I beckoned Molly's parents forward toward me.

"Oh my god," Lydia said, gasping. "Is that—?"

Horace slid to the ground next to us. "I never thought we would see you again, girl."

"Mom," Molly said, lifting her head. "Dad." She wrapped them tightly in her arms, and I let go of her and stood aside, giving them space to have their reunion.

"All right," I said, walking through the stunned new faces. "Welcome to Aziolith's cave. First thing's first, Aziolith is a dragon. He's not here now, but he is friendly." I stopped for a moment. "—ish. As long as you are polite and clean, then you will do fine with him and the rest of us." I stopped for a second to look at all the bewildered faces. "I know it's a lot, but I have so much to go through that it's best just to firehose you with the details, okay?"

They all nodded. "Good. So, second thing. You might not know this, but you all have pixie blood. I'm going to teach you how to use your powers to teleport in and out of this place like I've done with the others here. Does anybody know how to teleport or fly yet?"

No hands went up. "Well, you've got very important skills, especially for the Apocalypse. I'll teach them to you like I've already done with the others you see here. We've really turned this into a community.

"Third, you cannot tell anybody else about this place or bring anyone here without our permission. If I find out you have betrayed us, I will have no choice but to kill you and them. As you can see, there is enough money and treasure here to satisfy every one of us a thousand times over.

"Fourth thing, this is not your gold. It belongs to Aziolith. He has stated that each of you may fill up one chest with gold and treasures when this is all over, and you will never have to worry about money again. There is plenty for everyone, so no fighting over it.

"Fifth," I continued. "This Apocalypse will end. We are working to end it even now. Until then, our job is to save as many fairy folks as possible and bring some stability to the world. If you cannot fight, we will find something else for you to do, but everyone contributes. Got it?"

Everybody nodded and mumbled. "Good. Lastly, Aziolith is our very gracious host, and many hunters would like nothing more than to kill him for the legend it would bring them. We won't allow that to happen, which means we'll all be good about keeping our mouth shut, yes?"

They all nodded again. I moved to the side. "Good, now go eat. I'm sure you haven't had a decent meal in a long time."

"What about my family?" a fat, black man with a long beard said.

"We're trying to reunite families, but all we can do is try. We all know demons are not kind. They've slaughtered millions."

The new additions walked gingerly toward my mother and took the plates of food that the older residents held out for them. As they ate, I heard a plate drop and turned around to see Sabine standing, stunned, tears filling her eyes.

"Dad?" she said, shocked. "I thought I heard your voice, but—"

I spun around to the fat, bearded man, who smiled at her. "Hi, Beany."

They ran to each other, and the man picked Sabine up and spun her around, both of them laughing and crying at the same time. Another reunion and tears welled in my eyes looking at them.

Molly walked up to me, flanked by her parents. "Are you crying?"

I wiped the tears away. "It's beautiful, okay?"

"Good thing I told you to go back for them."

"Yes," I said. "Thank you. My head has been up my own ass for months now. I didn't know whether I was coming or going because I was looking for you."

"I knew you would come." She paused. "Though, you could have been quicker."

I smiled. "I literally chased you all over the world, from London to Turkey to Denmark and a thousand cities in between, but you were nowhere. Every whisper turned into a dead end. But now, look at you."

She looked down at the scars on her arms. "Yes, look at me."

I wrapped my arms around her. "You're free, and you're safe. In the Apocalypse, that's basically all we can ask."

She nodded, but her head was buried in my chest. "So, what's the plan for Thomas? Also, who is Thomas?"

I spun her around until she was cradled in my arm. "I'll tell you all about it after you eat. You're skin and bones."

"That's what I said," Lydia agreed. "We gotta fatten you up again."

CHAPTER 24

I only meant to close my eyes for a moment, but after she was fed, Molly and I lay in bed together for the first time in months, and the next thing I knew, four hours had passed. I woke groggy but satiated in a way I hadn't been in ages.

"That was nice." Molly stretched and dragged her arm across my chest. "Let me get this straight, now. We have to kill a demon prince?"

I stretched. "I don't know if we are supposed to kill him, but we need to get the Dagger of Obsolescence from him so he can't kill the Devil and rule over Earth, Heaven, and Hell."

"Right," Molly said. "But why don't we want him to kill Lucifer? I mean, won't that end the Apocalypse?"

I shrugged. "If Thomas gets the Devil's power, then he can take a run at Heaven, and that doesn't sound any better than an Apocalypse on Earth."

"So, how do we end this?" Molly asked.

"I don't know," I said. "I'm figuring this out as I go. I haven't had time to sit down and make a plan, but once we get that Dagger back, we will. You know how much I like a good plan."

Molly sat up. "And you trust Lilith to tell you the truth?"

I shook my head fervently. "Hell no, but she knows more about demons and the Apocalypse than I do, and she's been around Thomas more than me, so I at least trust her that he's the bad guy. Besides, she brought me to you."

I sat up and stroked her face. "And anybody who can do that can't be all bad."

Molly pushed up and grabbed her gun belt before pulling on her pants. She wrapped it around her hips and looked at me. "Well, let's go then."

"God, you are so hot right now."

I pushed up and dressed myself. I had found a second set of armor for Molly during the time she was gone and helped her put it on, running my fingers across her body as I did to remind myself she was real. Neither of us liked armor, but we also didn't like dying, and in the Apocalypse, you couldn't take any chances. I gave her a pinch of pixie dust and took one myself, both of us rubbing it on our gums.

"Should we wait for Aziolith?" Molly asked.

"No," I replied. "We've already kept Lilith waiting long enough. If Thomas really isn't sending more troops, then Clarice needs all the help she can get."

I closed my eyes, and we flashed into the sky above Buckingham Palace. Thousands of demons gathered around the front of the palace, cheering and hooting. As they did, the double doors of the balcony swung open. Thomas strolled out of the building, holding a wriggling Lilith by the hair in front of him.

"Friends!" he shouted. "I have helped you find glory in this new time, have I not?" The cheers echoed through the air. "Are you not happier now?"

Again, they all cheered. "And yet, in that time, one has been working to undermine me! And you! They call her the Mother of Demons, but she helped slaughter many demons in Christiania!" Boos. "She plotted to kill me and take for herself the Dagger that we need to kill my father! She works to end the Apocalypse and send you back to a crowded Hell!"

Thomas held Lilith over the balcony and pulled the Dagger from his belt, holding it up for all to see. "But do not worry, my friends, I have found the traitor, and I will use the power of the Dagger of Obsolescence to show my doubters what true power really means!"

"Oh no," I said. "Dive!"

Molly and I flew downward as fast as we could. Arrows and bullets fired at us from the roof of the building and the courtyard below, but demons were terrible shots.

"Now!" We vanished, appearing on the balcony of the building. I kicked Thomas off of Lilith and pulled her to safety. "Hi, Thomas."

"Thank you, my dear. I did not think I would have to keep him entertained for so long." Lilith brushed herself off. "You are here now, which is something."

"Treason!" Thomas shouted.

"It's not treason, ya dink," I snarled. "You aren't king. You are just a pathetic prince who daddy didn't love." I stepped forward. "Now, give me the Dagger. It's over!"

He put his fingers together, and I leaped forward to prevent him from snapping. Molly pulled his other arm, and Lilith walked over to take the Dagger. Before she could, the door burst open, and a group of demons streamed in, firing at us. We had no choice but to abandon Thomas as the bullets rained on us.

"You fools!" Thomas shouted. "You could have killed me!"

"Oh, please. Demons are terrible shots, and imps are worse. Something about their stubby fingers." Lilith said. "But that's not the point. These men don't work for you.

They work for me." She snarled at them. "Could have come sooner, don't you think?"

She rose to her feet and held up her hands. The demons stopped firing. "You have no power here. Give me the Dagger, and you can live the remainder of your life in miserable inadequacy."

Thomas looked down at the Dagger in his hand. "I think not." He snapped his fingers successfully that time. He was gone.

"Damn it!" I shouted. "Why did they fire on us if they're on your team?"

"I was about to be killed!" Lilith shouted. "Do you not remember that? They were trying to protect me, which was more than I could say about you."

I glared at her. "I did save you, or don't you remember a couple of minutes ago?"

She nodded. "I do remember. And yet, I needed a backup plan, didn't I?"

"What are we going to do about Thomas?" Molly asked, brushing herself off. "Or the demons outside screaming for your head?"

Lilith chuckled and gave a wave of her hand. "Please, demons are easy to manipulate. As for Thomas, he'll poke his head up again, and you'll be there to knock them down."

"Like a game of whack-a-mole?" Molly asked.

"Not the most elegant metaphor, but yes. Like a game of whack-a-mole."

"Can't wait," I grumbled.

EPILOGUE

Molly and I tracked Thomas for more than a year, all around the world from Jakarta to Mumbai and back to the Once Again Free City of Istanbul, following clues and hunches that Lilith helped us piece together until we finally ended up in the last place I would ever think to look— Overbrook, a tiny town in a nowhere part of Oregon. I would never have known it existed if I wasn't looking for it.

The poor town had been ravaged by the Apocalypse, but it still had working lights and water, which was a blessing compared to most of the burnt-out husks I had seen in my travels. Most cities weren't even hanging on by a thread. They had long since fallen into the abyss.

"Why would Thomas wind up here?" I asked Molly as we walked through the dead streets. Not a soul moved in the buildings or on the sidewalks, even in the middle of the day.

Out of the corner of my eye, I saw something speed through the street in a flash of purple. "Come on," I said, flashing forward with Molly close behind. We followed the streak throughout the town until it stopped in front of the ruins of the town hall.

"Stop right there, Thomas!" I screamed. But when the streak stopped, it wasn't Thomas at all. I couldn't believe what I saw. The same complexion, like she hadn't aged a day since she was sacrificed. "J-J-Julia?"

"Oh my god," she replied. "Is that Kimberly? I've been looking everywhere—"

She started to smile at me, but her eyes went wide in terror. A torrent of wind rushed through the street and lifted her into the air, pulling her away from us.

"Julia!" I ran after her.

She grabbed onto the side of a building, but the brick was in such decay that it flaked off into her hand, and she was sucked even higher into the air, though she struggled to fly toward us. From the buildings around the city, hellhounds, orcs, ogres, demons, and all manner of Hellspawn rose into the air with her.

Julia maneuvered around them as she reached out for my hand. I pulled her down, and for a moment, she collapsed into my arms.

"It's so good to see you, kiddo."

"It's good to see you, too," I replied.

"It's over, now," she said. "I feel it in my soul. All of this. It's over. You won. Now, it's time for me to go back."

I fought against the intense pull of the wind dragging her back like a magnet. "I don't want you to go."

"I know, kiddo. I know, but you have to. I'm not meant to be here."

"I'm so sorry," I said to her. "I'm so sorry I didn't do more."

She pulled back slightly to look into my eyes. "Don't ever think that. Working with you was the best time of my whole life." She cocked her head to the right. "Is this your new partner?"

"In every way you can intend those words," I replied with a grin. "Molly, this is Julia. My mentor. Julia, this is the love of my life, Molly."

Molly smiled. "It's nice to meet you."

"You to—" Julia screamed as the wind violently jerked her back, but I held on tight, slamming us both into the side of a brick building.

"You have to let me go," Julia said. "It won't stop until I return to Hell."

"I don't care. I don't care. I'm not letting you go back to Hell. I can't—"

"Hey, hey," she replied. "It's okay. Really. I'm okay down there. I really am."

"I don't believe you."

"Hey," she replied. "Have I ever lied to you?"

Tears started to fall down my face. "I don't want to—"

"I know." She unlatched my hands from behind her and floated up in the sky. "You did good, kiddo. Better than me. I'm so proud of you."

She pulled her hands from mine, and the wind pulled her into the sky as I watched her disappear into the ether. When it was over, the wind stopped, and Molly and I looked at each other.

"Is that the end?" Molly asked. "Is it really the end of the Apocalypse?"

"I think...so...? God, I hope so."

Molly rubbed my back. "She was nice. I can see why you searched so long for her."

I disappeared into Molly's shoulder, sobbing uncontrollably—for surviving the end of the world, for bittersweet reunions, and for Julia.

BOOK 3

"Death's Bargain"

CHAPTER 1

I had no idea how to be a god.

After all, I had only been one for less than a year, since killing Thanatos with his own dagger and becoming the god of Death to save the universe from Ragnarok. I was once the stuff of legend – the immortal pixie who fought demons. When I returned to Earth after Ragnarok, though, I had become a shell of myself. I felt like a stranger in my own skin.

I had the power of a god at my disposal, but every time I used it, something went spectacularly and uncontrollably wrong. I had been around the block, having lived for 21 years as a normal pixie and then over two hundred as an immortal one, but I felt more out of sorts in my whole existence.

Since I had been imbued with Death's powers, the voices of thousands of people assaulted my brain every second of every day, crowding out my thoughts. They screamed into the abyss, and I was a tuning fork.

The constant barrage made it impossible to keep the kind of focus I needed to do my work, so I didn't do much of anything. I wandered the streets of Los Angeles, bitter and alone. Without complete control of my senses, I didn't dare teleport. If I lost my concentration, I could be lost in the inky blackness of the universe forever, stuck between worlds.

The only two things that drowned out the constant cries from humanity were alcohol and narcotics. It also worked to numb the pain of being a pathetic loser who could barely tie her own shoes. It took a massive dose to affect me at all, and I was usually high on one concoction of drugs or another, which meant I had several drug dealers on speed dial as my godly metabolism burned through the hardest stuff available. I couldn't puncture my skin with needles, which meant I resorted to freebasing, snorting, and popping pills.

High as a kite, I would stumble between bars until the world stopped screaming at me, and I passed out. When I woke up, I did it again. The only thing that broke my routine was a case, but they were becoming harder to find. Few wanted to associate with a mess like me, even if I had the power of a god. It wasn't much of a life, and I had an eternity ahead of me.

"You look like shit," Lilith grumbled as she slid into the seat next to me at whatever bar I was drinking my sorrows in at the time. They all looked the same, and the drugs affected my short-term memory so that I forgot where I was most days. I could remember faces like Lilith's, my oldest friend and mortal enemy rolled into one.

I pushed back the hood on the black robe that came part and parcel with being the god of death. I hadn't found a way to take it off. "Thanks. I know."

"I see you are still wallowing," Lilith said. Her face was softer and less angular than it had been during our last encounter. She usually chose the face of a harsh and powerful mistress ready to destroy you with a moment's notice, but this night she took the visage of a softer type, dark-skinned like an iced mocha, with kind eyes and a bright smile that reminded me of my Molly.

Molly. The only girl I ever loved, taken from me over a hundred years ago by old age. The pain never dulled, no matter how many pills I took.

The only consolation of being a god was the thought that I would be able to see her again after I left Hell, but I'd never been able to return to the fiery depth. I was the god of Death, and I could not even enter Hell to see my love and make sure she was all right. *What kind of god was I anyway? What good was infinite power if you couldn't control it?*

"It's really unbecoming, you know?" Lilith said, taking the scotch and 7-up from my hand and taking a sip. "Foul."

I pulled it back and took a long swig. "You don't have to drink it."

She spun to me, her curly brown hair bouncing in the air. "You shouldn't be drinking it, either. You're a god, for Christ's sake. What do you have to be miserable about?"

"Everything. Nothing. I don't know."

She shook her head and let out a motherly sigh. She did that sometimes, even though I wasn't one of her ilk. "Well, I can't believe I'm saying this, but I'm in need of your services."

"That doesn't surprise me," I said, sucking a piece of ice. "You only come around when you need something. That's why I haven't seen you for months. Gods forbid you cared about checking up on me."

"Would you pull your head out of your ass and listen for once? One of my demons is in a bit of trouble."

"They are literally chaos incarnate, so again, that doesn't surprise me."

"Quite," she replied curtly. "But I still worry about them, every one of them, and I need you to check on him."

I grit my teeth. "What's the problem? He kill too many people? Get blood all over his nice, clean shirt?"

"He impregnated a pixie woman, and now their child is being hunted by a squad of demons who believe she is the key to opening the gates of Hell."

"A pixie is in trouble?" I set down my glass. "Okay, now I'm interested. Tell me more."

"Sober up," Lilith said, sliding a piece of paper over to me. "Then, go see the master of the house at this address. He'll give you all the details."

"Why can't you?" I asked as Lilith rose from her seat.

"My darling, I have a thousand things to do today. I'm asking for you to take one of them off my plate. Can you do nothing without me?"

I downed the rest of my drink and slammed it on the table. "I got this."

***

A large gothic manor stood at the address Lilith gave me, surrounded by a wrought-iron fence emblazoned with a large, golden M in the center of the gate. The emblem was the only part of the house that shone like new. Thick green vines twirled through the bars, and the shrubbery on the other side clearly hadn't been trimmed in a year or more. The grass grew to a foot high, and tree branches hung low, swaying ominously in the night breeze.

It was the kind of place I could have easily penetrated with my powers if I trusted them. At the moment, my only option was to press the button on a call box that rested crookedly against a crumbling brick pillar next to the driveway. It gave a wicked screech before crackling to life. A smooth, confident voice spoke.

"Whom may I ask is calling?" the masculine voice cooed.

"Kimberly," I replied. "Um, Lilith sent me."

There was no answer on the other line, just a buzz and a click as the gate swung open. I took the cracked concrete path that wound through the unkempt garden and up the stairs to the main house. Like the gate, the brick had been overrun by vines. A thick layer of grime caked every window. Whoever lived there needed a gardener and a maid, stat.

The door swung open as I approached, and an older woman with bright white hair stood in its frame. Her dead eyes belied the reserved smile she plastered on her unnaturally smooth face.

"Good evening," she said, tipping her head to me. "You are late. We expected you hours ago."

"Sorry," I said. "I took the bus."

She gave a disappointed grunt and eyed me up and down. "Follow me into the study."

I walked into the house, and the door creaked closed behind me. The inside of the manor was spotless; it was as if I had entered another world. The walls had fresh paint, and the floors gleamed like sparkling glass.

"My apologies for the appearance," she said. "We just moved in."

"Okay," I said. "I was wondering."

"Master was very concerned that it felt homey inside, so we have spent every moment readying it for his arrival. We'll be working on the outside next, should we stay for the duration."

"The duration of what?"

She didn't answer. Instead, she walked me down a long hallway, her heels clacking against the shimmering wood floors. I looked down at my dirty, sullied sneakers that squeaked like a cornered mouse and made a mental note to buy a new pair.

"Who is your master?" I asked.

She chuckled. "You don't know?"

"I don't. I was just given an address."

"I'm sure master had his reasons for not telling you, and if I know anything about him, it's that all will be revealed in time."

It was an unsatisfactory answer, but I knew better to push a drone for information, especially when they were on the clock.

The woman stopped in front of a set of light blue double doors. She knocked, and a smooth voice responded, "Come in." I recognized it from the call box. She pushed open the door and beckoned me to enter with the wave of her arm.

"Thank you," I said, this time bowing my head to her as I passed. She closed and locked the door behind me. The sound of the lock prickled the hairs on my neck. *Who was I locked in with?*

A crackling fire roared in the hearth at the back of the room, the aroma of burning wood replacing the unpleasant smell of paint from the hallway. Every inch of the study walls was filled with wood shelving and books, first editions, leather bound, the type of collection any library in the world would kill for.

In the middle of the room, a gruff, stern-looking man sat on a high back, red leather chair, smoking a pipe. In his lap rested a long, oak box that matched the floor and shelving in its splendor.

"Good evening, Kimberly." His voice was as smooth as silk. "It's nice to finally meet you."

"I wish I could say the same," I retorted. "But I don't even know your name."

"No, you don't." He placed his pipe on a small end table next to his chair. "I am Momus, and you killed my brother."

"I kill a lot of people."

"Yes," he replied. "But this one was a god. Thanatos. You actually killed several of my siblings, and I have to say, I'm slightly miffed about it."

I didn't know that Death, War, Famine, or Conquest had any siblings, but it made sense. The gods were ancient, and there was only so much you could do before the universe got boring and you resorted to procreation. "Your family was about to unleash Surt on the world. Their deaths were necessary to save the universe."

Momus sighed. "You sound like my mother."

"Your mother?"

"Nyx, goddess of the night, and keeper of death. She would have you believe that all death is necessary. I disagree. Death is not inevitable, least of all for us. I didn't care much for my siblings, save for my beloved brother, Thanatos. I wept when he was exiled from the universe and was elated when I heard he had returned. Then I found out you killed him and felt a strange emotion I had never had before. Sadness. As a god, I have very little occasion to be sad, and yet, the loss of my brother filled me with this emotion. I have not been able to shake it since."

"I'm sorry you feel that way, but Thanatos was evil."

"He was not!" Momus boomed. "Thanatos had a poet's soul. Plenty in my family are evil, but he was... possibly misguided, corrupted maybe, but he was not malicious or malevolent."

"You're wrong."

He gripped the edges of the box. "I will not argue with you. Your feelings about my brother are inconsequential to the task I require of you."

"And what task is that?" I said. "I'm just about out of patience."

"I want you to bring my brother back."

I let out a chuckle. Of course, a god would ask the impossible. "I can't. I killed him. I know you gods don't deal with death a lot, but dead is dead."

"Oh, my petite. You have not been a god very long. Otherwise, you would know that being a god means that anything can be fixed." Momus's voice was cold. "He is buried deep in your subconscious, begging for you to free him. Perhaps you have heard him when you are not in a drug-induced stupor." He smiled. "Yes, I know all about you. I have been following your woefully, pitiful machinations for a long time."

"Then why wait until now to contact me?"

"Several things needed to fall into place, and now they have. It took a lot of convincing and cajoling and a bit of torture, but I wanted to make sure you took me seriously." He thumbed the box in his lap. "Shall we show and tell?"

"If you must."

Momus flipped up two metal locks on the box and opened it. He pulled out the Dagger of Obsolescence, which contained the essence of my soul. It was literally the last object in the universe I wanted to see, and he held it in his manicured hands. He was right. The tenor of my mood changed immediately from nonchalance to deathly serious.

"By the look on your face, I assume you recognize it. It truly is a masterwork of construction." He ran his finger across the curved blade and the red-eyed gem that rested in the hilt. "I have been told that if I destroy this Dagger, you will break apart, along with any hope to save my brother. While this blade survives, so do both of you."

"What did you do to Aziolith?" I asked. "If you hurt him—"

"He's fine," Momus said, lifting his hand. "Maybe a little worse for wear. However, if you fail, I will make sure to wipe him from existence slowly and painfully."

I needed to play it cool. "What do you need from me?"

"It's simple. Find a way to separate yourself and my brother, and I will let you live in whatever miserable state you were in before you became a god." He noticed the look of dread on my face and cocked his head. "Honestly, you aren't equipped to be a god."

"And if I fail, you will kill me?"

"Oh, I will do more than that. I will wipe any memory of you from the universe, destroy everyone you ever loved, and mount them on my mantle. Aziolith, Katrina, Julia, and your beloved Molly will vanish from existence." Momus stood. "I suggest you do not fail me."

CHAPTER 2

"You son of a bitch," I growled at Momus.

I lunged toward him, but he didn't even flinch. He simply placed the Dagger between his fingers and bent the blade—just enough to show he had the strength to destroy it.

"Tell me I'm wrong. Tell me you are happier right now than you were before you became a god."

I stopped moving forward, convinced he would destroy me. "I...can't."

"Of course, you can't. Because you're only human."

"I'm not human."

"You're at least part human, and humanity isn't equipped for godhood. They screw everything up before long." He stopped applying pressure to the Dagger, and I exhaled. I hadn't even realized I was holding my breath until that moment. "We gods are molded with the divine right to rule. You can't just become a god and think you can withstand the tremendous power we suffer every day. As you know, it is a burden, a curse."

I crossed my arms across my chest. "Then why would you want to plague your brother with it?"

"It is better than the curse of nonexistence," Momus said.

"Are you even sure I can do this?" I said. "Separate the two of us, I mean?"

"Not specifically, or I would have come to you with a spell or a plan. I only know that our powers are limitless," he said. "As to how to do it…I have no idea, I'm afraid. But then, it's not my burden to carry; it is yours."

"What if there is no way to do it?"

His brow furrowed. "I don't think we should be so defeatist, do you? After all, you haven't even tried." Momus stopped for a moment. "Now, there is the matter of a timetable. I am not good at these, as a century feels like a moment to me, but I know you humans feed on them. Let us say, one week from now." He nodded. "Yes, that sounds right. Bring me my brother one week from now, or I destroy the knife and you with it."

"That's not enough time!" I screamed.

"How do you know?" he replied, cocking his head. "You haven't even tried. Run along, now. I will stay in this place for exactly one week from this moment. If you bring me my brother by that time, then everything will be wonderful, but otherwise…" He pressed his thumb in the middle of the knife. "You and everyone you ever loved will be gone with a flash."

I wanted to punch him, but before I could swing my fist Momus snapped his fingers, and I was outside of the manor flailing at air, the gate shutting in my face with a loud moan.

***

Lilith had no reason to fear me. After all, I was barely a fraction of my previous self, but I was surprised to find her within an hour of me leaving the manor, nibbling on a sandwich as she strutted down Hollywood Boulevard.

"You totally set me up!" I screamed.

"Oh, darling," Lilith said. She wiped a crumb from her mouth. "That is the nature of our relationship after all, isn't it? You can't blame a demon for following her own inclinations. Momus offered me an ungodly sum for bringing you to him, and I knew you would never go of your own volition if you didn't have a little push, so…I lied. It's how I get anything accomplished."

"You could have warned me," I growled.

"Then, it wouldn't have been a lie." She took another bite of her sandwich. "Seriously, best sandwich in the whole world. I don't even like chorizo, but this is delightful."

I slapped the sandwich out of her hand. "Not cool."

She held up her hand in protest but eventually simply sighed. "And that was not cool either, so I suppose we are even."

"Even?" I slammed my fist against my chest. "I got my life threatened. You lost out on a sandwich. We are so far from even."

"Well, you would have gotten your life threatened one way or another, whether I helped Momus or not. Had you not slapped that sandwich out of my hand, I would be enjoying it right now, so who is the real monster here?"

"YOU ARE!" I snapped. "It's impossible to talk to you when you are like this."

"You seem upset. Perhaps I can offer you guidance. What is the subject of your ire?"

"The subject? The subject is that I have a week to somehow rip a god out of my body, and if I don't, then I'm going to vanish from existence along with everybody I love."

"Excuse me for being crass…that doesn't include me, right?"

"No, mostly because I absolutely hate you."

Lilith exhaled. "I suppose this warrants my attention."

"And how are you going to help me?"

"I'm one of few who can. There are few gods left on this planet, and most of them are of the demi— useless variety. I'm thinking the only way to get some answers is to talk with the big man, and the only person I know who can do that is Katrina since she has a line right into Heaven from her castle."

"That would be great if I could figure out how to get into Hell. I've been trying for the past year, but no matter what I do, I can't picture it in my mind."

"Oh, honey. That I can definitely help you with. Or have you forgotten that I am the mother of demons?"

***

"The reason you're having trouble is because you're used to moving between places on the same plane of existence," Lilith said as we walked through the crowded streets of downtown Morocco.

"Obviously," I replied.

She spun to me. "Hell isn't on this plane of existence. It operates outside of time and space, as do all underworlds."

"All underworlds?"

"Of course, you have been to Hell, haven't you?"

"I have."

"And did you see any Globorians, or Anchatians, or Ponjerians while you were there?"

"No," I replied. "Should I have?"

"Not at all. They have their own underworlds, as do other planets run by other pantheons. There are thousands of underworlds, darling. We are a small part of a very large tapestry."

"This is blowing my mind."

"Of course, it is, darling. After all, you're high as a kite, and you're barely a god, which means most of what I'm saying is going over your head, but that's okay. The highlight is that we have to teach you how to jump between dimensions if you are ever going to get to Hell."

Lilith stopped in front of a warped and worn door. She knocked, and the bottom of the door protruded more with each rap. It wasn't really attached to anything. It sort of just leaned against the archway.

"Stop doing that!" a low voice growled from the other side. "Come in and mind the hinges!"

Lilith looked on the side of the door. "There are no hinges!"

"I know that!"

"Then perhaps you should say to mind the lack of hinges," Lilith sighed. "I suppose that doesn't roll off the tongue."

Lilith carefully pulled the door off and motioned with her head for me to enter. When I was through the archway, she entered and replaced the door. Runes were drawn in white chalk on every surface of the mud-lined hut. The lines curved and swirled together beautifully, creating a tapestry of movement.

"What do you want?" A candle lit and the square bottom jaw of a demon came into view. As the demon raised its candle, two bloodshot, bulging eyes were revealed. The eyes narrowed. "Oh. Hi, Mom."

Lilith kissed the demon's cheeks. "Wonderful to see you, Greta. It's been too long."

"Who is that?" I asked, pointing to the ancient demon.

"No need to point, darling. It's rude." She pushed my finger down as she crossed her legs to sit. "This is Greta, my daughter, and not in the 'Mother of Demons' kind of way. She's biologically mine. Unfortunately, her father was a human, which means she ages. How old are you now, sweetheart?"

"Four thousand, give or take a few centuries."

"It's so sad." Lilith turned to me. "She's probably only got two or three thousand years left."

"That's a long time."

"Not on the cosmic scale!" Lilith took in a deep breath. "Darling, Mommy needs your help. I need you to do that thing you do where you help broken demons open their minds and flash between Earth and Hell."

"Flash between? What?" I frowned. "You're teaching demons to come here of their own volition?"

"Of course, my love," Lilith said. "Katrina is no friend to us, and I offer them sanctuary."

I threw up my hands. "They're going to flood Earth, just like during the Apocalypse."

"I wouldn't say they are *flooding* here," Lilith said, shaking her head. "Would you say flooding?"

"I wouldn't," Greta said. "I would say a light trickle. I'm very careful with who I train. Demons won't teach the method to other demons. They're too selfish and self-involved."

"Still, even a few are too many."

Lilith stood up. "My love, the Apocalypse was a disaster, but some demons were wrongfully brought back to Hell, and with a new regime, it became impossible to negotiate to bring them to Earth. We had to make other arrangements."

"I don't like it."

"You don't have to like it. We're not asking your permission." She turned from me. "However, if you don't want our help…"

"No!" I shouted. "I do."

"Then there is only one rule," Lilith said. "No judging."

I hesitated. "Fair enough."

"There are actually many rules," Greta replied. "But since I doubt you are going on a rampage through Dis, I will skip them. Sit."

She gestured me to sit across from her, then reached into her pocket and pulled out a piece of white chalk. She grabbed my hand and drew a single line on it that continued across my shoulder and then looped around. "Place your hands together." I did, and she continued along the other side with the same motion. "Touch your forehead with both hands." I did, and the line continued onto my head, down each cheek, around my neck, and then back up to my jaw. She drew around my lips and then pushed what remained of the chalk into my mouth.

"Swallow."

"Seriously?" I said. "That's gross."

"This is nowhere near the grossest thing you've put into your body today," Lilith chided.

She was right. I coated the chalk in my spit and swallowed hard. The chalk cut the sides of my throat as it slid down.

"Open," Greta said, and when I did, she confirmed the chalk was gone she sat back. "Good."

"What does the chalk do?" I said.

"Nothing you need to concern yourself with now," Greta said, chuckling. "It proves you are malleable if nothing else, which is the most important thing about this whole process. You must have an open mind and an open spirit."

"Not building a lot of trust here," I grumbled.

"Trust is overrated," Greta said. "Now, the reason you cannot transport to Hell is because you are trying to create a portal when you need to be constructing a wormhole."

"What's the difference?"

"A portal is like knocking on a door. All you need is the right key for it to open. A wormhole, though, is like burrowing through clay to come out the other side. To make a portal, you need calm and concentration. To create a wormhole, you need force of will. It is grit, determination, and an unmovable spirit."

"That she has," Lilith said, watching me.

"Good. Now, close your eyes."

I was embarrassed to tell them that I hadn't even made a portal in almost a year for fear of winding up vanished from the cosmos. Instead, I simply closed my eyes. I wanted so badly to see Molly again that I would deal with the consequences if that's where I landed.

"Just like with a portal, you need to imagine where you wish to go in your mind's eye. However, unlike a portal, where you succumb to the ether, you must force your way through, like a jackhammer. The universe does not want to let you in, but you must tell the universe to go screw."

I closed my eyes and found only blackness. I tried to push through it, but it invaded everything.

"It's too hard!" I moaned.

"The Kimberly I know would never say that," Lilith snapped. "Try harder!"

I imagined the hole where I had come out of in Hell a year ago. From there, I pushed harder, and the rocks around the hole populated, followed by the cracked Earth. My hands and my brain soon ached, but the world of Hell had become clear in my mind.

"I see it!"

"Great," Greta said. "Now, push!"

It was against my nature to fight against the darkness. To teleport, you had to surrender, fall into it. But I pushed hard, and my stomach fell to my knees. Every hair on my body stood on end, and my brain felt like it was going to pop out of my head.

"I...can't..." I grunted.

"Look!" Greta said. I opened my eyes, and my arms were glowing purple, pulsating in time with the throbbing pain in my head. "It's working. You show the universe who is boss!"

I closed my eyes and focused with renewed determination. I didn't care about living. I didn't care about the quest I was on. I only cared about one thing, seeing Molly again. With the simple thought of her, my body fell into weightlessness, and I felt myself slide through the caress of the universe and jerk forward into the bowels of Hell.

I had done it.

CHAPTER 3

Hell.

It smelled just as I remembered, like a barbecue where the host left the meat on the grill for too long, and it became inedibly charred. The skyline of Dis rose in the distance. Molly lived within its walls, but I wasn't going there yet. Instead, I unfurled my wings and rose into the air. I was headed to the Dragon Caves to check on Aziolith and find out how he'd lost my Dagger.

I followed the jagged rocks along the edge of Hell, passing several small towns along the way until I hit the rocky hillside toward the tip of Hell, southeast of the Gates of Abnegation, where souls first enter Hell. At the caves, Dragons had dug holes into the very foundation of Hell to make their home. I flew until I saw the unmistakable bone crest hanging above Aziolith's cave and landed in front of it.

"Aziolith!" I shouted. "Az!" I stepped into the darkness of the cave. "Az. It's me. It's Kimmy."

My eyes adjusted to the darkness quickly now that I was a god, and after a moment, I saw perfectly the metal net that bound Aziolith to the back of the cave. I followed his long, red neck up to his face, where a black metal muzzle on his mouth prevented him from breathing fire.

"Hang on, buddy!" I called to him.

Several large, black metal spikes ground the net into the rock of the cave. I grabbed one and began to pull. It was enormous and barely fit inside my arms, but with my new and improved strength, I was able to free the post.

I followed the chain around, yanking up every post that embedded the net into the rock wall, and when I was done, the chain fell free, and Aziolith stretched his great leather wings.

"Hang on, buddy. I'm not done yet."

I unlatched the strap from his chin. Then I did the same with the one at the back of his head. When I was done, the muzzle dropped to the ground, and Aziolith let out a great yawn before blowing a stream of fire into the air.

"Thank you," he said and lit the bonfire in the center of the cave with a quick blow from one of his nostrils. "Let me get a look at you."

I hopped into the air and did a little spin for Aziolith and then beamed a big smile at him. "It's good to see you again."

"You smile, but there is a great sadness behind your eyes."

"Wow," I said. "You can't even let me enjoy seeing you for a second, can you?"

"No," Aziolith replied. "I assume you have returned because I lost your Dagger."

"I'm afraid so." I sat down next to him.

"Then, it is as I feared."

"What happened?"

"It was an ambush. I have never dealt with a coordinated attack by so many monsters at once. There must have been close to fifty, maybe more. I was able to fight off three squads of them, but eventually, I succumbed and ended up chained to the back wall. I am so sorry, Kimberly. I meant to protect it, but I failed you. I couldn't even keep it safe for one decade. Lucifer was right to keep the Dagger from me."

"Hey!" I said. "It's not your fault. That guy who attacked you was a god, the brother of Thanatos. You couldn't beat back a god. Nobody could."

"You killed four of them," Aziolith said.

"Not four, I'm afraid. By keeping the Dagger intact, I saved myself, but I think Thanatos is still alive."

"That is…incredible, if true."

"If true," I said. I was too high to hear anything right then. "I need to find Katrina and get in contact with God, but first, I need to get to Dis."

"What's in Dis?" Aziolith asked.

"Molly."

***

Bang. Bang. Bang.

Julia lived on the southern tip of the city in one of the few areas that weren't destroyed after Ragnarok. Most of the city was still a hovel, with new buildings sporadically peppered throughout. The demons I passed as I traversed Dis lived in makeshift tents and shanty towns. I hadn't seen Julia since the end of the Apocalypse, and butterflies rose into my throat at the thought of seeing her again.

"Coming!" I heard Julia shout from inside her apartment. She opened the door wearing a doily apron and holding a mixing bowl. It was very unlike her to play housewife, but she wore a smile also, and that was even more unusual.

"Oh my god," she said, dropping her bowl on the ground. It cracked against the hardwood, and dough splattered across the floor. "Where have you been?"

She wrapped me in a big hug. Even a tight hug from somebody without godlike strength barely registered against my skin, but I still appreciated the contact. "It's good to see you, Julia."

Tears filled her eyes when she pushed back from me, and she wiped them with the fringe of her blue-checkered apron. With her eyes cleared, she saw Aziolith, in his human form, tall and lithe, standing behind me. "And you, too, Aziolith!"

"He insisted on coming," I said as she pushed past me to hug him, too.

"I haven't seen you in weeks," Julia said, elated.

"Yes," Aziolith said. "I have been indisposed."

"Oh no," she said, looking from Aziolith to me. "What happened?"

"Is it that obvious something is wrong?"

"I mean, you do tend to only come to Hell when the world is about to end."

"That's not fair," I replied. "I tried to come a bunch of times, but I only figured out how to travel between dimensions today." I stopped for a moment. "But yes, everything is awful, and I am in deep trouble."

"Well, come in then," Julia said, moving away from the door. "Watch for the dough. I don't want you tracking it through the house."

Julia's house was everything she never wanted. Well-furnished and clean, complete with tiny decorations and touches that we used to laugh about in another life. It was the opposite of the Julia I knew, but then, the Julia I knew was from three centuries ago.

"Sorry for the mess," she said, scooting past me into the kitchen and grabbing a towel from the messy island to clean up the spill. "I was baking and—well, I got a little carried away."

"It's damn near spotless in here, Jules, at least compared to your old place," I said, looking around. "And there's so much light."

"Yes, Francis wanted to face the palace. He said there was better light that way."

"Who is Francis?" I dropped down to pick up pieces of the bowl with her.

Julia smiled coyly as she cleaned up the mess. "He's my...special friend."

"My, my, my, Julia," Aziolith said, not sullying his tailored suit by helping us clean. "In almost three hundred years, I've never seen you take a lover."

"Piss posh. I wouldn't say all that," she said. "Lover makes it sound like we're having a secret tryst."

"But you live together?" I said.

"We do." She blushed, broadening her smile. "It hasn't been that long, of course. I met him well after Ragnarok. Just a couple of months ago, actually."

"That seems...fast, especially for you."

"I know," Julia laughed. "I don't know, after...I was gutted for a long time. My house was gone. Most of my friends were gone. Dis was a nightmare, even more than usual. And in came Francis, like a calm breeze, and he kind of swept me off my feet."

"You sly dog," Aziolith said. "So, what does Francis do?"

"He's an architect. He's helping redesign this whole city from the ground up. Isn't that amazing?"

"Impressive," I said. "And you were baking for him?"

Julia shook her head. "No, not him. We are feeding some of the displaced residents today. I know it's stupid since we don't have to eat, but it's a bit of normalcy, you know?"

"I want to help."

"That would be lovely."

I had not had many normal days since I was eight years old, and a banshee kidnapped me, so it was nice to stand in a kitchen and bake cookies and pasta for other people. I had to become Death and bore my way into Hell to do it, but it was a nice change of pace to forget myself, even for an afternoon.

After we were done, we walked the food down to a local shelter and distributed it to the imps, demons, satyrs, ogres, goblins, and other monsters gathered in the streets like paupers during the Great Depression. After witnessing them rampage through the streets on Earth during the Apocalypse, seeing them grovel for scraps was something else. There are two sides to every coin.

When all the food was gone, Julia and I walked back to her apartment. Aziolith had stayed behind so as not to get any grime on his clothes, or at least that was his excuse. I also thought he wanted to give Julia and me some time alone, which I appreciated.

"I'm sorry we missed your beau," I said.

"Yes, well, he's very busy," Julia replied, walking past another corner of destroyed homes and broken buildings. "You would like him, I think. He's nice…and not just by Hell's standards."

"That is high praise. I hope I can meet him before I go."

"Francis would like that, I think." Then, her smile dropped. "Kimberly, my dear, as pleasant as this has been, I know it's not what you were here for. Why are you in Hell?"

"I need to find Molly," I said. "Are you still in touch with her?"

Before I left Hell, I reunited with Molly, and we spent what felt like an eternity together over the following week. I could have stayed in her arms forever, but there was already a Devil, and Katrina felt like having another god in Hell cramped her style, so I promised to return to Earth and keep things stable there. I thought I could come back to see Molly any time I wished, but, well, time made fools of us all.

Julia shook her head. "I haven't heard from her in months. We used to meet for lunch, but then she stopped calling."

My eyes widened. "When was that?"

"It was just about the time I met Francis, and you know how new lo—relationships can be all-consuming. I should call her."

"Do you have her address?"

"Up in my apartment."

We picked up the pace. A knot grew in the pit of my stomach. Molly wasn't one to stop calling her friends. She was the most social person I had ever met. It was one of her worst qualities.

CHAPTER 4

I asked Aziolith to wait with Julia while I visited Molly alone. We had a lot of catching up to do. Then, they would meet us at The Old Hat later in the evening. I wanted some alone time with the girl I loved, who I hadn't seen in over a year, and not for two hundred years before that.

I was legitimately nervous as I walked across the city. It was easy to tell I was nervous because I was walking instead of flying, and I certainly wasn't about to teleport in a place I didn't know.

As I walked through the broken streets of Dis, I couldn't help but think about the last time I had entered Hell. Dis was a metropolis, every bit the equal of New York, Paris, or Tokyo. It had skyscrapers, flying cars, and even overpriced coffee, the distinction of any great city by my estimation.

Now, it was as if a tsunami had swept through and destroyed everything, leaving the city rudderless. Surveying the damage, I wondered if I should have left in such a hurry. I was so confident that Katrina could handle it all. She was forceful and strong-willed and spoke with such authority, I believed wholeheartedly that she would change Dis for the better. Maybe I was expecting too much, or maybe Katrina had become a true politician, speaking out of one side of their mouth while masking the truth of the situation.

Either way, everywhere I went, demons, imps, and other monsters shambled around the city in shock, as if they had just been hit in the jaw. Perhaps two hundred years ago, living even in this squalor would have been an upgrade, but they were sold a bill of goods about technology. They were promised that it would make their lives easier, and when it did, they fell into the classic trap of any modern society: they became complacent with the status quo.

Our ancestors had very little, so they expected very little. When they rose above their station, they were pleasantly surprised. However, we built a world that gave us everything on a silver platter. We rose to heights our ancestors could not even imagine, and when we fell, we smashed hard into the ground. I saw it after the Apocalypse when the world tried to return to normal, and I saw it on the faces of every monster—they had been forsaken by the only god that ever delivered for them—technology.

When I found Molly after Ragnarok, we took up residence in an overturned building. We didn't need anything but each other, so we righted the bed and curled up together, but in the past year, she had moved out of the city to a little suburb on the outskirts of Dis that had seen a massive influx of monsters after Dis fell.

Her apartment was a converted ranch house that somebody had fashioned into a duplex, though they didn't do a very good job of it. There were no pretenses in the little street; no grass lawns, no plants, no frills, just a house plopped in the middle of clay. If there had been any rain, the dinky homes would have sunk into the ground. Hell didn't have weather, at least, so they sat precariously and precipitously above the cracked ground. Molly lived in unit B around the back of the house, and butterflies flapped in my stomach as I rang the bell.

"Molly!" I shouted. "It's Kimberly. Sorry, it took so long, but I'm back. Can you—"

It wasn't Molly that answered the door. Instead, a four-armed woman with long black hair, glowing yellow eyes, and two serpent tails slithered toward me, naked.

"Who are you?" she growled.

"Who are you?" I said, indignant. "Where's Molly?"

"Oh, you're friends with Molly?" She stretched, throwing her naked breasts in my face. Classic alpha-bitch power move. "She'll be home later. Sorry, I would tell you to come in, but it's a little messy in here. Molly's a bit of a nester."

She was right. Molly was a nester. At that moment, my heart cleaved in two.

***

"How could she?" I screamed out from my seat at the booth in the back of The Old Hat. Julia sat on one side of me and Aziolith on the other.

"I know it's tough, kiddo," Julia said, rubbing my back. "But maybe it's for the best."

"I'm not a kid! I'm almost three hundred!" I shouted. "And how could this be for the best?"

"Well," Aziolith said, "she is in Hell, and you are on Earth, and that's quite a difficult long-distance relationship. It's not like she could send you a card and tell you she moved on. Besides, if there's one thing I've learned in Hell, it's that anything you can do to make your life bearable…you take it…even if you'll regret it in the future."

"Amen to that," Julia said, clinking her bottle with Aziolith's wine glass. She pushed up from her seat. "I'm going to get another. Do you need?" She looked at my sullen eyes. "You need."

She walked to the bar of the seedy pub. As she did, Akta walked through the front door. She was a slight, little thing, though she worked with the purpose of one three times her size.

She saw us and made her way through the hordes of other patrons. "Kimberly! I barely bel—oh god, you look horrible. What happened?"

"She got dumped," Aziolith said.

"I didn't get dumped, not technically," I said. "I just found out my girl is cheating on me."

Akta furrowed her brow. "Molly? No way, that gal loves you. It's literally hard to talk with her because she gushes about you all the time. I actually thought about not coming because I'm so sick of hearing about you that I've been avoiding her calls."

"Calls?" I said, my ears perking up. "When was the last time she called you?"

"I mean, I bumped into her like two weeks ago, and she was still smitten with you, so I find it hard to believe that she got over you so fast, or that she got under somebody else when she—" She rubbed her temples. "—like literally can't stop talking about you. Sorry, it's frustrating." Julia brushed past Akta as she slid into the booth. "Ask Julia. She and I complain about it all the time."

I spun to Julia, who looked contrite. "Is that true, Julia?"

She sighed. "Yes, all right? I wasn't lying that I haven't talked to her in a few months, but I would be lying if I said I wasn't kind of happy about it."

"I asked you for one thing!" I shouted. "One thing."

"Yeah, one huge thing!" Akta said. "And we did look after her. We just did it from a distance." She placed another beer in front of me. "Something smells fishy. What did this new person look like?"

I took a long swig of my drink. "She was tall and beautiful and half snake."

"Wait." Julia stopped the bottle next to her lips. "Isn't Molly afraid of snakes?"

"Not afraid, but—" Oh my god. It clicked. She hated snakes more than anything. She would have never willingly dated a snake monster. "Yeah, this doesn't make sense."

"What kind of monster was it?" Aziolith said. "Snake bottom or top."

"Bottom."

"Hideous or beautiful?" he asked.

I sighed. "So beautiful."

"A lamia," Aziolith said. "Can't they mind control people?"

"Yeah," Julia said. "But we're kind of not supposed to use our powers down here, except for work."

"And when was the last time you teleported for convenience?" Akta asked.

Julia smiled. "I mean, this morning, I forgot to turn the stove off, so…then, I guess."

"Exactly," Aziolith said. "Nobody follows those rules, and nobody enforces them, either."

I slammed my beer down. "We have to save my girlfriend!"

I thought they would scream and cheer. Instead, they just finished their drinks and slid out of the booth. It didn't instill me with a lot of confidence, but they were all with me, and together Akta teleported us to Molly's house. I felt a little like a crazy ex-girlfriend, but with a god after my closest friends, I had to be sure Molly wasn't captured.

I knocked on the door just as I had before, this time with the drunken forcefulness of a woman who had downed twelve drinks an hour for the last four hours. Even for a god that self-medicated often, that was a lot, and I wobbled from one side to the other.

"Coming!" a recognizable voice came from the other side of the door, and when she opened it, my broken heart nearly ripped out of my chest when I saw Molly smiling at me. She was just as beautiful as the last time I saw her, if not more so. Perhaps the distance made my heart grow fonder, but the grooves time bore into her face accentuated her vibrant brown eyes and high cheek bones.

"Oh," Molly said, dropping her voice and her smile. "I thought you might come back. Sysestia told me you stopped by."

"Molly, I want you to know that I'm not mad." I caught a burp in my mouth and swallowed it. "I'm really not. We have to do what we have to do to survive, right? And we all gotta survive. It just sucks, you know? I was so excited to see you—and look at you, you're beautiful—and this is the greeting I get? I haven't seen you in a year."

"Exactly. A whole year you've been gone."

"I've been trying to get back here since the day I left."

Molly crossed her arms. "Is that all?"

"I—um—yes?"

"Then I think you should go."

"Wait!" Aziolith said, stepping forward. "Would you indulge me for a moment, Miss Molly?"

Her eyes narrowed. "Why should I?"

"Under the auspices of old friendship. It'll only take a second."

She sighed. "Fine."

Aziolith pointed to me. "What's her name?"

"How dare you ask me that as if I wouldn't remember the name of my ex-girlfriend!" She went to shut the door. "Goodbye."

Aziolith grabbed the door before it slammed closed. "I know it's stupid. Please, humor me."

"This is really stupid," Molly said. "That's Kimberly, my ex. Good enough?"

She went to close the door, but Aziolith stuck his foot in the jamb. "And who are those two?" He pointed to Akta and Julia with his free hand.

Molly rolled her eyes. "Akta and Julia. They are friends of mine, or I thought they were friends, until today."

"Where are you going with this?" I whispered to Aziolith.

"Just trust me." He smiled back. "And one more question…who am I?"

She scoffed. "I don't have time for this."

"Of course, you don't, but I just seemed to remember that lamias are expert shapeshifters, and while you may have seen the others before, I haven't seen Molly for a year." Aziolith moved closer to the door. "So, who am I?"

I watched Molly's face. First, her cheek twitched, and then, her eye blinked, and I saw for a second a purple hue behind her eyes.

"Lamia!" I screamed. "You're the lamia!"

"That's preposterous!" she shouted.

I pushed past her into the apartment, where it looked like there had been a bare-knuckle boxing match inside its walls.

Finally, the Molly doppelganger sighed and changed back into her lamia form. "Fine, you got me. Come in, I guess."

CHAPTER 5

"Where is my girlfriend, Sysestia?" I screamed. "Where is Molly?"

Sysestia scoffed. "Like I know. That wasn't my part to play in all this. I was just supposed to capture her and hold her until somebody picked her up and then stay here in case anybody came looking for her."

I stepped forward. "Then who would know where she is?"

Sysestia shrugged. "I don't know, man. I do have a message for you, though, Kimberly." She cleared her throat. "Shit, how did it go?" She thought for a second. "Oh, yeah. You really should be working to save Thanatos instead of chasing old flames. I promise that your beloved will be fine, as long as you do what I say. If not, none of those you love will be safe."

"Momus," I growled.

"What's a Momus?" Akta asked.

"A very annoying god," I said. "He trapped Aziolith, stole the Dagger of Obsolescence, and is threatening everyone I love."

"By the way," Sysestia said. "That was a good trick, saving the dragon. I was not prepared for that. We thought for sure you would come right here if you got into Hell. Kudos for unpredictability."

"Thank you?" I said, confused. "Do you have anything useful to say, or should we kill you now?"

"You're the good guy," Sysestia said. "I can smell it a mile away. You're not going to kill anyone."

"If you truly believe that," Julia said, "then you don't know us very well at all."

"We don't have to kill you to torture you," Akta added. "I've learned a lot of tricks from the pits while I've been here. The things I could do to you…"

"And I'll just set you on fire, over and over again," Aziolith finished off the conversation. "Trust me; I'm aching to."

"Long story short," I said, getting in her face. "We're the good guys, but we're not that good." I took a deep sniff. "I smell the fear on you, and that's the right emotion. You should fear us more than Momus because once I kill him, I'll be back for you and everyone else who touched a hair on Molly's head. I'm going to slice you into little strips while you beg for my mercy."

"All right, I get it!" Sysestia grumbled. "You are all very scary, congratulations. And this is Hell, so that's really saying something." She shifted in her seat. "We all met once to go over the plan and make sure there weren't any muck-ups."

"How many were there?" Akta asked.

"Ten, plus Momus, who is a stone-cold fox, by the way."

"Did you recognize any of the others who were there that day?" Julia asked.

"No, they were just run-of-the-mill monsters."

"What types?" I asked.

"A couple of imps, a few demons, and a Dullahan."

Julia's eyes went wide. I had seen that look before like she had just finished snapping together a piece of a complicated puzzle. And then, it dawned on me, too. Julia's boyfriend was a Dullahan.

"Wait," Julia said. "The Dullahan. What was his name?"

"Frank, I think, or Francis." Sysestia thought for a moment. "No, it was definitely Francis."

"Son of a bitch," Julia said. "That's my boyfriend's name."

"Funny, he was the one Momus assigned to neutralize you. Probably not the same Dullahan, though. I mean, what are there, ten in all of Hell?" Sysestia laughed. "Can I go now?"

"Oh, no." I turned to Aziolith. "Do we still have those chains?"

"Yes, we do," Aziolith replied with a smile.

***

After talking Julia down from a murderous rage, we agreed to confront Francis together at her apartment while Aziolith kept Sysestia as our prisoner. When we got to her apartment, though, Francis was nowhere to be found.

"He must be at work," Julia said.

"What do you think he actually does?" Akta asked.

"Arch—shit, I don't know. He's probably some sort of scumbag or another. You know, just a general douchery artist."

I sat down on the fine leather couch to wait. "Can I ask you something?"

"No," Julia said. "But okay."

"A Dullahan…they are headless, right? So, was that the appeal?"

Akta laughed despite the icy glare from Julia. "I'm sorry, but I had the same question. Actually, it all kind of makes sense. You hate people and small talk, so having a headless boyfriend is kind of perfect."

"He's not headless," Julia said. "He just doesn't have a head that he consistently wears. It's like dating dozens of people at once, which keeps me from getting bored."

"Explain, and please use small words because I want to make sure I understand this clearly."

"It's not that complicated. In our bedroom, there's little closet with a dozen or so heads that he rotates between depending on his mood. Keeps things interesting."

"That is brilliant," I said, sliding off the couch. "I have to see this."

I ran down the hallway toward the back room. Akta rushed forward to join me. As I reached for the door, though, Julia flashed in front of me to guard it. "I can't let you do that."

"Why not? Is there freaky sex stuff back there?"

She paused. "Yes."

"That just makes me like you more," I said. "I just assumed you were asexual, not that there's anything wrong with that, but this is blowing my mind. Come on, you have to let me see."

As we struggled for the knob, the front door creaked open. "Honey, I'm home!" a rough voice bellowed.

"Not now." Julia blew past me into the living room. "Hi, sweetheart."

I moved forward to watch the spectacle. Francis was tall with a wide build. I don't know about his other faces, but this one was square-jawed and had a real Clark Kent spirit to it, without the glasses. His face was slightly too big for his body, though it wasn't noticeable unless you looked closely. I wondered how closely Julia looked at his face and which one she liked best.

Francis went in for a kiss, which was his second mistake. His first mistake was being a lousy, spying crook. Julia spun away from him, placed her foot behind his, and dropped him to the ground in one smooth motion. She unloaded on him with both of her fists, and by the time we wrestled her off, Francis's face sagged on one side, and the other had swelled to twice its size.

Julia popped off Francis's mangled head. "Bring him to the couch."

She disappeared into the back room and came out again with the head of a black man with a long beard. As we laid him on the couch, she twisted a new head onto his neck. I realized that the rest of his body was gray until the head snapped on, and then it morphed into the same coloring as the head. His shoulders even shrank slightly to better fit the proportions of his new persona.

"OW!" Francis said. "What was that for?"

"We know you're working for Momus," Julia said, sitting down.

"Shit," Francis said. "Who told you? It was the hobgoblin, right? That stupid little cheat."

"Hey!" Akta snapped. "You're all cheats as far as we're concerned. We want names and addresses of everybody who's working with you."

He chuckled. "Please, I'm just a cog. My job was to keep Julia distracted until the boss called for me, and then I would deliver her."

"Whose job was to get me?" Akta asked.

"Nobody," Francis replied. "I didn't even know you existed until this moment. I knew about the Devil, Julia, her mother, and the girlfriend. Who are you?"

"Ouch," Akta said, glaring. "That kind of hurts."

"I—need a drink," Julia said, standing up and moving to the kitchen.

"Watch him," I said, looking at Akta.

"Of course. That's all I'm good for." Akta shook her head. "What are friends for? Oh, wait. We aren't friends."

I didn't answer. I didn't have time for a temper tantrum. I walked over to Julia.

"Akta's really upset," Julia said. "I didn't even know she had feelings."

"I did. I saw how she was when Sven betrayed her and when they took you. She's not a robot."

"No, she's not," Julia said, fighting back tears.

"And neither are you," I added. "Are you okay?"

She shook her head. "No, I'm not all right. This is all so screwed up. I've been barely hanging on since Ragnarok, and I was finally—stable, in a way. Maybe that's why I fell for Francis in the first place. He's as boring as milquetoast, but he had something that I didn't, something I haven't seen in all my time in Hell—he was stable. I grabbed on with both hands. Stupid."

"It wasn't stupid," I replied, grasping her hand. "It was his literal job to trick you. You can't be pissed at yourself because some dickhead did their job well, any more than they can blame us for doing our job well." I turned away from her. I needed to change the subject, and there was no way not to be callus about it. "I'm sorry to do this, but I have to go."

"Of course you do."

I spun back to her. "Look, I can stop this if I just give Momus what he wants. If I can find a way to rip Thanatos out of my body, then this will all be over."

"Do you really think he's going to let you go after all this?"

"I have to."

"Then you are dumber than me," she replied. "Gods don't do nice things to people who succumb to them. They are heartless dickbags out for no one but themselves. Haven't you ever read any mythology or the Bible?"

"Yes."

"You killed his brother. What if Thanatos wants revenge for his death, or the death of War, or Conquest, or Famine? Ever think of that?"

I was taken aback. "No, I didn't. I'm not really thinking two steps ahead."

"I taught you better than that."

"The shit you taught me to do three centuries ago isn't really relevant now." I sighed. "You didn't have any lessons about how to deal with a vengeful god."

"That's true." Julia stopped. "Just promise me you won't trust any gods, okay? Don't trust anyone."

"What about you?"

"Well, okay, trust me, but don't trust any scummy gods, okay? No matter how silver their tongue."

"I promise." I took a deep breath. I didn't want to go, but I knew I had to. I couldn't ask anyone to carry this burden for me, and there was still a god threatening my life.

"Will you work to find Molly while I go and try to end this?"

"Of course." She hugged me. "You can trust us."

"I know," I replied. "It's one of the few things I know for sure in this crazy universe."

"Don't die, okay?"

I smiled. "If I do, I know where to find you."

CHAPTER 6

Katrina's castle was due south of Dis. It would have been more convenient to simply fly straight there, except that the Black Gate protecting her castle from the rest of Dis was magical, because of course it was, and it could extend to the far reaches of Hell, across the complete expanse of the underworld, and even down to the magma river that fed into the lake.

The only way through was the gate granting you access.

I landed high above the cliffs of Hell, near its southernmost tip. Katrina's castle lay far beyond the gate, sitting on an island in the middle of the molten lake. Akta once told me that from the highest tower of the castle, you could see all of Hell.

"Drop your weapons," something squawked from high above me. I looked up to see two harpies perched on either side of the gate. They looked like vultures with glowing, red eyes on their human heads. They expanded their wings and flew down to meet me.

"Drop your weapons," one squawked again.

I shook my head. "Yeah, I'm not doing that."

"Then you'll die," the other chimed in.

The first one spoke again. "Only weaponless may you hope to see the queen."

I pushed back my black robe, revealing the daggers hanging from my belt in their sheathes. "You can certainly try to take them."

"Not us you have to worry about," crowed the second harpy.

"We're just trying to help." The first one flapped her huge wings until she returned to her perch with her sister. "Be ready to meet your doom."

I stepped toward the Black Gate. "What do I do?"

"Now you want our help?" the harpy cawed. "Just stand there. It will judge you unworthy."

Everybody who had ever judged me unworthy was long dead, and I wasn't afraid of a stupid gate. As I waited, a red gem situated at its center began to glow. A bright light shot out of it and scanned me for a long moment.

"Screwed," the second harpy laughed.

After a minute, the big gem began to rattle, and the beam scanning me grew hotter until it sizzled on my skin. Then the light fell silent and receded into dullness above the gate.

"Alive?" one harpy crowed.

"How?" said the other.

"I'm a frigging god," I said to them. "Do you really think a little laser would hurt me?" I looked up at them. "I really don't have time for this."

I pushed on the gate, and it swung open for me. I grinned at the harpies as I walked through it. I had heard tell of Charon, the boatman who sailed people across the lake, but I was pleased to see that there was no boatman when I reached the dock. I didn't feel like talking to anybody. There was just a little gondola with a pole sitting atop it. A sign was nailed to a post next to the boat. *Those worthy may cross. Otherwise, piss off.*

There was no way I was worthy, but I stepped onto the boat and grabbed the gondola's oar. It burned and tingled in my hand slightly. It certainly wasn't enough to deter a god. I pushed the oar and made my way across the lava.

Halfway across the lake, I saw a boat pass in the other direction with no boatman. It was a nice touch connecting the two boats to each other like funiculars and meant no monsters had to wait on the shore all day—a genius bit of magical automation.

After rowing the boat for an hour, I arrived at the dock on Katrina's island. My hands were throbbing and red, but after a few moments, they returned to their normal coloring and the pain subsided. Some parts about being a god were okay.

A thousand or so steps separated me from the entrance to the castle, and three dozen soldiers blocked my path. I flew right past them without a second thought, heading toward the entrance of the castle. When I landed, the soldiers on the steps grumbled and began to climb in my direction. I paid them little mind, instead pushing on the malformed black skulls and bones that made up the door. It moaned while opening.

"STOP!" a giant troglodyte screamed at me.

I wheeled around. "I swear you do not want to mess with me today." I don't know if it was my power or my voice, but the monster believed me and backed down. "That goes for all of you. I will end you."

"Katrina will deal with you herself," the monster said. "It has been so long since she had a plaything."

"Oh, I'm real scared." I rolled my eyes and walked into the castle.

The inside was much as I remembered. The human bone aesthetic continued from the door and up every wall into the ceiling and along every column. It was excessive and overkill. Probably one bone would have done, or maybe two, but millions definitely screamed, "I am not secure." It would have been much nicer if they played against type and made it feel homey like springtime, but then I wasn't an interior decorator. I could just tell I hated everything I saw.

A black velvet carpet extended from the door along the hallway, lined with suits of ancient armor. Each held a weapon of some type. I wondered if an imp cleaned every suit or they were magically enchanted not to get dirty. It didn't really matter. It was just another bullet point in my insecure Devil thesis.

I continued down the hallway, still lined with black bones until it broke into a magnificent throne room, the walls lit with blue torches and covered with paintings of demons. I nearly tripped over an extension cord that snaked into the center of the room, where Katrina was seated on a throne made of bones, holding a controller. The imp Carl, her right hand, sat in front of her with another one.

"I'm kicking your ass, Carl!" she shouted.

"Yes, ma'am."

I stepped forward, watching the blue light from the television bounce off Katrina's pale skin and brown hair. She was dressed in pink flannel pajama pants and a white tank top, which looked decidedly un-regal. It was the first thing I had seen since passing through the Black Gate that I liked.

When Katrina caught sight of me, she dropped her controller. "Who are you?"

I stepped into the light of one of the torches. "You don't recognize me? It's only been a year."

Katrina laughed. "Shit, is that Kimberly?"

"That's right."

She hopped off her throne and stood up. "I thought I would never see you again. Frankly, I hoped I would never see you again since you bring trouble everywhere. How are you?"

"Still bringing trouble everywhere," I said.

"Shit," she replied. "Well, come on. Tell me all about it. Do you want to play some video games? We've gotten kind of good at making them now. Definitely PlayStation 2 quality."

"I'll pass," I said. "I'll watch you play, though."

"Groovy."

CHAPTER 7

I watched Katrina play video games for a couple of hours, and then she insisted we watch an all-demon remake of *Bill and Ted's Excellent Adventure,* which was surprisingly entertaining.

My stomach was rising in my throat, though, so I couldn't enjoy it. With each second that passed, my doom approached. When I tried to tell Katrina my frustration, she simply said, "time moves differently in Hell. You'll be fine."

After our third tin of stale popcorn, I stood and brushed myself off. "All right, now about—"

She waved her hand dismissively. "Look, I know you want to talk about some deep shit, but I'm just not there yet. Can we please just watch *Mean Girls* and chill out?"

"You have *Mean Gir*— No!" I narrowed my eyes. "What's with you, anyway?"

"Nothing!" she replied. "I'm fine."

"No, you're not. This is not the Katrina I remember. The Devil I remember was imposing, unrelenting, and a force of nature. She wasn't…this…neutered, jammie-wearing…nothing."

Katrina sat up. "You're toeing a real fine line. Watch it."

"I'm not scared of you." I balled up my fists. "You look like you just went through a bad breakup. When was the last time you even left this stupid castle?"

"I don't remember." Her voice faltered.

I stepped forward. "Have you been out of here since Ragnarok?"

"DON'T. Say that word." Katrina pointed a stiff finger in my face. "Nobody gets to say that word to me. Ever."

"What word? Ragnarok?"

Fire blazed in her eyes. "Watch it."

I grabbed Katrina's finger and twisted it around her back before kicking her to the floor. "No, you watch it. Not only am I more powerful and better trained than you, but I'm also a god. I could rip you apart with just a thought."

"Yeah!" she screamed, rolling to stand. "Then why don't you do it? If you think you can beat me, then come at me. Come on. I rose from a simple human to the Devil. Look at me. Just look at me!" She rushed toward me. Her belly was full of fire, but she had no technique. I spun out of the way and pushed her into the wall behind me, shaking the paintings from their moorings.

"This is stupid. You cannot beat me."

"If I had a nickel for every time I heard that," Katrina said. Fire filled her hands, and she shot it at me. I ducked her attack easily, and they did little more than set fire to the paintings behind me, which were hideous anyway.

"I don't want to hurt you," I said as Katrina rushed me again. I grabbed her by the throat and threw her to the ground. "But I will."

"Do it!" Katrina screamed. She stopped struggling for a moment and looked me in the eye. "Do it! Kill me. That's all that anybody wants anyway, me dead."

I let go of her neck, and she hopped up. She rubbed her throat as I turned to her. "You don't believe that, do you?"

"Of course I do. I did everything for this place, and they tried to kill me. They're still trying to kill me, Kimberly. Every day, I'm looking over my shoulder, trying to figure out where the next dagger is coming from. My own generals turned on me. The dukes of Hell are still plotting, I just know it. They're polite to my face, but I know they're planning something." She rolled onto her side, crying. "I might as well be dead."

I crouched next to her. "I was just in Dis, and do you know what I saw?"

"A bunch of pitiful demons."

"Well, yes, that, too, but what I saw were demons who had lost all hope. They were miserable, Katrina."

Katrina looked up at me. "You're not making me feel any better."

"They're miserable because they lost something they didn't know they missed. They loved their old life, and they're looking for something to believe in, a leader. Even if they didn't know they were supposed to believe in you, I think they will if you give them a reason."

"That's a lot of thought," Katrina replied. "But what do you know?"

"A lot," I stood. "Before the Apocalypse, we were docile and content. We complained about the simplest things. We complained that the internet took three seconds instead of one. I was there for the Apocalypse and its aftermath. After the shock wore off, people banded together like never before. Once we knew what we missed, we cherished it, and we lauded those that brought it to us. That could be you, Katrina. Right now, there is a power vacuum, and you're leaving yourself open for somebody else to fill it. You could fill it, but not if you're playing video games and holing away in this stupid castle." I reached my hand out to her. "You'll do it by being out on the streets."

"You're right." She wiped her eyes with her shirt and grabbed my hand. "If you ever tell anybody that I broke down, I will kill you."

"No, you won't. But I won't tell anyone about this."

Katrina rubbed her eyes to get the last of the tears out of them. "What did you need, now?"

"Well, you remember that Dagger?"

"Of course, I think about it every day."

"We kind of lost it."

"What?" Katrina screamed. "Are you kidding me?"

I held up my hands. "Hang on, now. I know where it is, and the god who stole it said he would give it back…but I have to do something for him first."

"Oh, good. Bargaining with a god. That always goes well."

"Look, I don't know any gods, but I need to talk to one. As far as I know, you have the only direct communication with a god in this galaxy. Can you help me speak to the god of Earth?"

"I can't do that," Katrina replied, shaking her head. "I pissed him off something fierce with the whole Ragnarok situation. But I can probably get a message to Lucifer to meet you at the cliffs in front of the Gates of Abnegation."

"You think?" I said. "Well—I need you to do more than think you can because, not to put too fine a point on it, if I can't get him what he wants, he's going to kill me and then kill everybody I care about, including you."

"Ha!" Katrina replied. "That's funny. And you said I should leave the castle." Katrina sighed. "I'll get Lucifer a message for you. Get to the Gates of Abnegation, and I'll have him meet you there in an hour."

"What if he doesn't come?"

"He'll come."

***

Katrina snapped me to the entrance of Hell, a dark void of the abyss that I couldn't see past. I pressed against it, but my hands met a solid, black surface.

"It's not the best system."

I spun around to see Lucifer, just as overweight as I remembered but more slovenly than our last encounter, dressed in shorts and a t-shirt. He continued, "Tartarus could have been designed better. Of course, it was designed at the beginning of time, when humanity was barely a nascent speck, and now, look at them." He pointed to the millions crowded into the path below me. "Like locusts."

I landed beside him on the cliff. "Thank you for coming."

"Usually, when Katrina asks me for a favor, it's to save a lot of lives, and I hate that, so this is a nice change of pace. What is it you need?"

I told him everything from the beginning, probably too far from the beginning, and when I was done, he stroked his unkempt beard. "That...is quite a dilemma."

"I know," I replied. "And I need to figure out how to fix it in the next couple of days, or I'll be toast, along with a bunch of my favorite people—and Katrina."

Lucifer chuckled. "Nice distinction."

I rubbed my neck with a grimace. "I mean, I love her as much as I hate her."

"I think that's the consensus reaction," he said. "All right. I have good news and bad news. Which do you want first?"

"Um, the bad news, I guess?"

He pressed his lips together. "I don't think God is going to be able to help you. He's a bit of a twit and a lush. I honestly don't know how he got assigned here. So, there's that."

"Can you at least ask him?"

"I don't think so," Lucifer replied. "He's been sleeping one off for the last hundred years. We tried to rouse him a couple of times, but he's as comatose as Odin during one of his famous naps."

I frowned. "Then what's the good news?"

"There is an organization that can help you, but I am reluctant to tell you about them due to certain…confidentiality standards."

"What is it, Fight Club?"

"I don't understand that reference, but no. It's an organization that helps gods with their problems."

"Well, I'm a god, and I have a doozie of a problem."

He looked me up and down. "How good are you at keeping a secret?"

"Very."

"Excellent. Be at the Holy Quinninella Church in Burbank tomorrow morning at three am Pacific Time. If you're late, then you're on your own."

"I'll be there."

***

I burrowed through dimensions using the techniques I learned from Lilith's daughter Greta and arrived back on Earth with just enough time to grab a shower before I had to be at the church. When I finally found a clock, I learned that I had been in Hell for three days. More than half my time was already gone. *Time moves differently, my ass, Katrina.*

The Holy Quinninella church wasn't anything special, not even the biggest church on the block, easily dwarfed by a Baptist monstrosity across the street. But I'd learned not to question magic. It was like questioning the very fabric of reality itself.

The clock above the church struck three, and the bell at its steeple rang three times. It must have been very annoying to live in the neighborhood behind the church. When the ringing stopped, the door glowed white and pulsated, then swung open with a huge gust of wind. Out walked an old man, wrinkles grooved into his face so deeply they folded into each other, wearing a maroon robe that hung loosely over him. A pendant of an all-seeing eye encrusted in jewels hung from his hunched face.

"Are you Kimberly?" he asked.

"I am."

"Then follow me, dear girl."

"Who are you?" I said.

"That's inconsequential."

I paused, trying to articulate my thoughts politely. "To you, maybe, but I don't tend to get into strange magical doors with old men I don't know."

He touched his chest. "My name is Angus. I'm afraid you'll have to trust I'm here to help you."

I stepped up the stairs. "Trust has never been my strong suit, but I can try."

"That's nice," Angus replied. "Welcome to the Godschurch."

CHAPTER 8

The Godschurch was full of more of that opulent bullshit I couldn't care less about, more than even Katrina's castle. High ceilings, beautiful reliefs, intricately painted columns, and about a billion pews for worshippers, even though they were completely empty.

"What do you think?" Angus asked cheerfully.

I really didn't want to get into it with an old man, so I just smiled and swallowed my contempt. "It's beautiful."

"Thank you." His lips sagged and covered his teeth when he smiled. "It nearly dates back to the origin of the universe."

"Wow. Crazy."

The uninspired and unimpressed feeling in my gut must have translated to my tongue because Angus smacked his lips together and sighed. "Come." He waved me forward. "The masters are about to discuss your case."

He shuffled down the center pew toward the front of the church, where the gaudy all-seeing eye hung over three golden high back thrones. On each one sat a man in a similar red robe to Angus's. They looked like they hadn't heard a joke in about a million years.

The one in the middle had clearly just eaten a lemon raw, and when we approached, he pursed his lips even tighter and stood. "You are the God of Death for Zeus's pantheon, yes?"

The two behind him had short, trimmed goatees, and when I looked closer at the standing man, I saw that he had one too, but it was completely blonde. The men sitting behind him didn't speak, only cocked their heads.

"I'm Kimberly. I don't know anything about Zeus's pantheon."

"Oh," he said, disappointed. "We three are the masters. We run the Godschurch for the different pantheons of the universe, protecting them and carrying out their will throughout the cosmos. I'm sorry for missing your transition of duties. Frankly, your Earth is in such a backwater we rarely ever have reason to look in its direction, and the analyst in charge of your quadrant isn't our best."

"Who are you?" I asked.

"I am Headmaster Fizzle." He pointed to his right. "This is Master Hilmos." He then pointed to his left. "And that is Master Gilbarge."

"Do they talk, Mister Fizzle?"

"Master Fizzle, please," he replied. "Now, it says here that four gods were killed last year during Ragnarok. Do you know what happened to them?"

"They all died by my hand, and I have no problem killing more."

"There will be no need for that, I hope."

"Me too. So, are you going to help me?"

He held up his finger. "Once we finish protocol, of course. Your mistress Nyx has extended her membership to you, should you choose to accept it, until such time as you can refill your coffers, so that is nice."

"What are you talking about?" I asked.

"Your dues, of course. Our services don't come free, unfortunately."

"I have to pay you now?" I chuckled. "No chance of that."

He waved me off. "Not now. For the time being, you are a probationary member, as long as you agree to never speak of the Godschurch to any others."

"And if I don't agree?"

He sighed. "Then we can't help you."

"But if I do, then you will?"

"Of course," Master Fizzle said. "It is our sworn duty, should we be able. This is the finest force in the whole galaxy, culled from the very best of the best."

"Except for the analyst assigned to my quadrant."

"Yes, there is always a bell curve, even here. The worst of the best is still one of the best."

I was torn between my hatred of being part of any organization and my desire to get help for my problem, and they certainly looked like they could help, if nothing else. "All right. If all it takes is for me to shut my mouth about this place, I can do that."

"Excellent," Master Fizzle said, his voice never modulating regardless of the timber in his voice. "Angus will lead you downstairs into the base, where you will meet with Director Verford. He is a fine example of the Godschurch's best and brightest."

Angus waved me toward him. "Come, dear." He pushed open a small wooden panel, revealing a set of stairs, which he started down gingerly. I followed him into the bowels of the building. At the bottom, he slid open a door and led me into a big, open room that had the opposite feel of the church. Upstairs was stuffy in an ancient way, but the base downstairs had a completely sterile and sanitary, modern feel to it.

Hundreds of people dressed in gray, spandex jumpsuits hustled through the station between dozens of different hyper futuristic-looking workstations. It was like *Star Trek* barfed all over *Farscape*.

Angus led me past a large window that looked out into the universe. In the center of my view was a massive oblong oval of pure white light that dominated the horizon.

"Wait, are we in space?" I asked.

"Of course, dear. The center of the universe. Or, to be exact, slightly outside the center, circling around it."

"And what is that?" I said, pointing to the white light.

"That's the Source, my dear."

"What is it?" I asked, unable to take my eyes from it.

"Everything in the universe comes from the Source and will return to it. It is creation, plain and simple, and it is our job to protect it, with every bone in our bodies, for the rest of eternity."

"I thought you helped gods here."

"That is our stated mission, but the Source is our real charter. The gods are just the manifestation of it since they can so easily change the balance of the universe." Angus turned from the window. "Besides, the Source doesn't pay, and running an organization of thousands doesn't come cheap. Come now."

He led me across the floor of the station. We swerved between stations until we reached a door that said Director Verford on a brown plaque with gold lettering. Angus pushed the door open and turned away. "I will leave you to it."

"Thank you, I think."

Out of the office walked a strapping, light-skinned man with a clean face and amber eyes. His jaw was clenched tight, and I mentally bet his asshole was the same way, with a stick jammed so far up it that he stood completely at attention. He towered over me.

"Kimberly?" he said, holding out his hand. "It's nice to meet you." I shook his hand. "Won't you come in?"

"Lead the way," I said. "Hopefully, you can give me some answers."

CHAPTER 9

"And that's my story," I said when I'd finished explaining myself to Director Verford.

His expression hadn't changed the whole time I was speaking, but now his face scrunched in consternation. "That is very upsetting for several reasons."

"I'm aware."

"Did you file permissions to kill the four gods you mentioned?"

"I—no—what permissions?"

He leaned forward and typed into his computer. "You can't just kill a god. There are steps and procedures to be foll—oh. Well, it looks like none of the four gods you mentioned were under the protection of the Godschurch. Never mind."

"But I am, right? Under your protection?"

He nodded. "On a probationary basis, yes."

"So, then, how can Momus kill me? Did he file some bullshit special permission?"

Director Verford typed into his computer. "As a matter of fact, he did. The permissions took some months to be approved by the proper authorities, but it looks like approval came through six weeks ago. Everything is in order."

"Wonderful." I let out a deep sigh. "And I'm supposed to be okay with that? Since he filed some stupid papers? I'm just supposed to lie back and accept it?"

He shook his head. "I'm not saying you should accept it. However, in reviewing his claim, your death is a measure of last resort should you not be able to separate yourself from Thanatos."

"This is some grade-A bullshit. But if it's what I have to do, how do I do it? What's the secret to separating me from his brother so I can get this over with?"

"That's the tricky part," he said. "Have you heard Thanatos speak to you at all?"

"I don't know. I hear thousands of voices screaming in my head all the time."

"First, we must calm them, and we can see what we have to work with." Director Verford bit his lip. "I should tell you now that I have never successfully seen a being separate from a deity when they have been fused for so long." He stood. "We're going to do everything in our power to help you."

He led me out of his office and down into the bullpen, where hundreds of drones were typing on their computers. We stopped in front of a mousey girl with a black bob, who turned obediently. "Hello, Director. What can I do for you?"

"Charzarine, is Hypnos still in your quadrant?"

"Absolutely. He's helping the gods stabilize Flortho Seven. Big project."

"Stabilize?" I asked, but they continued talking like I wasn't there.

"Can you send a message that we are requesting an audience with his majesty?" the director asked.

"Of course," the girl said with a smile. "Who will you be bringing?"

"The new god of Death for his line, but don't tell him that," the director said. "Just say Mags will come with a new god. I don't want to be the one to tell him his brother Thanatos is dead."

"Absolutely, I'll just say a human has become a newly enshrined god and has some questions. Does that work?"

"Perfect, Char." He turned to me. "Just one more stop."

He led me up a set of stairs into a glass-enclosed hallway. We passed a cafeteria with a half dozen Godschurch drones munching away, talking to each other as if working on a base that spiraled the nexus of creation wasn't frigging weird.

We walked through another door into a shooting gallery. The woman shooting wasn't dressed like the others. She had a long black coat and thick boots. Her hair was pulled back into a long ponytail, and her face was scarred down the right side, making her bottom lip sag slightly.

"Mags!" the director shouted. The woman lowered her weapon and turned to us before removing her earmuffs.

"Hello, Director," she said, her tone even. "Something wrong?"

"Isn't there always? I have an assignment for you. Should be an easy one for a change."

"Shoot."

The director tilted his head in my direction. "This is the new God of Death for Zeus's line. Unfortunately, not everyone is happy with how she was appointed."

"By murder, I assume?"

"Justified murder." The director nodded in agreement. "They are threatening her life unless she can separate herself from the consciousness of her former—"

Mags eyed me up and down. "How long has the new god been fused?"

"*SHE*," I said, stepping forward. I was sick of being talked about like I wasn't standing right there. "Killed Thanatos about a year ago."

"Oof," Mags said. "Not gonna be easy."

"So I've been told."

The director continued speaking with Mags. "Char is setting up a meeting between you and Hypnos. You've worked his detail before. Can you try to make sure they don't kill each other?"

"How can we kill each other?" I said, rolling my eyes. "I haven't filed the proper paperwork."

Mags laughed. "That was funny."

"It wasn't meant to be," I snapped, wheeling on the director. "Can you please put in an order to kill Momus, just in case?"

He held out his hands. "It will never clear in time."

I placed my hand on the director's shoulder and gave it a firm squeeze to let him know I wasn't asking. "I have faith in you."

***

Mags brought me up the stairs back to the Godschurch proper. Aside from the three masters, the only person in the church was Angus and a weird-looking blue monster with eight arms and a face like a bonobo monkey who sat at a switchboard in the rafters high above the pews of the church.

When Angus saw us, he rose from his pew and smiled. "Good evening, ladies. Where are we going this fine day?"

"Flortho Seven," Mags replied.

Angus pulled out a tablet from his long robe and typed into it. When he was finished, the blue monster started turning knobs and slamming his hands down on the switchboard loudly. Less than a minute later, the front door of the church began to glow white, and Mags walked toward it without another word.

"Bye," I waved to Angus as I followed her into the white.

I stepped through the church and entered a barren desert filled with nothing but dirt for as far as the eye could see. When I turned to Mags, she was wearing a gas mask.

"Sorry for the mess," she said. "Flortho Seven isn't quite ready for humanity yet. They're still building it out."

"You are going to have to explain that slower," I said as I followed her across the desert. When I turned back, I saw that there was no church around our portal. It was simply a hovering ball of white light. "A lot slower."

"It's not that complicated," she said, stomping through the sand. "The gods created every world in the universe. Most of the time, the planets they create can't support habitable life, at least not human life, and they are abandoned. Occasionally though, like one of every thousand planets, they get it right, and life is born."

"And this is one of those planets?"

"Hard to tell yet, but Zeus is sure putting a lot of resources into it, so there's a good chance. When life catches hold, the gods stick around to make sure it fosters human life. Once it does, they start the next project. If you ever wondered why there were all sorts of god sightings in past civilizations but very few in your modern world, that's probably why. They leave one regent in charge of each system that can sustain life."

"Who did we get?"

"Bacchus."

I chuckled. "In all the stories about him I've ever read, Bacchus is a vain drunk. The last three hundred years makes a whole lot more sense now."

"Some regents are good. Some are bad. Yours is a big bowl of awful. Luckily, your Earth is a backwater hamlet that is culturally insignificant, so they don't care much how it's run."

"How is that lucky?"

"Well, if they cared, they would have scrapped your whole planet right after that Apocalypse you had a few hundred years ago. I mean, eventually, Bacchus will have to answer for it, but who knows when they'll get around to it."

"How do you know any of this? I haven't seen you look at a computer since we met."

Mags tapped on her ear. "Char is feeding me information as we speak. It's a real time saver."

"Wonderful," I said. "So, Apocalypses are bad?"

"So bad. Not to mention you absolutely can't have monotheism. Religion is meant to worship all the gods and not just a vain drunk, as you so admirably put it."

"Interesting…I think."

"Hey!" Mags said to a group of humans, or human-like beings, that were crouched down in the middle of the desert. They all wore white gowns. I assumed they were angels that didn't have any wings. "Where's the portal up to Mount Olympus?"

One of them pointed into the distance. "About a thousand meters west. Can't miss it."

"Thanks!" she said, walking toward where they pointed.

"Who were they?" I said, catching up to her.

"Gorbs. The grunt workers of the universe. Not powerful enough to be angels, they basically go sector to sector doing grunt work for the angels until they can get their wings."

I looked back and waved at the gorbs, who turned away from me quickly. "Skittish little buggers, aren't they?"

"They aren't treated very well and aren't used to kindness." Mags squinted into the distance. "Ah, there it is."

We stomped forward through the dust, dirt, and sand until we came upon a long, blue streak of light that climbed from the sand up into the sky. "I've seen one of these before, on Earth."

"Of course, you have. They are great for little conveyance vehicles," she replied. "They'll be invisible when construction is finished, of course, but until then, it's easier if everybody can just see them. Watch out before you step inside. The ride tends to mess up my insides."

She stepped inside the blue portal and shot up into the sky. I followed, and as I rose into the air, my stomach fell into my knees. I watched the ground fall away from me, noticing that there was no water on the whole planet yet. It was like seeing the Earth hollowed out. It wasn't even quite a sphere. More like an apple with several bites chewed out of it.

I rose through the clouds until I shot out into the top of them. When I looked down through them, I could see the entirety of the world floating underneath me.

"Wild, huh?" Mags asked. "Mount Olympus is a trip."

"Totally."

As we passed through Mount Olympus, angels worked hard constructing buildings and carrying materials between the different work crews that littered the clouds. I had only ever seen angels after a world had been built, and it surprised me how blue-collar their work was during the start of a new world.

"This is the advance team," Mags said. "They're here to build out the majority of Mount Olympus before the gods arrive. I mean, some gods are here now, but this will all be cleaned up before Zeus and the upper echelon of the pantheon arrive."

"Zeus is coming here?" I felt eager, suddenly, even though I didn't know why.

"Of course. He comes to oversee every new planet once the angels get past the initial stages. He's kind of a control freak." Mags pointed to a golden man dressed in a toga, with one wing protruding from the middle of his head like a third ear. "There he is. That's Hypnos."

Hypnos had his eyes closed, cross-legged in meditation. When we approached him, his eyes opened slightly. "I have strict orders not to be disturbed while I'm meditating."

"You're always meditating," Mags said it like they were old friends.

"There's a reason for that. I do not like being disturbed ever, Magzarlenia."

"Ew," Mags said, sticking out her tongue. "I haven't been called that in years. Please stop." Mags sat down across from the god without a hint of the fear that gripped me looking at him. "Did you get Char's message?"

"Of course, I did. Otherwise, you never would have been allowed access to this place." He looked up at me with one eye. "This is her?"

"Yes, I am Kimberly, mister…majesty." I held my hand out, and he took it carefully. "I'm sorry. I'm nervous."

"As you should be. Few humans can withstand the power of a god. Sit."

I did, and the clouds were springy against my butt. "Thank you. I'm not quite human. I'm not quite a pixie either. I'm a bit of both, and I guess now I'm a god."

"So," Hypnos said, turning to Mags, "what aren't you telling me? You Godschurch folks are always playing two sides against the middle and keeping things close to the chest. What is it that I'm missing here?"

"You know, don't you?" Mags said.

"Of course, I know," Hypnos said. "I can smell my brother's power all over her, but I want you to say it."

"I killed Thanatos!" I screamed. The work stopped for a moment, then resumed. "I'm sorry."

And then, I waited to be pummeled by a god.

CHAPTER 10

I clenched my fists, ready for a fight, and shifted my weight so I could dodge an attack, but instead of taking a swing at me, Hypnos simply laughed.

No, it wasn't a simple laugh. It was a guffaw that lasted for five minutes. When he was done, the god looked at me. "How wonderful. I hated that little brat."

My jaw unclenched, but I was still frowning. "Your brother Momus doesn't share your opinion. He wants to kill me."

"Of course, he does. He and Thanatos both got the gloomy gene like most of my mother's children. They are too much, too somber, and too impetuous for me. I, for one, am thrilled he is gone from the universe. Thanatos tortured me for my whole existence…until he was exiled to the nether realms. Hearing he's dead brings a big sigh of relief."

"Then you aren't going to like what we came here to ask," Mags said.

"No, I won't. Still, I'd like to hear what it is, so I can reject it formally."

"We need you to help separate Thanatos and Kimberly, relieving her of her godly burden."

This time, Hypnos did not smile. "It's impossible. Even if it weren't, I would say no."

"You're a god," I replied. "How can anything be impossible? I thought your powers were limitless."

"Yes, that's what we would like you to believe, just like humans think monsters are limitless in their power.

Anything that exists has limits. Our limits are just less limited than yours."

"If I don't get this power out of me, Momus is going to kill me and everyone that I love."

"Well, you shouldn't let him do that."

"I can't help it. He has the Dagger of Obs—He has a weapon that has been infused with my power. He has threatened to destroy it and me in the process."

"I suggest you find a way to uninfuse it instead of trying to separate you from Thanatos." Hypnos closed his eyes. "I have looked into your soul, and Thanatos does not exist inside of it. Any thread of him has been merged with your essence. You cannot pull him apart any easier than you could separate hydrogen from oxygen in water…sure, it's possible, but you would cause a massive explosion in the process, killing everyone and everything in the vicinity."

"Please." I sighed. "I don't want to be a god. I was already an immortal being on Earth, and I didn't like that much. I hate being a god even more. The last year has been the most miserable of my life."

"You must learn how to use your powers." Hypnos grabbed my hand. "You have done me a great service in killing my horrible brother, so if I can help you, I will."

I began to cry. "Make the voices stop, please. They have been pestering me every moment of this past year. I cannot sleep. I cannot think. The only thing that helps me is drugs."

"Ah!" Hypnos said. "I can help with that." He turned back to a slight creature holding a golden jug. "Wiftail. Ambrosia!"

The gaunt, gray creature with arms longer than its body and skin stretched tight across its ribcage ambled forward, barely able to hold the enormous jug in front of it to hand it to Hypnos, who took a great drink.

"The prayers of humanity are hard to ignore, but this helps." He handed me the jug. "The only other thing that helps, of course, is answering them, but that is a lot of work."

I took the jug. My eyes ping-ponged between an eager Hypnos and a consternated Mags for a moment. Finally, I took a sip. It smacked me in the face, the taste of honey and lavender, but when I was finished, the voices in my head had stopped completely. Even my pills didn't silence them completely. They simply drowned them out until they were a dull whisper, but now, everything was quiet for the first time in months.

"It worked."

"Not forever. That's why so many of us are lushes, of course. Keeps our head right." He turned to the creature, its spindly arms straining as Hypnos placed the jug into them. "Go fill a leather with some of this for my sister."

Mags huffed, folding her arms across her chest. "Isn't there anything you can do to help her without getting her wasted?"

Hypnos shook his head. "Momus doesn't like me. You would have to appeal to Nyx herself, and she has been gone from the universe for some time."

"Gone?"

"She is the darkness, and she has lived inside it the whole length of eternity. However, in the last million years, she abandoned the universe to live in the crevices that none can enter without losing themselves."

"How do I enter it?" I asked. "How do I find Nyx in the darkness?"

"You don't," Hypnos said. "That description was supposed to turn you away."

"No way." I shook my head. "I need to find a way, any way. If Nyx can help me, then I'll search her out. Please."

Hypnos stroked his clean face. "You'll need to entreat with Zeus. If any would know how to reach her, it is he. There are none stronger or wiser."

"That is a bad idea," Mags said. "Zeus has a mean streak a mile long, and he hates women."

"I don't care," I replied. "If that's what it takes, I'll take on a misogynistic prick any day at any time."

The creature came back with a leather pouch filled with ambrosia. Hypnos took the pouch and passed it on to me. "I think we will have a very strong friendship, Death. If you do end up kicking Zeus's ass, please take pictures. I would pay a godly sum to see that."

***

"You can't punch Zeus," Mags said after we arrived back in the Godschurch base.

"Why not?"

"Well, for one, he's under our protection, so we would have to stop you. That would cause a lot of paperwork, and I hate paperwork. More importantly, he's more powerful than you."

"How do you know?" I asked as we blew past Angus. "I feel pretty powerful. I once crushed a townhouse by just leaning against it wrong."

"Every god has a power level. You're all more powerful than humans and monsters, sure, but listen. Zeus is an Omega-level god, as powerful as anything in the universe that we have tested, except maybe the titans, but we haven't seen them in a long time."

"Oh, I fought one of them. Kind of a pussy, actually."

"I'm going to pretend I didn't hear that," Mags said as we descended the steps toward the base. "You, on the other hand, are a Kappa-level deity. You're pretty powerful, but only when you're doing what you do."

"Killing people."

Mags halted for a moment and looked at me. "Death isn't about killing people. It's about shepherding them to the afterlife. It's being the last comfort of humanity before they reach the great beyond."

"That doesn't sound fun."

"No, it sucks. People are whiny babies when they die."

Inside the base, I turned to the large window and toward the Source. "So, it's my job to take them there?"

"Ha!" Mags shook her head. "No. That is for clean souls, every sentient being in the universe is dirty on some level. You take them to the underworld for processing and cleaning."

"Come again?" I said. "The underworld, where people are tortured for an eternity, is for cleaning souls?"

"It's to torture the bad out of them so they can return to the Source, cleaned. I really shouldn't be the one telling you this." She pulled me from the window. "I'll bring you to Zeus, just don't make a scene, okay? You might survive his wrath, but I certainly won't."

I nodded. "I'll be good."

She pulled me toward Char's station. "Can you help me find Zeus, please? You're the best at it."

Char looked up at Mags, furrowed her brow, and then went to her screen, typing furiously. "Sure. I had nothing else to do today than track down a dirty, old god."

Mags rubbed her back. "Thank you, baby."

"Anything for you, my love." She finished typing. "He's on Felonious Three. Oh god, he's doing his swan thing again."

"Men," Mags said, rolling her eyes. She kissed Char and then turned to me. "Why can't they keep it in their pants?"

***

"Let's just hope he's done by now," Mags said when we reached the grotto from Char's coordinates. "I absolutely hate when he does this."

"What is 'this'?" I asked, confused. "What is he doing?"

"Zeus likes to…seduce…women…"

"I know that. I've read mythology."

"Yeah…and that's bad enough. I mean, he's like four billion years old…but…he likes to do it…as an animal…"

"Ew, why?"

"To prove he can, I guess…I don't know. Gods are gross. Every one of them. Zeus just takes the cake for lechery and debauchery."

We pushed through the trees and stepped into a grotto filled with flowers and a babbling brook, just as a beautiful brunette with dark skin finished buttoning her pants. When she saw us, she skittered away, her face red.

"Still got it!" a swan squawked at us. "You want some too, ladies?"

"Gross," I said. "No."

"Then what good are you?" the swan bellowed. "Just kidding. I love you, too." It paused for a second. "Who are you?"

Mags stepped forward. "Your majesty, the exalted one, Zeus the Creator. This is Kimberly. She is the god of Death now, taken over for Thanatos after the unfortunateness of his death last year."

"What unfortunateness?" Zeus asked.

"Surt came back to Earth, and to stop him from taking over the universe, Kimberly and her friends killed Thanatos and three other gods."

"In fairness," I replied. "I killed them all. It's just that only Thanatos's power remains."

"What a wonderful story," the swan said. "Thank you for stopping Surt for us. He's quite a nuisance. We should have handled it, but we didn't. Could have, had we been there."

"That's fine. We handled it."

"And he's back down below?" the swan asked, a note of fear in his voice.

I nodded. "Yes, and we plan to make sure he stays that way."

"Good, good. Fine job, then. Kudos all around." We all stood around in silence for a couple of seconds before the swan added, "Is there something else?"

"Yes," Mags said. "We need your help."

"Hrm. Well, this is the right time to ask, I'll give you that. I am in quite a glowing mood right now."

"Do you know how to reach Nyx?" I asked.

The swan honked, flapping its wings violently. "Why would you say that name?"

"I'm sorry," I said. "I'm new and—"

The swan rose into the air, annoyed. "And nothing. Nobody shall ever say that name around me. A horrible witch. If I could kick her out of the pantheon, I would. Unfortunately, she outranks me."

"Outranks you? Aren't you the head of the pantheon?"

The swan settled back on the ground. "In a way, but in another way, she is above us all, every god in every pantheon. She has been around since the beginning and created many of my best gods—some of the worst, too. A heinous shrew. I hate her so much."

"So, you can't help us?"

"Oh, I can help you…but I won't. I will leave that contemptuous harpy in the darkness where she belongs. I suggest you leave before I get angry and do something I will regret."

"But—" I started, but Mags pulled me away.

"He's not kidding," she said as she dragged me out of the grotto. "He will absolutely end you if you say anything else. Don't worry though, I have another idea."

"Let's hope it works because we are running out of time."

"Technically," Mags said. "You're the one running out of time. I have plenty of it left."

I chuckled. I wasn't sure, but I was starting to like her.

CHAPTER 11

"You cannot tell anybody at the Godschurch about this," Mags said as we exited the portal into a quaint Viking village. "Especially not Char, okay?"

"Okay." I shrugged. "I mean, I hate all of you, so that won't be a problem, but even if I didn't, then I wouldn't say anything. Promise."

"Good."

I had been to Denmark and traveled around the ancient Viking villages that people toured like we in America once toured Jamestown and Williamsburg, but I didn't ever expect to see a working one with my own eyes.

"What's got you spooked?" I asked, noticing the dread plastered on Mags's face.

"I'm not spooked," she said. "It's just that the Zeus line hates the Odin line, and they hate the Godschurch. The two pantheons split a long time ago, and if they found out my ex was one of their enemy's gods…oh, boy, it would be a mess."

"Who is your ex?" I asked.

"You'll see," she said, pushing through a group of women wearing heavy furs. "Please don't laugh."

Two men sat on the edge of a lake, scraping fish out of their nets. A blacksmith hammered an anvil outside of her thatch-roofed hut. Smoke billowed from the chimney of another, and the pleasant scent of bread wafted through the air.

"Where are we?" I asked. "When are we?"

"This planet started about eight hundred years after yours, so it's a bit behind. You're looking at your past, and they're looking at their future. That's why they're staring."

She was right. Everybody in the town was glaring at us. Mags stopped in front of a large hut at the end of the dirt path. She knocked on the door and let out a deep sigh.

"Bragi! Are you home?"

"Ya, ya. Coming." A pudgy man with a long beard and shiny, rosy cheeks threw open the door. When he saw Mags, he smiled and wrapped her in a hug, lifting her high into the air. "I knew you would come back to me, my muse."

Mags grunted. "Put me down, Bragi."

Bragi slid her down, and he beckoned us inside. "Come on in. You and your weird, robed friend."

The inside of his hut was plain and simple, except that every surface was covered in musical instruments and hides filled with writing. A writing desk sat in the back of the hut with an inkwell and hide drying on top of it.

"How are you, Bragi? Freya said you went native, but I didn't believe it."

Bragi took a lute from a chair and a stack of hides off another and pushed the chairs toward us. "I'm fine. Fine. Better than ever, actually. I'm writing again. Can you believe it?"

Mags smiled. "I'm glad. I know how important that is to you."

"Not just me, but the whole pantheon. Without music, Asgard is a dreary place, you know, full of mean drunks."

"Wait," I said. "Are you a god?"

He turned to me, his teeth yellowed, with large gaps between them. "That's right, deary. And who are you?"

Mags stepped between us. "She killed Thanatos and now has his power."

"A Zeusian!" he shouted. "Here! How could you?"

"Hey!" I said, throwing my hands in the air. "I don't align myself with that creep. I'm my own god, and I need your help."

"You must be out of your mind, my love. If Odin catches a whiff of it, it will cause a war that would rip the universe apart."

"It's a shame you say that, Bragi," Mags said. "Because I need you to take us to him."

"No way. He's already pissed at me for a series of—incidents. I'm not at liberty to discuss it. Let's just say I absolutely cannot risk getting further on his bad side."

"Come on, Bragi." Mags's voice changed. It was soothing. She rubbed her finger up his sweaty chest. "For me. For old times."

That was the reason she didn't want me to tell anybody. She was flirting with him to get what she wanted. I didn't blame her for wanting to keep it silent. It was embarrassing to watch.

"I—can't—"

"Come on." She cocked her head, stepping even closer to him. "Do it for the good times." She rubbed her scarred lips. "And if you won't do it for the good times, do it for the bad times."

Bragi pushed her away. "Cursed woman. It's not my fault you have that scar. That was your own doing."

Mags straightened herself, and her tone changed back to the hardened agent who gargled with nails. "We both know that's not true. Idun was not happy when she found out about us, and this was my punishment."

"We both made our mistakes," Bragi said.

"Yes, but only one of us wears it as a mark of disgrace every day. You know I've tried a dozen healers, and they can't fix me since it was from a weapon of the gods. I'll be marked like this until the Source takes me."

"You wish me death, is that it?" Bragi sneered. "Because that is what you are asking. Why do you think I'm here in this town? I am out of favor with Odin. Bringing one of Zeus's ilk to them…would seal my fate."

I piped up then. "Or it could set you free. I may have Zeus's magic flowing through me, but I am not beholden to him. I can do anything I want and make up my own mind where my allegiance lies. Wouldn't someone like that be valuable to Odin?"

Bragi raised an eyebrow. "Are you saying you would turn spy for the Odinson line?"

"No," Mags said. "She's not saying—"

"I can speak for myself," I snapped before turning back to Bragi. "I am saying my allegiances are my own. If you refuse to help me, I have no choice but to crawl back to my own pantheon. However, right now, I am a free agent."

"It's an intriguing idea, my dear," he said, rubbing his chin. "You will fit right in with the duplicitous scum of Zeus's line. Still, it's an offer I have trouble passing up. To see the halls of Asgard again is something I very much desire."

"Does that mean you'll help me?"

"Aye," Bragi said after rubbing his face for several moments. "I suppose death is better than being stuck in this place for one day longer." He hobbled across the hut and opened the door. "Let's just hope it's quick for all of us."

***

Asgard. I had read about it in stories but never thought I would see it with my own eyes. It sprawled across the cosmos, a glimmering city, its skyline every bit the sparkling jewel of any I had seen, and yet so much more beautiful. Every building gleamed in the light of a thousand colors, reflected from the million stars shining down upon it.

We teleported on a cloud across from the magical city. A tall, gruff man with a permanent sneer and bulky arms stood in front of us, preventing us from moving further. What he protected was a mystery to me, as there was nothing between us and the city except miles of space.

"Heimdall!" Bragi hollered. "You old cuss. Still protecting the rainbow bridge, are we?"

"Bragi." Heimdall glared. "Didn't we banish you?"

"Not quite," he replied, stepping up to the bulky god. "Odin said if he ever saw me again, he would incinerate me. He didn't outright banish me."

Heimdall grunted.

"It's an important distinction, really. It's the difference between you letting us into the city and turning us away, yes?"

Heimdall grumbled but eventually relented, turned, and pressed down on a golden lever that had been hidden behind his back. As he did, a sparkling bridge made of every color in the rainbow appeared.

"Die well," Heimdall said, a mean smirk crossing his face.

Bragi headed onto the bridge, and I followed, looking down at the universe under me. It was a sight that even Mount Olympus couldn't rival.

"It's been a long time," Bragi said, with an apparent lump caught in his throat. He was looking, too. "Since I've seen the shimmering spires of my homeland."

Mags patted his back. "It's going to be okay."

"What did you do?" I said. "To warrant banishment?"

Bragi glared at me, his eyes red with tears. "I wasn't banished!"

I held up my hands. "I'm sorry. I didn't mean to imply…you're right. I misspoke."

"You're damn right you did," Bragi said, wiping the snot from his nose. "I'll be the first to admit I don't live up to Odin's vision of a god. He wants us to be strong and powerful—regal, even. But I just want to write and play music. It makes me a bit of a black sheep." He wiggled his belly. "I just don't quite fit the mold, if you catch my drift."

"I do." I offered a small smile. "I think it's great that you carved out your own path."

"Aye," Bragi said. "You haven't been a god for long. There's a bit of expectation on us. You'll learn soon enough."

He led us through the city. We passed angels like I had never seen before, nothing like the soft faces I'd seen on Mount Olympus. These were hard and battle-tested.

"Don't make eye contact with the Valkyries," Mags whispered. "They take it as a personal affront, and they are always looking for a fight."

"It's not the most insufferable thing about them," Bragi murmured as we passed a particularly mean-looking Valkyrie. "But yes, they will fight at the drop of a hat."

At the end of the main road that Bragi led us down stood a castle, bigger than any I had seen on Earth. No less than a hundred spires formed its base, and they grew as they moved from the outside of the edifice toward its center, almost like the whole building was giving you the finger.

With every step I took upon the stairs leading to the main door, an explosion of colors followed the pressing of my shoes on the ground, radiating out and combining with the footsteps of my companions. At the top of the stairs, two of the biggest Valkyries I had seen up until that moment crossed their lances across the entrance.

Bragi puffed out his chest as he addressed them. "I, Bragi, son of Halfdan the Old and Frigg, have business with the Allfather."

The Valkyrie gave him a dismissive look and said, "Weren't you banished?"

"No, gods damned it, I wasn't banished. I just left!" He stomped his foot. "Now, I have important business with the Allfather that cannot wait. Let me through or face my wrath!"

The Valkyries looked at him for a long moment, then at each other, then laughed uproariously until they fell over themselves. Bragi grumbled and walked past them into the great hall. Platinum sculptures a hundred feet tall lined either side of the throne room, dominating each platform between stairs that led up to a platinum throne. Two metal crow reliefs squawked at all who entered. Bragi followed the stairs toward the throne, stopping at every platform to stare at the sparkling statues.

"My mother always wanted me to be as brave as these heroes. She hated that I wasn't." He gathered himself and continued.

As we neared the throne, I saw someone sitting on it. He was an old, one-eyed man adorned with armor, jewels, and wearing a winged helmet made from the same shimmering metal as the rest of the city. When he saw Bragi, his lip twitched.

"How dare you show your face again in my hall, Bragi?" Odin scowled. "I told you that if I ever saw you again, I would incinerate you. Do you wish to test my resolve?"

Bragi dropped to the ground, pulling both Mags and me with him. "No, Allfather. I left to find my worth to you, and I believe I have done so."

Odin's lip curled, and he sneered. "I doubt it. You have always been worthless."

Bragi looked up. "I bring you one of Zeus's line who claims to have no allegiance to him. She wishes to pledge allegiance to you."

"A damnable lie if we prove her deception," Odin said, staring at me with his eye. "But worth consideration nonetheless, I suppose. Very well, Bragi. I will not incinerate you until this matter is resolved. Introduce me to this god."

"Thank you, Allfather." Bragi stood and beckoned me to do the same. "This is Kimberly, slayer of Thanatos, new god of Death."

"And Zeus pissed me off something fierce," I added. "I really, really hate that god."

Odin smiled. "Then you and I have something in common already."

CHAPTER 12

"So," Odin said, glaring at me. "You expect me to believe that you wish to collude against Zeus."

"I believe her," Bragi said.

"That means nothing," Odin growled.

"You don't have to believe me," I said. "I don't believe myself, really. I don't like any of you. I have a deadline, and Zeus is being a twat, so I'm exploring my options. I'm desperate."

"And what is this deadline for?" Odin asked.

"Well, it's—" Bragi started, but Odin made it clear with his eyes that he should shut up.

I continued. "I only have a few days left before a god named Momus kills me and everyone I hold dear. I have to find a way to separate myself from Thanatos before then and bring him back to life."

Odin stared at me quizzically. "You must know that is impossible."

"I have been told that it is impossible but that Nyx might be able to help me still."

He laughed. "I can see why Zeus wouldn't help you. He hates Nyx. I, on the other hand, have a different relationship with her."

"Then you can help me?"

"I can help you." He sat back on his throne, staring at me with his cold eye. "Before I do, I wish to know how this god, Momus, hopes to kill you."

"You must know of Ragnarok, Allfather," I said.

"Of course. It was one of the last times I fought on the side of the Greek gods before I discovered their duplicitous nature."

"Then you must also know how that war ended."

"With Surt bound in Hell for eternity, and four gods bound to their duty to keep Surt sealed in the Earth."

"Thanatos was one of those four gods bound to protect him. His essence was bound to the Dagger of Obsolescence."

Odin scratched his chin, nodding. "Binding their souls to their weapons was the only way to make them powerful enough to fight Surt. Once Surt was interred in the ground, Zeus became wary of the power the Four Horsemen possessed and cast them out of this universe. It was the final straw that caused me to break from his clan. I have not regretted it since."

"Surt returned and nearly destroyed the universe again, with the help of the Four Horsemen," Mags said. "It was Kimberly and her clan who fought them back and rescued the universe."

Odin raised his eyebrows. "If that is true, then we are forever in your debt."

"I wish everybody saw it that way," I said. "Unfortunately, by killing Thanatos, I was bound to his power, and the dragon I entrusted with the Dagger lost it to Momus, who is holding it ransom for his ends. If he breaks it, it will sever from my soul and kill me."

"As you are at war with one from Zeus's line, I am inclined to help you. However, my help has a cost."

"Powerful men never give up something for nothing," Bragi added, almost despite himself.

"That is so true," I replied.

"Your request is a steep one, so I must ask for a steep favor in return." Odin stood. "In the Godschurch, there is a list that tells the location of every god in the cosmos, including those of my line. My price is that you wipe the names of my line from that database so that we can live in peace and freedom."

"What you're asking is treason!" Mags screamed. "I won't allow it."

Odin sneered. "I allowed your human voice to infect my ears once before. If you open your mouth again, I will rip it from your body and feed it to you." His eyes flashed with fire. "I care not for your pitiful Godschurch or for the humans that run it. My people have been kept in check for eons because of that list. That all ends today…" Odin snapped his neck to face me. "Unless you wish to die, which I can accommodate as easily as Momus."

"I am not good with computers," I said, holding my hands out. "And I'm not much for espionage."

"My dwarven coders will give you simple instructions. All you have to do is load it into the system from any computer, and it will do the rest."

"How can I be sure that it won't destroy everything else?"

"You can't," he said. "But I give you my word; we only want our privacy. That is my price. You can choose to die by Momus's hand, die by mine—or live and make a powerful ally in me."

I looked into Mags's eyes and saw her begging me not to do it, not to betray everything she believed in, but I didn't care about her. I cared about Molly, and Julia, and my own little life.

"Okay," I said. "Give me the code. I'll plant it."

Mags' head collapsed into her chest, her face bowed, defeated. For the second time, I felt like a true god. I was out for my own interests, even if I destroyed everything and everyone that I touched.

***

A thick, stumpy dwarf held up a shimmering disk, no larger than a quarter, and placed it in my hand. "All you have to do is place this inside any port on a computer in the network, and it will do the rest." He pressed something tiny into my other hand. "When it's done, go somewhere safe and press this button. It will bring you back here."

"It won't destroy the whole system, right?"

He shrugged. "What do you care?"

I didn't, really. But I cared for Mags. I didn't want to destroy her whole life. Odin ordered that she be held in a prison cell underneath the castle so that she couldn't notify the Godschurch of our plans. Before I left the castle, I stopped by her cell.

"I'm sorry," I said.

"I've worked with gods long enough to know that you can never trust them, even for a second. I just thought you might have some humanity left."

"Don't you think it's a little screwed up that you're tracking them, though?" I asked. "I mean, it's very 1984 of you."

"No," she replied, shaking her head. "I don't. Our job is to protect gods, and that includes protecting them from each other. We need to know where our greatest enemies are."

"That's some messed up, police-state bullshit."

She turned away. "Tell yourself whatever you have to do. Just don't get Char involved, please."

"I won't," I replied. "Who should I get involved, though? Who is the absolute biggest shitburger in the Godschurch?"

She thought for a second. "Kib. He's some weasel, always making passes at Char, saying that she just needs a good deep dicking to get over me." She turned to me. "If you have to send anybody to their death, make it him."

I clenched the disk in my hand. "Let's hope it doesn't come to that."

"It will." Mags took a deep breath. "You're going to make a great god."

She didn't mean that as a compliment, and I didn't take it like one. It was no use belaboring the issue, though, so I left the prison and walked out of the castle and across the rainbow bridge to Heimdall.

"Where to, god of Death?" he asked.

"I need to get back to the Godschurch."

Heimdall shook his head. "That I cannot do."

I narrowed my eyes. "Then send me back to Earth, my Earth. I can take it from there."

He nodded. "So be it. Close your eyes and imagine where you wish to go, and I will send you there."

I closed my eyes and tasted mint jelly just before I vanished into the abyss. When I reappeared, I was in front of the Holy Quinninella Church in Burbank. I ran up the steps and opened the door, but it didn't take me to the Godschurch. Instead, I was inside a dusty, rundown church that looked like it should be condemned.

"Can I help you?" an old woman said, emerging from one of the confessionals with a dirt rag.

"I don't thin—you don't know how to contact the Godschurch, do you?"

"I'm sorry, sweetness," she replied. "I just do the cleaning."

"I don't believe that for one minute unless you are very bad at your job. This place is a sty."

She shrugged. "Lots of people are bad at their job, sweetness. Doesn't mean they're hiding something."

"True, but you are." I stepped forward. "I am Kimberly, God of Death. I am in desperate need of the Godschurch."

The woman laughed, walking away. "Sure you are, and I'm Hera, sorcerer supreme of the multiverse."

She disappeared into the back of the church, leaving me alone in the dirty pews. There was only one place left that might be able to help me. I really didn't want to go there, but I didn't have much choice. I called a cab, and when it dropped me off, I was in front of Momus's manor.

The gate swung open for me after I pressed the call button, and I breezed right into the house, past his maid, into the study. I was surprised to see him sitting, twirling the Dagger in his hand, waiting for me.

"Ah, my sweet. You are back, and with so little time to spare."

"Cool it. I'm not done yet. I need to get back to the Godschurch."

Momus looked at his watch. "You still haven't figured it out? Just a couple hours left now."

"I need to get to the Godschurch. Now. No long speeches, just please get it done."

Momus laughed. "I will send a message to Angus. I assume you know the church where he will meet you— What am I saying? Of course, you do."

I spun on my heels. "I do, but I'm having a portal problem right now. Can you please just snap me there?"

"Of course," he said. "I want you to succeed, after all. Your glory benefits us both."

I flashed to the church, and two minutes later, I saw whiteness pulsating behind the doors. Angus stepped out softly. "Welcome b—"

I didn't have time for his introductions and platitudes. I brushed past him into the church, ran down the pews, and hopped the stairs into the base. I passed the large, gaping window and ran to Char, the only person I knew inside the base besides the director.

"Hey," I said. "Remember me?"

"Of course. Where is Mags?"

"She had business to attend to. You know Mags. She said there was a computer I could use here. Do you know Kib?"

Char grunted. "I hate that guy. He's on break, thank god." She pointed to a computer at the end of her row. "He sits over there. Go for it. I don't know how you're going to figure out the keyboard, though. I know thirty-six languages, and sometimes I still get lost."

I looked down at the keyboard and saw what she meant. It was like nothing I had ever seen. Five hundred different keys and only about a hundred I recognized, plus knobs and levers of all types and shapes. I pressed one, hoping for the best, and the screen popped on, asking for a password.

I chose to take the dwarf at his word and simply inserted the disk into the only port I could find that would fit something so small. I heard the machine catch and accept the disk, bringing it into the mainframe.

Without another word to anyone, I walked out of the room, hoping that I hadn't just doomed the Godschurch to utter destruction. Stepping into an open closet, I pressed the button and vanished, the taste of honey wine on my lips.

CHAPTER 13

I reappeared in a shining room with the same dwarf that had given me the button and the disk. "You're back. That didn't take long."

"I work fast."

The dwarf spun into a chair and started typing onto his computer, though it was like no computer I had ever seen, with dozens of extra keys and symbols I didn't recognize. After a second, the dwarf nodded. "Good, good. It just broke the encryption key. In the next hour, it should be done."

"What will happen?"

The dwarf turned to me. "Once it's wiped the database clean, the disk will disintegrate, causing the computer to crash and wipe itself clean. The terminal will need to be replaced because it will crash, but the rest of the Godschurch will remain intact. Your friend's job is safe."

"Wonderful."

"I wouldn't go that far, but you are an adequate spy."

"Glad you approve." I took my leave of the dwarf and found Bragi outside the door, waiting for me. "Did it work? Did you do it?"

"I did, but I don't really want to talk about it. The thought of betraying the Godschurch makes me queasy."

"I don't like deception, either. It's probably one of the reasons I haven't been banished. I never had a taste for lying, to anyone, at any time. Truthfulness is a trait that Odin respects above all others, along with bravery and loyalty."

"That's funny because I just lied to betray people."

"Yes, but you showed enough bravery to make up for the others, and that is what matters to Odin most, in the end. If you are brave, you can just about get away with anything. If you bring glory to Asgard, you will be lauded above all others. Glory is built on bravery, you see."

He led me down the hall into a dining room with a large silver table and several dozen high back chairs around it. Odin stood before a crackling fire, holding a goblet.

"Allfather," Bragi said. "Kimberly returns victorious."

Odin turned, smirking. "You have done well, my dear, better than any other of your ilk. They do not deserve you."

"I am not bound to them any more than I am bound to you, for better or worse."

He took a sip from his goblet. "The universe is a big place with many dangers. Without gods to look out for you, it will gobble you up. We could—"

"I'm sorry," I said, holding up my hand to stop him. "I appreciate you trying to recruit me like some blue-chip linebacker, but I'm on a deadline. Can you please tell me how to get to Nyx?"

"It's rude to interrupt, my dear. Given your situation, I will allow it." Odin took another sip from his goblet and held up a finger. "This once, and only this once, I will tell you how to get to Nyx. First, though, I will do you a great favor, one none other in the universe can give to you because none know it."

"What is that?"

He touched my shoulder. "I will unbind you from the Dagger. Otherwise, any lesser being will use it to control you."

"You…can do that?"

"I can." He moved his hand to my chest and closed his eyes. "Who do you think bound Thanatos's soul to the Dagger in the first place?"

Warmth filled my chest. When I looked down, Odin's hand glowed orange, and that power splintered through my body. Everywhere it touched, I felt a simmering heat. He muttered words under his breath that I couldn't understand, and I smelled the sizzling of my flesh. Pain streaked through my whole body. I took a great breath in, and cold filled my lungs, then dropped like a weight to the floor.

"None other but those in this room know you are not bound to the Dagger, and I would keep it that way. One day, you will need to reveal that secret. If you do so at the right moment, it will save your life, and maybe even the universe."

My chest heaved, sucking in as much air as I could gather. "Thank you."

"Of course, I always pay my debts in multiples."

"And Nyx?" I said, struggling to stand.

"I cannot bring you to her. However, I can tell you how to find her. She lives in the ether—the darkness—between space and time." He took another sip from his goblet. "I believe you know how to get there…unless I have mistaken the pixie blood I felt course through you."

I nodded. I knew exactly what I had to do. I had to intentionally do that thing I had always avoided: I had to embrace the void and become lost in it.

CHAPTER 14

All right, Kimberly.

All you have to do is think of somewhere and remember it wrong when you teleport. You'll be stuck between universes, trapped in the darkness, forever. But maybe, just maybe, you will find Nyx, and then, you can get her blessing to kill her son, and—this is all so messed up.

I closed my eyes and remembered the Eiffel Tower as it had been two hundred years before, before I was immortal. No flying cars, no reconstruction after the Apocalypse. I made it real in my mind and then fell into the darkness. It felt like home to me.

I had no mooring; I was nowhere and everywhere at once. I hoped that Odin was right. It would have been so easy for him to lie about how to find Nyx and be rid of another troublesome god, but he was honorable, right? That's what Bragi said. I had to believe Odin was trying to help.

"Hello!" I shouted. I looked down at my arms, and though they were a dark brown against the black of the oppressive abyss that surrounded me, I could still make them out. "Nyx?"

Why would she answer to that? I had jumped through the abyss hundreds, thousands of times, and never, even once, did I see Nyx there. Think, Kimberly. *What would entice a powerful god to entreat with you?*

"I killed your son!" I screamed. That was a bad idea. I knew it when the words flicked off my tongue, but I needed to say something that would get her attention if she could even hear me.

"WHAT!" a booming voice echoed.

Looks like I got her attention.

"Speak carefully, child, for I can break you in less than an instant."

"He was trying to destroy the world, and, well, things happened. I didn't mean to kill him. I'm not proud of it, but—yes, it's true."

"And you have a death wish?" the voice said, more subtle than before. "Why else would you be here?"

"No, ma'am. I very much want to live."

"You sound like my children." Two purple eyes popped open in the darkness. They glowed brightly but illuminated nothing. "Then tell me, which of them did you kill?"

"Thanatos. The god of death."

"Things have been erratic since Zeus locked him away." A great gust of wind whipped through me. "You smell like him."

I chuckled nervously. "Smelling like death isn't a compliment where I come from."

"Death has a sweet smell to it, with acidic overtones. People have the wrong opinion of death. It is an inevitability, integral to keeping the universe spinning." Another gust of wind blew through my hair. "Did he die well?"

"Does anyone?"

"Yes, many."

"I don't know about that. He died quickly and painlessly."

"I felt his presence tug on the universe for this past twelve months, but I thought he would come to me when he was ready. I never imagined he was dead and that his essence had transferred to you."

I closed my eyes. "I'm sorry."

The darkness sighed. "I have other children."

"About that…one of your kids is trying to kill me now. It's a whole thing, and it's really eaten up my week."

"That also sounds like my children." The eyes peered closer to me. "Which one?"

"Momus?" I said, my voice faltering. "No offense, but he's kind of a prick."

"I should have guessed. They were very close, those two, and Momus was always protective of his brother. I'm afraid revenge flows deep in our blood, theirs and mine."

"He's threatened to destroy everything I love if I don't give Thanatos back to him, but…I can't. I have been around the universe, and you are the only one who could help me. Maybe, you can even bring him back."

"I can see into your soul. My son has not lurked there for a long time. There are still traces of him, but every bit of his power flows through your veins now. If you had found me sooner, then maybe…but now. There is nothing I can do."

My head dropped to my chest. "Then there is nothing to do."

"There is everything to do," Nyx said, her words whipping me like wind. "You have a great destiny ahead of you. First, return to Yrowet and rebuild it. Your quadrant of the universe is in utter disrepair; millions of souls desperately scream for help while their voices go unheard. They are begging to be cleansed. Devils are making a mockery of the afterlife. The Source has been in chaos for eons, and now, it will have stability because of you."

"I can't do much if I am dead."

"I cannot reason with Momus," Nyx said. "But you must live. He cannot take the mantle from you. He is not built for the role of Death. You are. The mantle suits you, as it suited my Thanatos."

"What are you saying?" I asked.

"I believe you know what I am saying."

"You are saying that I have to kill your son before he kills me."

"No," Nyx said. "I am saying I must do so. I will absorb him back into me, and then you will work for me, for death."

"I don't work for anyone," I replied. "I've already been recruited by Zeus and Odin this week, and I have no love for either."

"Petty men, both. Their squabbles are inconsequential to all but them. At my side, you can right a great wrong that has left the universe out of balance for generations." She stopped. "Do you hear them screaming for you?"

I shuddered. The effects of the ambrosia had long since worn off. "Unless I medicate heavily, they are ceaseless."

"I can help you calm them. I can give you peace. If you help me, I will help you."

"And what about those I love? Will I have time for them?"

"You will be very busy," she said. "But we always make time for the things that matter to us. The arc of the universe is long. You will not have much time for them, but time is in your favor."

"I understand you are not giving me a choice. I appreciate you framing it as one."

"We all have choices. They just might not be good choices. If you do not help me, I will leave you here in the ether, drowning, until you change your mind."

I took a deep breath. "Very well. I will help you."

"Good," she said. "Now, I will show you how to return to the universe." I felt a light weight on my elbows. "Bring your hands to your face and make a square with the index finger and thumb on both hands."

I did and then followed her instructions to press the square on my right eye.

"Close your other eye and unfocus your vision. Then, pull your hands away from your eye slowly, never breaking the fingers apart."

I slowly pulled my hand away from my eye, but I didn't see anything…until I did. As I pulled my hands away from my face, I started to see tiny strands of light lining the darkness, thousands of them, millions of them shimmering everywhere, so beautiful my eye started to water. "What is that?"

"The fabric of the universe. Threads of light in the darkness, two sides of the same coin. They lead everywhere. You simply have to grab one and pull."

I reached my hands long until I felt the fabric of light in my hands.

"That one will take you home."

I pulled them apart with my hands, and the light overwhelmed my senses. When my eyes refocused, millions of stars shimmered in my vision. I felt the ground under my feet, and a cool breeze filled the air. I was in front of Momus's manor, and the gate was wide open.

"Earth," I whispered, grateful to hear my own voice on the familiar air.

I was home. Now, to end this.

CHAPTER 15

I stood outside of Momus's manor for longer than I should have, given the ticking clock of his ultimatum. I needed my strength for what would come next, especially if Nyx did not fulfill her end of the bargain.

I pushed open the front door and stomped into the study to find Nyx, sitting in Momus's leather chair, toying with the Dagger of Obsolescence. She was cloaked in the shadows of her darkness, nothing but an opaque shadow of a woman, only her bright purple eyes defining her amorphous shape.

"There you are, my dear," Nyx said. "I thought you would never arrive. I'm afraid all the action is done."

"What happened to Momus?"

"I told you." She stood. "I have reabsorbed him into myself. It is unthinkable for a mother to kill her own child, and yet, what must be done is done."

The Dagger disappeared inside of her body for a moment. All the light whipped out of the room, and then a bright explosion of color filled the sky. When Nyx removed the Dagger, it was a black-bladed scythe, replete with a long, black handle.

"Here," she said, handing it to me. "The god of Death needs an appropriate weapon."

I took the scythe in my hand and felt an immediate kinship to it. "Thank you."

"There is much to do," Nyx said. "When you have finished here, meet me on Yrowet."

"Where is that?" I asked.

"The Godschurch will know. It is your home planet."

"Earth is my home planet."

She tsked. "Oh, poor girl. There is so much to teach you."

And then she was gone. She did not know that Odin had loosed my bond with the Dagger, and I would never tell her. Some secrets were better kept hidden, as he said. I gripped my scythe and walked out of the house.

"Finished already?" I tilted my head up, and I saw Mags, cross-armed, in front of me at the bottom of the stairs. "Did you kill him?"

I thought for a moment. "I didn't kill him, but he is dead."

"You didn't have the kill authorization for that."

"I didn't kill him," I repeated. "If you have a problem with his death, then you should bring it up with Nyx herself."

Mags uncrossed her arms. "Nyx killed her own son?"

I nodded. "It would seem that way, or at least that's what she said. Either way, the threat to my life is over."

"Good."

"I'm really sorry, about all of the…but I had to—"

"It's okay." She chuckled almost lightheartedly. "If there's one thing I can count on, it's that a god will always betray you given the chance." She held up the disk. "Luckily, if you plan properly, you can use it to your advantage."

"You sneaky little—how did you—"

She tapped her ear, and I remembered the microphone. Char had been in communication with her the whole time.

"I'm a woman living in a god's world. The only thing that I have is my guile. Now, we have insight into the Norse gods that we never had before."

"And now they hate me, too. Thanks for that."

"That would presume they know you betrayed them, which they don't. Our first job is to protect gods, including you. So, Odin will never be the wiser. This is a win-win."

"For the police state."

She put the disk back in her pocket. "For the protection of the universe."

"I want very badly to be mad at you, but I can't be too upset at you for double-crossing a double-cross."

"You always have to think six crosses ahead. If you don't mind, I think you should go so I can make my final report."

"Are we…okay?"

Mags passed me as I walked down the steps. "Does it matter? You're my charge now, and I'll be there if you need me, no matter what."

"Thank—"

"Don't thank me. This isn't because of some misplaced sense of duty or love for you. It's my job. And my job is thankless." She stepped into the house. "Oh, and I think you should go to Hell, and I mean that with only an iota of venom."

I didn't wait another minute. I knew exactly what she meant. *Molly.*

***

I bored through the universe and ended up in the city of Dis, in front of Julia's building. I rushed up the stairs and banged on the door. The door cracked open, and I pushed through into the apartment.

"Where is she?" I asked.

"It's good to see you too," Julia said.

I scanned the room and saw Akta and Aziolith on the couch. "Hi."

"Hi," I said. "Sorry, but…where is she?"

"She's here," I heard Molly say behind me. I turned to see her walking down the hall, and I ran to her, wrapping her in my arms and squeezing her. I couldn't stop the tears cascading down my cheeks as I kissed her again and again.

"It's good to see you, too," Molly said, laughing and stroking my face.

"Where did you find her?" I asked the others when I had wiped the tears from my eyes.

"My asshole ex-boyfriend told me they stashed her in a pit about a hundred miles outside the city," Julia said.

"I wanted to smash through and get her out with a show of force," Aziolith said.

"But I convinced them to go to Katrina and have her release Molly," Akta added. "It was actually all very boring and bureaucratic."

"The pits," I said, cupping Molly's face in my hands. "Are you okay?"

She nodded. "It was only for a little bit. I can't believe that people endure torture for eternity. Something really should be done about that. It's inhumane."

I couldn't tell them that it wasn't for eternity. They couldn't know anything that I had learned. A deep heaviness settled in my heart. I never wanted to keep anything from my friends, but as a god, I realized there were things I couldn't tell them. A pang filled me, just for a moment, and I choked it down.

"I'm so happy to see you again."

I was filled with joy and a newfound sense of peace, even if those feelings were mixed with the complications of my new office. There would be millions of things I would see in the universe that no one could know about. It would draw me further away from everyone as time went on, and eventually, I would be alone.

At the thought of it, another tear fell down my face. I wiped it away and looked around the room, filled with love. Julia, Aka, Molly, and Aziolith, four of the most important people in my whole life, and I was reunited with them.

That was a worry for another day, I decided. Today, I wanted to be awash in the joy of seeing my friends, the only family I truly cared about. They made life worth living.

Death could wait.

***

If you loved this, keep reading after the author's note for a sneak peek of *Chaos,* a team-up book featuring Kimberly, Katrina, Akta, Julia, and Rebecca, as they try to prevent the end of the universe.

CHAOS

Book 11 of The Godsverse Chronicles

By:
Russell Nohelty

Edited by:
Leah Lederman

Proofread by:
Katrina Roets & Toni Cox

Cover by:
Psycat Covers

Planet chart and timeline design by:
Andrea Rosales

CHAPTER 1

Kimberly

Location: Opsidious 7

Ten thousand years ago, I became Death.

Or, well, an incarnation of Death.

This day, I was summoned to a job which had stumped a half dozen of my best reapers, of which I had thousands, across the universe, doing my bidding. Honestly, it made me more a bureaucrat than anything these days. Every pantheon had its own version and its own claim on the universe, but I became Death for my Earth and a million Earths like it, which made me a busy celestial being.

"Where is she?" I asked a black-robed fairy waiting for me when I finally landed on the white sand beach of Opsidious Seven. I had trained Muriel myself a millennia ago. She wasn't one of my best reapers, even after a thousand years of experience, but she was competent enough that when she asked for my help specifically, I took a personal interest in this soul.

She pointed down the coastline. "She washed up last week, but she refuses to leave her body. We've tried everything, and she's injured three of us already. Even in death, she's too powerful for us to—"

"I got it." I rolled my eyes beneath the hood of my robe. "Thanks."

I walked down the sandy beach toward the point where Muriel had directed me before she vanished off for another case. I could only be at one place at one time. Even an immortal being had to account for time and space, which was why I assigned reapers across the endless cosmos, so I wouldn't have to do it all myself.

Opsidious Seven was far from my office on the far side of the galaxy from where I once lived on Earth. It was in a small pocket quadrant protected by the Greek Gods, sandwiched between a galaxy protected by the Hindu Gods and the Norse ones. Of course, they didn't call themselves that, but it was easier for me to think of them that way, the way I'd learned of them when I was still on Earth. They called themselves by the name of their most powerful gods, the Brahman line and the Odin line, respectively.

In the distance, I saw the body of a young woman, the tide lapping against it. It amazed me how similar each habitable world was, and they had made millions, though there were trillions more which had no life on them—or at least no life that was touched by the gods. The banal similarities of every Earth showed an innate lack of imagination on the part of the creators.

My job was to deliver to the underworld those who clung too tightly to their mortal coil. Most souls left their bodies willingly and without incident but sometimes, every thousand or so deaths, a soul clung to the last vestiges of their lives. That's when they called me in, the arbiter between the land of the living and land of the dead. It was not glamorous work, more akin to a counselor than any other role I'd taken on in the thousands of years since I became a god.

The sun shone on my face as I pulled back the black robe from my face and let the sand fill my sandals. The robe was part and parcel of my look. It was bestowed on me when I became the god of Death, and I forced the other grim reapers to wear it for camaraderie and consistency, even if the robe was a bit on the nose. Everybody needed a brand. The black robe distinguished us from other gods and bestowed us with a sense of austerity.

I approached the woman's body, bloated and waterlogged, near an outcropping of palm trees. Next to the body, a blue, shimmering apparition sat looking out at the water, holding the corpse's hand. She looked over at me with hollow eyes.

"I'm not going," the apparition said to me flatly. "I shouldn't be dead. This is all a mistake."

I nodded. "They all say that."

"You don't understand," the apparition said. "I'm—you know what, I've tried to explain this to every one of you, and I'm not going to do it again."

"I get it," I replied. "You were a god, and you think the rules don't apply to you. You wanted to speak to a manager, right?"

Her eyes narrowed. "Are you a manager?"

"In a way, I guess. I am Death incarnate. My name is Kimberly. Who are you?"

She chuckled. "You expect me to believe you are the god of Death, and your name is Kimberly."

"Can I sit?" I asked. She shrugged. "Frankly, I don't care if you believe me, but I am the god of Death. I don't consider myself much of a god, though. I'm more of a bureaucrat than anything."

She looked over at me, squinting under the beating sun. "If you are the god of Death, then how did you get your powers?"

"Do you know of the Four Horsemen?" I asked.

She nodded. "Conquest, Famine, Death, and War, chosen to protect the end of the universe from Surt, the demon god."

"That's right. Well, they were called forth about ten thousand years ago, but they had turned against the universe, so I killed them—every one of them, including Death—to stop Ragnarök. And for my troubles, I was left with this burden to carry for the rest of my days."

"So you kill gods, then?" she asked, acerbic.

"Not as a rule," I replied. "But when the need arises, sometimes a god needs to die. We should all have the option to die."

"Gods aren't supposed to die," she said, looking out at the water.

"No, they aren't, but they do. Now more than ever."

"Yes, I know that," she said. "And I did, didn't I? Die, I mean."

There was no way for a mortal to deny one of my reapers. Each of them was endowed with a bit of my spark, making them as close to a god as one could get without being gods themselves. I didn't generally get calls like this about a deity, though. They required a more delicate touch.

"You did," I said softly. "What was your charge when you were alive?"

"They once called me a siren, but I soured on that name once humanity bastardized it and made us villains. Imagine acting as if a group of women protecting themselves were the bad guys."

"I don't have to imagine it," I said. "I've seen it too many times."

"I just wanted a simple life, to live out the end of time."

"How did you die?" I asked.

"My three sisters and I were attacked. They threw a bright blue ball at us, and when it exploded…my sisters took the brunt of the explosion and vanished instantly. It still killed me. My body didn't vanish, nor did my soul, like theirs, but I died all the same. My soul drifted across the ocean, tethered to my body until I wound up here."

"That's horrible," I said. I'd become pretty good at commiserating with souls over the last few thousand years. Being Death meant being dispassionate about any deaths while empathizing enough to bond with the people you must shepherd. "And what were you called?"

The siren turned to me. "Molpe."

I held out my hand. "Nice to meet you. I'm Kimberly, again."

"It's horrible to meet you." She didn't take my outstretched hand, instead dropping her haunting eyes to the ground. "There's nothing you can do to put me back in my body, is there?"

I shook my head. "Even if I could, your body is gone, bloated and waterlogged. I would not wish my worst enemy to live in that body."

"Where will I go?" Molpe asked.

I shrugged. "Frankly, this doesn't happen every day. I would like to take you to my boss, who has been around since the beginning. Perhaps she will know, and if not, then the Godschurch, I suppose."

"Piffle," Molpe said. "A group of ineffective and incompetent dolts."

"I don't disagree with you," I said. "But they also protect gods, and if you have died, then they will want to know and hopefully be able to figure out what to do with you."

"I don't know why," Molpe said after a few silent moments, "but I trust you."

"Well, I am very trustworthy." I held my hand out to her. "Will you take my hand? It's okay. You can touch it."

"You won't abandon me?" Molpe said.

I shook my head. "I would never do that. My job is to shepherd you to the end, and I take my job very seriously."

Molpe nodded and placed her hand in mine. It was cold, and I squeezed it to warm it. "Would you like to stay here for another moment, or are you ready to go?"

"Can you ever be ready?" she asked.

In ten thousand years, I had never met a person who was truly ready to leave. Even the most stoic and ready to die still clung to at least one aspect of their lives. "No, but you can look forward to the next thing. Those who are most content think of the end as a new beginning, with new challenges. I imagine that, like most gods, you haven't had a challenge in a long time."

"I have not," she said, letting go of her body. "A new challenge sounds nice."

I pushed up to my feet. "Then let us go, Molpe."

"Yes," she said, rising to join me. "Let us go."

CHAPTER 2

Rebecca

Location: Antigone Three

It felt good to be out in the field on an assignment again instead of stuck behind a desk, even if the circumstances weren't ideal. Training new recruits shouldn't be the purview of the director of the Godschurch, but there weren't enough senior agents to go around since losing 90 percent of our people to the Godless. I had to step up.

"Julia!" I shouted as she strafed down the hallway across from me. "Eyes forward."

"I know, Director," she replied. "I've only done this a couple thousand times before."

"Yeah," I said. "But never with the Godschurch."

Julia Freeman was one of Katrina's recruits. After the Godless destroyed the Godschurch and thinned our agents to almost nothing, Katrina and the other gods gave me lists of their best people to train. While the recruits made decent clay, they had a long way before they were molded into something worthy of the Godschurch. The gods under our protection had dwindled, and if we had any hope of getting more pantheons to join the cause, then we needed highly-trained agents.

"You go around back in case they run out that way. I'll go in hard and flush them out to you, okay?"

Julia nodded. "Got it."

We were on the tail of a terrorist selling old Horde weaponry to the highest bidder. We had done a decent job of snuffing out the remaining Godless cells in the decade since the Battle of the Obelisk, an epic confrontation between Dolos and his people and the Godschurch joined together with the gods.

Of course, in the old movies, that's where the story ended—with a glorious victory. I was living in the aftershock of the destruction wrought by the Godless. We destroyed their infrastructure, but they destroyed ours in kind, and we'd never truly recovered.

On top of that, the Horde were still out there, and their tech could still kill a god. Every time we snuffed out one of their cells on one planet, another would pop up again. They used different names in different galaxies and with different cells. This one went by Projekt Kaos. With over a hundred thousand planets to govern and a fraction of our previous might, it meant that at any one time, thousands of planets were left unprotected.

I pressed my shoulder up to the door of an old, run-down house, gripping my pistol tightly in my hand. We'd tracked a group of arms dealers selling Horde tech to this house three days ago, and with any luck, they were still there. Our thermal heat maps showed two people inside, and nobody had come or gone in the past day. The odds were good. Even if they were inside, though, they would likely be heavily armed.

Godless tech was unstable. It could explode randomly in even the most careful hands, and most arms dealers weren't very careful. One side benefit of this was that often, Godless cells blew themselves up. We couldn't always wait for that. Every cell we took down was another story to help us earn the gods' confidence.

I tapped the bug in my ear. "You ready?"

I heard the crackle in my ear from Julia, on the other side of the house. "In position."

We really needed this operation to go well, so the gods would hire us back to protect them. At one time, we had over 2,000 dues-paying gods, but that had dwindled to less than a hundred. It didn't help that by the time the Battle of the Obelisk was over, almost all our dues-paying members had been killed, which didn't instill much confidence with other gods that we could protect them.

We tried to explain that they died defeating Cronus, the biggest threat to our universe in a million years, but nobody wanted to hear it. Many asked for refunds. Some sued. In the end, we could barely survive.

I took a deep breath at the door. "Please go well."

I raised my leg and kicked the lock off the door before sliding inside the house. Two young men wearing cloth face masks sat on a dirty couch watching cartoons. Heaps of Godless tech glowed green underneath them.

"FREEZE!" I shouted. "Hands up!"

They both hopped up and rushed toward the back of the house. Of course, they did. They always ran, even though they rarely escaped. I chased them down a narrow hallway, flushing them toward Julia at the back door. One of the boys opened the back door and rushed outside.

"Now!"

A forearm came out of nowhere and clotheslined the perp, sending him to the ground. There was a flash and then a purple cloud of smoke. Julia appeared behind the other man, and she pulled him over her shoulder, flipping him onto the ground.

Both of the terrorists writhed on the floor in pain.

"I told you I could do it," Julia smiled at me. "I don't need training. Just let me loose."

One of the men pulled a handgun from a holster on his leg.

"GUN!" I shouted.

Julia dove away from the door, and I disappeared, using the fairy blood coursing through my veins to jump forward. When I appeared in a flash of my own purple smoke, I was in front of the door, aiming my pistol right at the man's head. "Don't do it."

His finger twitched for the trigger, and I fired two bullets, sending blood and brains splattering through the grass in the backyard. I whirled on Julia. "You don't need more training? Really? You almost died right there and put me in danger on top of that," I said. "That was sloppy. You can't just fall back on your pixie powers all the time, Julia."

"You did," Julia replied.

"That's different," I replied. "I was very careful to use them—"

"Listen, I appreciate what you're saying." Julia cut me off. "But I'm over 10,000 years old and I think I know how to use my powers better than you know how to use yours."

I scoffed. "Then prove it next time."

"I don't know why you're complaining." Julia walked over to the other man. "We still got one. Was there any tech out front?"

"A bunch of it," I said.

She nodded. "Then we got that, too. Pretty good for a first mission, I think."

My eyes narrowed. "Don't get cocky. Pick him up, and let's call it in. It'll take hours for Zalnir to open a portal for us."

I was satisfied with the new prospect. Julia could handle her own. She had an attitude of superiority, even though she was brand new to the Godschurch. And she was infuriatingly flippant. Of course, what else did I expect from a Katrina recommendation, the single most cocky being I've ever met in my life?

***

If you enjoyed this preview, make sure to pick up *Chaos* today!

ALSO BY RUSSELL NOHELTY

NOVELS
My Father Didn't Kill Himself
Sorry for Existing
Gumshoes: The Case of Madison's Father
Invasion
The Vessel
The Void Calls Us Home
Worst Thing in the Universe
Anna and the Dark Place
The Marked Ones
The Dragon Scourge
The Dragon Champion
The Dragon Goddess
The Obsidian Spindle Saga

COMICS and OTHER ILLUSTRATED WORK
The Little Bird and the Little Worm
Ichabod Jones: Monster Hunter
Gherkin Boy
How NOT to Invade Earth

www.russellnohelty.com

1000 BC – BETRAYED [HELL PT 1]
/PIXIE DUST

500 BC – FALLEN [HELL PT 2]

200 BC – HELLFIRE [HELL PT 3]

1974 AD – MYSTERY SPOT [RUIN PT 1]

1976 AD – INTO HELL [RUIN PT 2]

1984 AD – LAST STAND [RUIN PT 3]

1985 AD – CHANGE

1985 AD – MAGIC/BLACK MARKET HEROINE

1989 AD – DEATH'S KISS
[DARKNESS PT 1]

1985 AD – EVIL

2000 AD – TIME

2015 AD – HEAVEN

2018 AD – DEATH'S RETURN [DARKNESS PT 2]

2020 AD – KATRINA HATES THE DEAD
[DEATH PT 1]

2176 AD – CONQUEST

2177 AD – DEATH'S KISS
[DARKNESS PT 3]

12,018 AD – KATRINA HATES THE GODS
[DEATH PT 2]

12,028 AD – KATRINA HATES THE UNIVERSE
[DEATH PT 3]

12,046 AD – EVERY PLANET HAS A GODSCHURCH
[DOOM PT 1]

12,047 AD – THERE'S EVERY REASON TO FEAR
[DOOM PT. 2]

12,049 AD – THE END TASTES LIKE PANCAKES
[DOOM PT 3]

12,176 AD – CHAOS